Nineteen Seventy-Four

THE SEVEN BOOK FOUR

SARAH M. CRADIT

Cover Design by Sarah M. Cradit
Editing by Lawrence Editing

First Edition
ISBN: 978-1-958744-27-7

Publisher Contact:
sarah@sarahmcradit.com
www.sarahmcradit.com

Preface

If you're here, you've hopefully started with *1970,* followed by *1972*, and *1973.* If you operate best with order, you're in the right place! If you like to jump into the middle of something with blind excitement, then you're also in the right place.

By now, you've suffered through three of my disclaimers that remind you, the reader, that I was a child of the eighties, not the seventies. That my imagining of this period is a combination of the remnants of the mindset of the seventies that lingered into my generation, as well as leveraging feedback and ideas from those who lived through it, and lived through it well. Because of this, any errors or misrepresentations are my own.

This series is, first and foremost, a character-driven narrative about the "founding mothers and fathers," so to speak, of the future House of Crimson & Clover heroes and heroines. I'd always wanted to tell this story, because origin stories have a way of becoming so much more. As much of the past was written when I wrote the future, piecing together what was missing revealed that their lives were even more rich and intoxicating than anything I could have imagined. In writing their stories backwards, if you will,

I had the pleasure of watching who they'd become unfold before my eyes. Writing has a way of taking on a life bigger than the writer, and this series has been one incredible revelation after another. To say the seven have surprised me would be selling the experience short.

I mention this, because, while the time period in which this series is set was an important consideration for me (my playlist, since I started writing *1970* has been completely immersed in nothing but seventies music), being true to the seven Deschanels, and those who shaped their lives, for better or worse, was always my foremost goal.

As the series crests the hill and begins the descent toward the finish, I hope you continue to find the journey rewarding.

Also by Sarah M. Cradit

KINGDOM OF THE WHITE SEA

Kingdom of the White Sea Trilogy

The Kingless Crown

The Broken Realm

The Hidden Kingdom

The Book of All Things

Blackwood Cycle

The Raven and the Rush

The Poison and the Paladin

Southerlands Cycle

The Sylvan and the Sand

The Flame and the Forsaken

Guardians Cycle

The Altruist and the Assassin

The Belle and the Blackbird

Darkwood Cycle

The Melody and the Master

The Hand and the Heart

Sceptre Cycle

The Claw and the Crowned

The Duke and the Disciple

THE SAGA OF CRIMSON & CLOVER

The House of Crimson and Clover Series

The Storm and the Darkness

Shattered

The Illusions of Eventide

Bound

Midnight Dynasty

Asunder

Empire of Shadows

Myths of Midwinter

The Hinterland Veil

The Secrets Amongst the Cypress

Within the Garden of Twilight

House of Dusk, House of Dawn

Midnight Dynasty Series

A Tempest of Discovery

A Storm of Revelations

A Torrent of Deceit

The Seven Series

Nineteen Seventy

Nineteen Seventy-Two

Nineteen Seventy-Three

Nineteen Seventy-Four

Nineteen Seventy-Five

Nineteen Seventy-Six

Nineteen Eighty

Vampires of the Merovingi Series

The Island

and more

The Dusk Trilogy

St. Charles at Dusk: The Story of Oz and Adrienne

Flourish: The Story of Anne Fontaine

Banshee: The Story of Giselle Deschanel

Crimson & Clover Stories

Available as a single collection, The Shorts

Surrender: The Story of Oz and Ana

Shame: The Story of Jonathan St. Andrews

Fire & Ice: The Story of Remy & Fleur

Dark Blessing: The Landry Triplets

Pandora's Box: The Story of Jasper & Pandora

The Menagerie: Oriana's Den of Iniquities

A Band of Heather: The Story of Colleen and Noah

The Ephemeral: The Story of Autumn & Gabriel

Bayou's Edge: The Landry Triplets

For more information, and exciting bonus material, visit www.sarahmcradit.com

The Seven in 1974

Children of
August Deschanel (deceased) &
Colleen "Irish Colleen" Brady

Charles August Deschanel, Aged 24
Augustus Charles Deschanel, Aged 23
Colleen Amelia Deschanel, Aged 22
Madeline Colleen Deschanel, Deceased
Evangeline Julianne Deschanel, Aged 20
Maureen Amelia Deschanel, Aged 18
Elizabeth Jeanne Deschanel, Aged 15

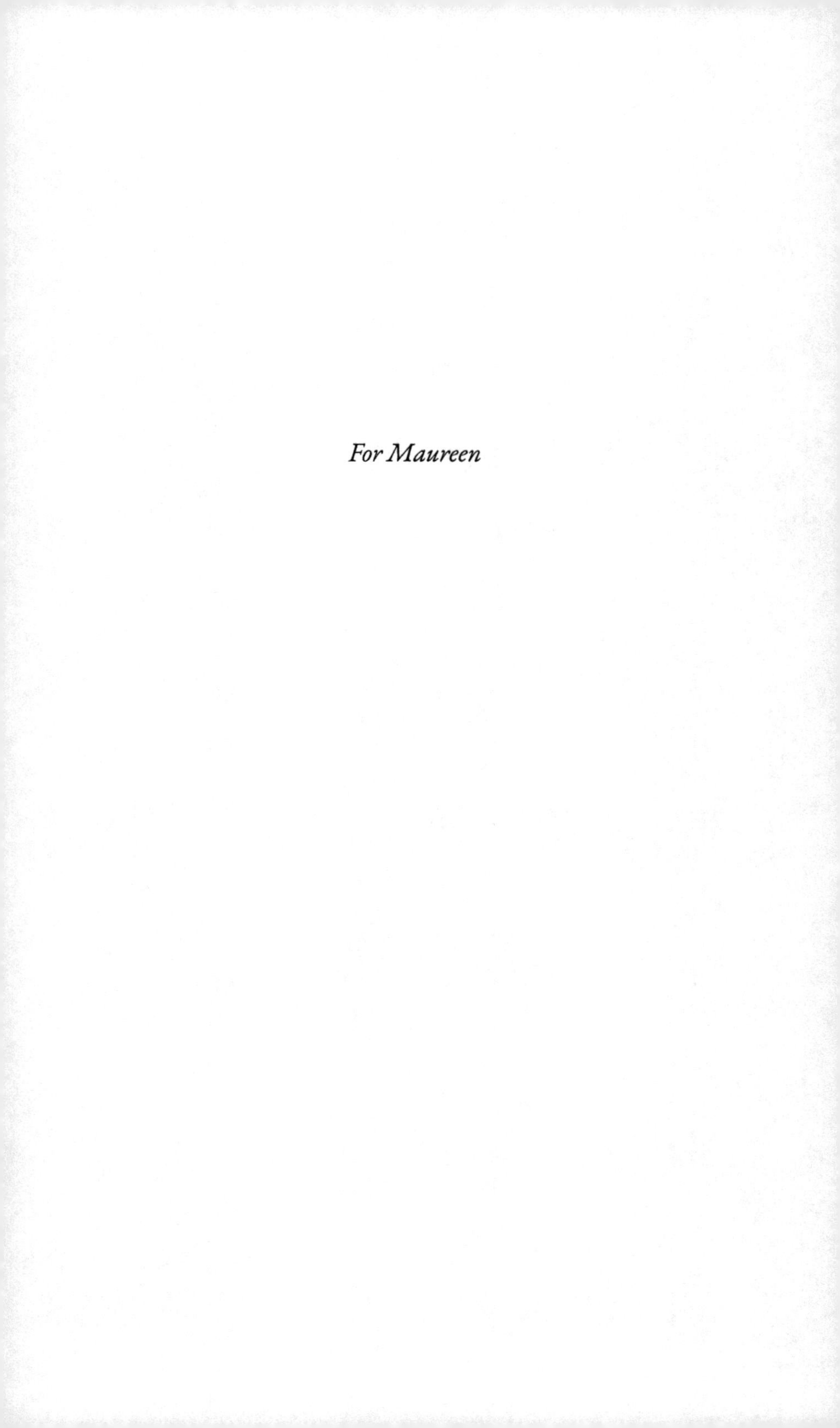

For Maureen

SPRING 1974

VACHERIE, LOUISIANA
NEW ORLEANS, LOUISIANA

Prologue: Irish Colleen and the Seven

Colleen Deschanel, known as Irish Colleen to her family and friends, walked past the faces of her seven children, as she did every night of her life.

All seven of her children lined the marble mantle of the townhouse that was her home now, and possibly always.

She hardly saw any of them anymore. Their lives had recently ceased to be an extension of hers, and her days of actively mothering any of them, even young, sweet Elizabeth, were almost entirely at an end. They didn't need her meticulous preservation of their father's world. They didn't need her heavy hand, or even her soft one, though she had always been more natural at the former than the latter.

Charles lived alone at Ophélie, sulking around the property like a specter, awaiting his marriage to Cordelia. He'd resigned himself to the union born upon a terrible secret between the fathers of the not-so-happy couple, and that showed an unexpected level of maturity from her reckless oldest son. Yet Irish Colleen could not help but feel bitterness that his future unhappiness was what finally brought upon him the need to act like a man. She'd chided him for growing to this point too slow, and now he would settle into this space with all the expected bitterness of a man wronged by an unfair world.

Augustus, on the morrow, would take his own bride and bring her back to his Magnolia Grace. Irish Colleen didn't know whether he was happy about this or not. He displayed none of the joy of the newly fiancéd. His signature, perpetual glower of sourness, the way one might look if their taste buds were tuned inappropriately, dimmed only a little with the pretty, if odd, Ekatherina on his arm. Irish Colleen quelled her suspicions at the young woman's motivations. Surely, she wasn't marrying him for their unbridled passion for one another? There was no evidence of that, or of any binding attraction. But Ekatherina would bring none of her own people to the wedding, and therein that fact lay the answer Irish Colleen had been avoiding.

Augustus was no fool. If she was after him for his money or connections, then he already knew this and was running toward the fire, not away.

Colleen's plane for Edinburgh left the day after Augustus' wedding. Both Irish Colleen and Ophelia had reminded Colleen that the family had access to a private jet, but she insisted her life in Scotland wasn't going to be about who she was, but what she could do. No one there would know the name Deschanel, she said, though Irish Colleen thought her eldest daughter was underestimating the power of the family influence. Even in Scotland, she'd find those who would pander to her for favor, and doors would open because of this connection, even if she never understood the link. *I want to start this season of my life right,* Colleen insisted, and although it was a delusion, it was important to her, and Irish Colleen hadn't pushed. Colleen said she'd be back once a quarter for her Collective Council meetings, and of course in the summer for Charles' wedding, but Irish Colleen had the strong sense that once Colleen fell in love with Scotland, those visits would taper off, and her commitments back home would wane. Irish Colleen still remembered the rolling hills of Erin, which she'd been told were so like the Highlands of Scotland, and keened for them. Places like this were a place of rest for the soul. She'd daydreamed of returning when all her children were grown, but not all souls were worthy of rest.

Spring was the time for decisions, and Evangeline, as with the prior two years, was faced with a decision of her own. Each year, she said she would leave for MIT, and each year, she found a reason to stay. This time, she claimed she was doing it for Colleen, who would need to know the family was cared for in her absence. Did neither of her daughters understand how hurtful this insinuation was? She'd borne it from Colleen since she was a child, because she chalked it up to a personality tic, but now Evangeline spoke as if their presence alone was required to keep the solid bond running through the family. She tried not to think too much about this, because the underlying truth was enough to shatter the façade she kept around the walls of every house they'd lived in. To them, she was a mere steward, like the wretched Denethor in that book Elizabeth insisted on reading, *The Lord of the Rings.* She was just here until the rightful king of Gondor appeared, or whenever Colleen finished college, whichever came first.

She supposed this was how her late husband had seen her, as well. Having failed to produce children with the love of his life, he'd resigned himself to marrying a baby-maker, and giving her the means to produce and produce until there was nothing left of her except a shell.

Irish Colleen closed her eyes in prayer after they passed over the face of her beautiful Madeline, who was now God's child more than hers.

She started up the stairs, to where the bedrooms lined the hall in a neat row.

Maureen was sound asleep. Irish Colleen didn't know her daughter well enough anymore to understand the change, but she'd noticed Maureen had found more peace in recent months. This started at Ophélie, and though Irish Colleen had worried coming back to New Orleans would reverse any progress made, it continued. Was it her eighteenth birthday looming around the corner?

Maureen had always talked of the day she could fly with her own wings and leave the nest, even if none of her plans ever involved the specifics she'd require to make it happen. Details had always been unimportant to Maureen, who responded more acutely to emotional need than the ones logic commanded. How long would she stay? The pang in Irish Colleen's gut told her Maureen wouldn't have many more nights under this roof.

She blew her daughter a kiss and moved on.

Irish Colleen found Elizabeth standing at her window. One hand peeled back the lace curtain, and the other lay pressed against the glass, fingers spread. Beyond, rain peppered the panes. Elizabeth seemed lost to the process.

"It's late, Lizzy."

"I'm not five anymore, Mama."

"Yes, of course. I know that, smarty pants." Irish Colleen longed for the days where her baby *was* five, and she could hold her, a simple mother's touch washing the pain away. That window had been so short and was now closed forever. At fifteen, Elizabeth was almost a stranger to her now. She recoiled from even the slight touch of her mother pressing her hair aside. Scowled at the mild attempts at tenderness.

"Charles and Augustus are both making mistakes."

Irish Colleen flinched at the blunt transition. "Charles has his challenges ahead, but love is not the most important part of marriage, Elizabeth. They'll find their balance. As for Augustus, he chose his bride."

Elizabeth's lips curled in a smirk. "Choice is an illusion."

"And what, pray, does that mean?"

"Aggie chose Ekatherina about as much as Charles chose Cordelia."

Irish Colleen wrapped her arms around her, pulling her shawl tighter. "What you're saying makes no sense, Elizabeth."

"It wouldn't to you. You've always been so black and white."

Irish Colleen took a step forward, slighted by the observation. "That's not fair, Lizzy. I live my life according to the Lord's direction, and if that seems to be a method that leaves me making clear choices, then so be it."

"Did you ask yourself why Augustus left when he did?"

"He was a grown man. It was time."

"Was it?"

"Stop with the questions and make your point."

"He's punishing himself," Elizabeth said. She ran her finger down the glass, chasing a rogue drop outside. "For Maddy."

"Madeline made her choices, and they had tragic results. Augustus was a wonderful brother to her."

"Augustus was the only one who cared about what was important to her, and then he gave her the money and the way out that killed her within hours."

Irish Colleen drew in a sharp breath. "I know that, but it would be foolish to blame himself for something he wasn't even there for."

Elizabeth half-turned with a grin far beyond her years. "And when is guilt fair?"

"You're too young yet to understand."

"It would be easier for you if I was, I guess." Elizabeth shrugged. She let the curtain fall and turned to her mother. "Ekatherina is more like Madeline than even he realizes. She's alone in the world, and misunderstood, and in need of something he can give. Now do you see the connection?"

"He must love her," Irish Colleen insisted.

Elizabeth shrugged. "He seems to. Only Augustus knows for sure about that. But any relationship that starts on the wrong terms has a way of ending on them."

"What are you saying?"

"I don't know anymore," Elizabeth replied. She bounced down onto the bed and flopped into position on her pillow. "I don't even know why I bother to open my mouth."

"Lizzy, that isn't what I meant. You know you can tell me anything."

"Can I? Even if I can't tell you everything?"

It was a fair question, and one with no satisfying answer. "You can't be cross with me for wanting to understand the things you see and say, my darling."

"Then you can't be cross with me for not knowing everything."

Irish Colleen nodded. "Very well. I'll prove to you I can leave you well enough alone, from time to time. Tell me something I don't know right now, and I promise I'll ask no further questions."

Elizabeth laughed. "Okay, how's this? Charles and Augustus aren't the only ones who will be starting an unhappy marriage this year."

"What?"

"You said no questions."

"Well, yes, but—"

Elizabeth turned her face away and buried it in the plush fold of her pillow. "Good night, Mama."

CHAPTER 1

Augustus Takes a Bride

Ekatherina's lips were even softer than he'd imagined. He should have kissed her sooner. It wasn't as if he hadn't found a suitable occasion. This wasn't the nineteenth century, where chasteness ruled all. Still, so much about their relationship was a careful dance of interpreting intentions, and Augustus would be horrified if he misunderstood hers. Even for a kiss.

She had a small, but generous mouth. Augustus once heard Maureen telling one of the other girls about how she'd been pinching her bottom lip in order to give herself a "feminine pout," and while he had no actual idea what that was, it seemed Ekatherina had this naturally. She never wore lipstick—something he was only certain of by the frequency of which she chewed her lips, and the unchangeable color of the surface—but she didn't need to, and even today, on her wedding day, he was happy not to taste the waxy blend that reminded him of kissing Carolina.

When he pulled back, Ekatherina was smiling, and that was enough to restore his heartrate to normal.

He pitched forward as his brother, looking both dapper and out of place in his bespoke tuxedo, clapped him hard on the back.

"Congratulations, my man." Charles stepped around Augustus and kissed Ekatherina on both cheeks. "Welcome to the family, sister."

"Thank you." Her timidity in the face of Charles' intensity caused Augustus' anxiety to reappear as he agonized over whether or not she would ever be happy as a Deschanel, in a family so unlike hers.

Or was it? Augustus didn't know, but he intended to find out. For her.

Irish Colleen had grudgingly agreed to a small wedding, after Augustus threatened to elope, but she insisted all his siblings be represented in the wedding party. This was the first wedding of the generation, and the family *would* be a part of it. Augustus didn't mind this part so much. He loved his siblings, and when he'd declared he wanted a small wedding, he of course meant they should be there. But this posed a problem, because he had a disproportionate number of sisters.

Colleen paired with Charles as the maid of honor, but that left his three younger sisters needing groomsmen. Augustus didn't have friends, only business acquaintances, a fact that never bothered him until faced with deciding who should be at his side on the biggest day of his life. Now, it was a bleak reminder that the life he required to keep himself focused on what was important was also no life at all by the standards of most.

In the end, he chose the Sullivan brothers. They were practically family, and ready-made for the task. Colin, Rory, and Patrick were all too happy for the honor.

Was Ekatherina resentful of having four women she hardly knew stand at her side as she married? Was she thinking of her own sister, Anasofiya? As a wedding gift, he planned to present to her a copy of his letter to the Soviet Embassy, making a formal request for her family to join them in New Orleans. By Christmas, she'd be reunited with her beloved family, and all would be well. The last of her tension would slip away, as would his, and they could begin anew.

Evangeline pressed through the small crowd gathering at the

altar. The taffeta bulging at her arms set off her wild hair with even more of a feral look than usual as she stomped in her platform heels.

She shook Charles aside and took Ekatherina's tiny triceps into her hands. The cornered look in Ekatherina's eyes put Augustus on edge, but he trusted his sister not to murder her new sister-in-law on the day of her wedding.

"We didn't get off to the best start, Ekatherina," Evangeline said. She released her hands temporarily to tug at the hem of her dress, shuffling her body around in very obvious discomfort. "But you're the first person to make my brother happy, since... well, since. So welcome to our family, sister."

Ekatherina dropped her eyes, but not before Augustus witnessed the tears brewing. She'd so far said one thing and only one thing about the family she was marrying into, and it had come days before the wedding. *You have many sisters. They will not want another.*

They will if they see me happy.

Are you happy?

Augustus had taken her diminutive hands in his and turned them over, studying the lines in her palms. *I think this is the happiest I've ever been,* he said, not adding that he didn't really know what happiness felt like so he wasn't sure he'd recognize it in any case. This must be happiness. Perhaps he just didn't feel it at the decibel of most.

"Well, I need a drink!" Evangeline declared and, lifting her skirts, stomped off in the direction of the bar set up just beyond the parterre garden.

Maureen appeared and slid her arm through Ekatherina's. "Welcome to the family, Catherine!"

Augustus breathed out, relieved at least one of his sisters remembered how sensitive his bride was about her traditional name. Even if he couldn't bring himself to use it.

"Seems to me you don't know very many people here, do you?" Maureen asked. She laughed. "Hell's bells, I didn't know you until Christmas. Don't you be letting Augustus hide you away, okay? He's too private for his own good, but you don't have to be."

Ekatherina looked at Augustus for direction. He smiled, and then Ekatherina smiled at Maureen.

"Brother, can I borrow your bride for a bit? I'll introduce her to the people you failed to. Heaven knows you'll have her all to yourself tonight." Maureen winked.

Augustus flushed and nodded. In an awkward series of starts and stops, he leaned forward and pecked Ekatherina on the lips before watching them disappear into the small crowd of close friends and family.

"She's smoking hot," Charles noted, pulling up at his brother's side with his arms crossed. "I mean, not in a way you'd notice right off the bat. But Russia sure does know how to make 'em. No wonder we're at war with them."

"That's not what the Cold War is about," Augustus replied, channeling Madeline. Today, of all days, seemed the occasion to take up her cross. Her absence rarely felt so acute as it had seeing his beautiful sisters lined up to celebrate his day. All his sisters but one. "People are starving in the Soviet Union, Charles. Her family included."

Charles nodded and a slow realization spread across his face. "Is that... what this is, Aggie?"

Augustus shook his head, not only to dispel his brother of this, but also himself. He couldn't pause on this thought long enough to consider that Ekatherina's affections might not be as in earnest as his own. "No, but I'll bring them here if it's the last thing I do. Ekatherina came to this country to make a place for them. Why shouldn't I make that easier?"

"Yeah, right. Of course." Charles nodded into the crowd. "Fucking Cat. My Cat, that is. Or *not* my fucking Cat, not anymore. Look at her."

"What am I looking at?"

"That dress. Girls don't wear dresses like that unless they're wanting someone to notice them. That's a *fuck me* dress, if I've ever seen one."

Augustus thought Catherine's dress was modest, if flattering to her figure, but Charles was looking for affirmations, not reality. It was easier for him to believe Catherine was miserable, crying into her pillow every night for the love that got away. "And just whose attention is she trying to get, do you suppose? You know, being a married woman, with her husband at her side."

Charles reached into his tuxedo jacket and pulled out a pack of cigarettes. "Won't give her the satisfaction," he muttered as he slipped one between his lips. "Not now. Not ever."

"Your fiancée is around here somewhere anyway," Augustus pointed out.

The cigarette bobbed in Charles' mouth as he gave his brother a powerful sideways glare.

Augustus stifled a chuckle, but not well. "I don't understand why you're marrying someone you clearly despise."

"You know why."

"Mama?"

Charles tilted his head as if to say, *bingo.*

"You've never listened to Mama about anything. Why this?"

Charles took a deep exhale and held the smoke in his lungs for a theatrical intermission. He released it in two streams from his nostrils. "You don't know the half of it."

"She figure out you moonlight as a murderer and hold it over your head?" Augustus realized how much things had changed since Madeline died, that he could joke about something so horrific.

Charles rolled his tongue around, across his bottom lip and inside it. "If you only knew."

"I could talk to her."

"Mama?" Charles released another cloud of smoke. "Or Lucifer?"

"Lucifer? Jesus, Charles. No, Mama. I don't think she realizes what she's doing. She wants you to settle down, of course, but this is only going to make matters worse, forcing you into a marriage."

"Thanks, but please don't. I don't want to get into it here, but I've made my decision, and I'm going through with it."

"She's not ugly," Augustus offered.

"If this is your idea of a comforting thought, don't quit your day job."

Augustus shrugged. "I won't lie and say she's pleasant. We both know she's a touch different."

"A touch?"

"There's still time to call it off, Charles. You don't have to throw your life away for some misguided idea of honor."

Charles shook his head and gripped his shoulder in a quick squeeze. "We can bitch about life later, Augustus. Today's your wedding day, and I'll be damned if you don't finally enjoy something for a change."

Augustus played the gracious host, greeting each of the guests individually as he thanked them for coming to his special day. Even Carolina, whose belly was so swollen with pregnancy that it overwhelmed her small frame to the point he was certain she would tip over and be unable to get back up.

"You're glowing," he said as he kissed both her cheeks. Rory hovered protectively at her side, one arm steadying her from behind. The white rose pinned at his breast, denoting his role as groomsman, had already begun to wilt and curl in the spring heat.

"You are too, Aggie." She pressed both her hands into her lower back and winced. "You look happy, and I'm glad to see it."

"Thank you. I am."

"Catherine seems lovely."

"She's a tiny little thing," Rory remarked. "She reminds me of the dancers in that ballet you like, darling."

"Swan Lake. Tchaikovsky was Russian, too."

"Catherine is American now," Augustus said. "We'll be starting the citizenship process first thing."

"Of course," Carolina said, her words rolling forward in a rush. "But, then, we're all a little of something else, aren't we?"

"Can you believe, there will be two big Deschanel weddings this year?" Rory said. "I might as well keep the tux for a bit. You think it will work for Charles' as well? He hasn't said." He laughed and looked off into the distance, his eye catching something.

Augustus followed and saw immediately the target of Rory's gaze: Colleen, huddled together with Colin, Cat, and Patrick. He diverted his own attention before Carolina wised up.

But Rory dug himself into the hole on his own. "I suppose I should say hello to Colleen. When does she leave?"

"Tomorrow," Augustus said, and it hurt him to see the flash of pain in Carolina's eyes.

"So soon?" Rory chuckled, but his anxiety on the matter was plain as day, written across his face. "What about Huck's wedding?"

"She'll fly back for that, but she wants to get settled in Edinburgh as soon as possible." Augustus had a sharp urge to reach forward and touch Carolina in some soft, subtle way. To push her hair behind her ears, or run his finger across her cheek. He shouldn't be thinking of another woman on his wedding day, but he felt it a great injustice that the one man who should be thinking of her—and the child growing within her—was instead fixated on another. She deserved to be loved wholly, and to experience tenderness. Augustus' odd desire to give it to her wasn't born of his own love for her, but of a detached but intense fondness for the young woman who had tried to save him.

Instead he found a more appropriate option. Augustus pressed a hand to her belly, ever briefly, and smiled. "Do you know what you're having?"

"A boy." Her cheeks flushed. "We've decided to name him Clancy."

"Well, we don't *know* he's a boy, of course, but we believe he might be," Rory added.

Augustus smiled wider. "A fine Southern name."

Rory kissed his wife's cheek and excused himself, in an odd, distracted manner, and jogged off toward Colleen.

Tears welled up in Carolina's eyes. She looked away, ashamed of them, and then explained them as a byproduct of her overworked emotions.

Augustus squeezed her hand. "You can't let that bother you, Carolina. I know what you're thinking, but you're wrong."

She sniffled. "And what am I thinking, Augustus?"

"I won't dignify it with words. He adores you, and he will adore your son. First loves are powerful, but they end. All things not meant to last do."

Carolina wrapped her palms over her swollen belly and grinned. "Listen to you, talking of first loves, on your wedding day, with your own first love."

Was she his first love?

He supposed she was.

Augustus leaned in and kissed her cheek again. "Rory is a lucky guy," he said. He beckoned Chelsea over. "Look after your sister-in-law, Chels. We both know she's stubborn. Don't want her running up the levee or something."

Carolina's smile that followed him was grateful.

AUGUSTUS TRIED TO RETRIEVE HIS WIFE, BUT EVERY TIME he spotted her, she was on the arm of one of his sisters, and much as he ached to be near her, in search of some reassurance that she ached for him too, he accepted this fire drill initiation into her family was good for her and would only help her become a Deschanel with greater ease.

The sun crested over the Mississippi, and, one by one, their guests filtered away to their own lives. Colin and Cat were the last to leave, and Augustus went to join them when he felt a soft hand tug him back.

Irish Colleen wore a beautiful lace dress that had been in her family several generations. From the high neck and veil, to the trim grazing her toes, it was an incredible show of detail and he only realized, as he turned to face her and really *see* her for the first time that day, that she had worn it because of her own love, for him, and in that love she was absolutely beautiful.

"You look so much like your father, Augustus."

"Mama," he said. "Thank you for a beautiful day."

"My sweet boy." Irish Colleen wrapped her hands around his forearms. She was too short to reach much higher. "Today is as good a day as any to tell you how proud I am. I know I don't say it to you, and I should."

"Mama."

"No, don't comfort me on my own failings, darling. I had seven children, nine if you count those who were in God's hands before they drew breath, before I could even take a breath and decide what it means to be a mother, and I haven't always been everything you need, but 'tis not for lack of love. I love you more than my own life, my son, and though I was doubtful of the girl when I met her, I see now that your wife loves you and is worthy of you, and that is all I could ever want for you."

Augustus could not recall a time his mother had spent so many words on him in one sitting. He didn't know what to say, or if he even should. "You look beautiful today."

Irish Colleen smiled and patted his arm. "Tell me in the summer when I wear it to your brother's wedding."

CHARLES HAD TO GIVE AUGUSTUS CREDIT. FOR A HERMIT in the making, his little brother handled the host duties at his wedding with surprising finesse. *He turned himself on*, Evangeline said, and when Charles remarked that Augustus' permanent switch must be set firmly on "off," she reminded him he hadn't become a successful businessman by retreating into his shell.

Knowing Augustus was a rookie in the bedroom, Charles had found his big brother usefulness by proffering some advice on how to delight Augustus' new wife. Some of the advice brewing, that he wanted to give, was no longer appropriate now that they'd reached the wedding day. He'd only dipped his toe into expressing his concerns over the bride's motivations; there was no use saying anything now. If he was right, Augustus was already married and the damage done. If wrong, he would plant the seed of doubt that could harm their already odd marriage.

For it was truly odd. Somehow the Deschanel least likely to be married had been the first to do so. That Augustus had taken an interest in *any* woman was weird enough, but this particular woman could not have much to offer a man who was hard to impress to begin with. She was a shy, diminutive thing, who deferred to Augustus like they were landowners in the nineteenth century. Yet behind her eyes was pure fire, and Charles had a suspicion that when it came out to play, no good could come of it.

Augustus thanked the last of the guests, and Charles decided it was high time to get the fuck out of his tuxedo. He made his way to the back door of Ophélie, the servant's entrance by the kitchens, where he could come and go without fanfare. Before he reached the door, a familiar, but unwelcome, voice called his name.

"Darwin," Charles said tersely as he turned. "I thought you'd left with your father and sister."

"You mean your father-in-law and wife?"

"Future."

Darwin pressed his lips into a tight smile that made him look as if he required prunes. "Family is family, is it not?"

"Until she's signing her name on checks with my name and money, we're not family."

"Semantics."

Charles' muscles tightened. All this talk of family could mean only one thing. "I don't loan money to family. It's bad business. Bad blood." *Also, I hate you and your vile sister.*

Darwin forced a laugh. "I'm not here for your money."

Yet, thought Charles.

"My father isn't himself, as I'm sure Cordelia has told you."

"What does that have to do with me?"

"Family, as I said—"

"What's your point?"

"He's spiraling. The reasons don't matter so much, but the outcome will. The business is failing, Charles, and we need to work together to protect it. I know our fortune is nothing to you, when compared to your own, but this is Cordelia's legacy, which will be the legacy of your children as well."

"This sounds an awful lot like you're about to ask me for money."

Darwin grunted under his breath. It was evident even talking to Charles was a pain to him, and Charles found great satisfaction in this. "I can handle the business side of things, thank you. I'd never ask you for help with that... not when your social calendar is so daunting."

"What can I say? Being an heir is tough work."

"For me, it certainly will be, as I work to save this business our father built and is now so damned determined to run directly into the ground."

Charles wasn't buying this poor attempt at misdirection. There was no doubt Darwin wanted in on his sister's future family's fortune, but Charles had not yet sussed out how he intended to accomplish it. "So, what, then?"

"Our reputation is as valuable to us as the money earned," Darwin went on, with all the airs of an aristocratic espousing the virtues of name. "I can be sure that Cordelia and I will do our part to protect our name in this delicate time, but I need to know you, as well, can be counted on."

"Meaning *what*?"

Darwin cleared his throat. "Everyone knows of your... proclivities. Your predilections. Now that the engagement is public knowledge, and the wedding imminent, I'm asking you to put that behavior on hold."

Charles wiped his hand across his mouth, grinning. "You want me to stop fucking around."

Darwin shifted in clear discomfort. "If you want to say it like that, then yes."

"And why the hell would I do that?"

"It would create an unnecessary scandal that could only hurt both families. Not just the Hendricksons, Charles. Society has forgiven and maybe even encouraged your dalliances because you were a bachelor. They will not so easily forgive you making a cuckold out of your fiancée."

Charles laughed. "Dalliances? Cuckold? What language are we speaking here? What are you, a returning soldier from the Revolutionary War?"

"Charles, I know you're not fond of me."

"I don't trust you as far as I can fucking throw you, if we want to be specific."

"Have I earned that?"

"One word: Elizabeth."

Darwin paled. "That was clearly a mistake, and in retrospect—"

"Speak English, will you?" Charles shook his head. "You might think, because of my reputation, that I'm all fun and games. I don't care about much, but my family is off fucking limits. And if you think time, and your sister popping out some of my kids, will dull that, then you're in for a rude surprise. So you want me to do you a favor? Really?" He spat at the ground, missing Darwin's feet by an inch. "Sure, no problem. Why not?"

Catherine, his Catherine, in that *fuck me* dress and simpering smile, stepped out from the shadows. "Is everything okay, Charles?"

Charles licked his lips. Laughed. "Yes. You were both just leaving."

He whipped around and disappeared inside.

CHAPTER 2

The Ocean

Colleen couldn't decide how she should feel about her own actions. She'd come to terms with moving to Scotland for graduate school, but even with the greatest of mental gymnastics she couldn't find a selfless reason for leaving so early… even if she had moved the date back from her original insane idea to depart right after Christmas.

Her need for self-punishment came entirely from within. All of her siblings, and her mother, had happily seen her off after Augustus' wedding. Evangeline promised to look after the family, as Colleen once did. Maureen promised to stay out of trouble. Elizabeth said only that Colleen leaving was where she was meant to go, and that she should move happily forth in that knowledge.

Charles said she was wise to get "the hell out of New Orleans, and as far away from the Sullivans as possible."

Augustus had offered more words than usual. "We have to find ways to live, Colleen. All of us. Don't you dare feel a lick of guilt in leaving. Not one of us has done more for this family than you have, and it's time to do for yourself."

Colleen had embraced him, overcome with her own fears. She had a bad sense of Ekatherina, something she'd dismissed when Evangeline first expressed hers. Colleen couldn't pinpoint the source of her discontent; it wasn't that she thought her brother's bride was evil, or necessarily bad at all, but the energy surrounding her, and them together, was palpably malevolent. But Colleen was a healer, and this was the only ability of hers she could trust to guide her true. "A bad feeling," wasn't enough to send her brother's happiness crashing down around him.

Instead, she'd made him a promise. "Aggie, you call me. For anything, right? Anything, and I'll be on the next plane home."

He'd grinned. "I thought I was the family fixer."

"For those things troubling us from the outside world, yes..."

Augustus paused long enough to take her meaning, and then waved the thought away, pushing it back to the place where all things unwelcome to him must go. "You'll be here in the summer for Huck's wedding. I'll see you then."

"Of course."

Sullivan & Associates had used their connections, whatever they might be, to help her secure an apartment on Blackfriars. They offered to have pictures taken, but the least of her penance would be showing up to her new home sight unseen—though she knew they would've never secured her anything less than what she was accustomed to. Even if she'd insisted they find her a hovel, they would've laughed it off.

She wasn't disappointed. The apartment was two stories, and from her upstairs window she could see both Edinburgh Castle and Arthur's Seat, as well as the start of the famed Royal Mile. The smell of freshly baking bread carried through her upstairs windows as she watched the morning come alive behind a dense fog. Shopkeepers appeared from the narrow closes, sweeping the remnants of the prior day into memory. All around her, on Blackfriars, young businessmen and women appeared on the street and disappeared into taxis, off to begin their days at the office.

Colleen yawned, then again, and then once more. Here in Edinburgh, the day was coming to life, but her body was still on New Orleans time and would be until she adjusted. And adjust she would, because this was home now. She was home, at least for the next few years.

That heavy realization mounted on top of her lack of sleep, and she decided a nap wouldn't be any harm.

Dearest Colleen,

You will be shocked to death to hear this, but the world continues to turn in New Orleans in your absence. I know... impossible. Impossible!

I miss you, though. But enough of the fuzzy stuff.

Poor Charles. He goes back and forth between accepting that he's marrying an evil hag and being a complete spaz. I worry about him all alone out at Ophélie (don't take that as an invitation to come back, now!), but he'll figure it out. I still don't understand why he's marrying Cordelia to begin with, but I stopped asking when he kept taking my head off. Honestly, I'm more worried about the whole Cat thing coming to a head. Chelsea told Maureen that Cat has been acting weird ever since Charles' engagement party, and she didn't outright say she thinks something is going on with them, but if Chelsea starts putting things together and Rory already has put it together, then it's only a matter of time before Colin gets wise. He's a square, but he's no fool.

For what it's worth, I don't think Charles is encouraging any of this. Baffling, I know. He seems like he wants nothing to do with Cat. Maybe he's growing up.

Hah! That'll be the day.

Maureen got a job! I repeat, Maureen got a job! She's working for some old recluse businessman. A Blanchard. I think he's an architect or something? She dresses up every day and goes into the office, like a respectable woman about to come of age. I hesitate to predict she'll stay out of trouble, but the forecast looks promising.

Augustus is... well, Augustus. I've been thinking I should move out, but he's downright insistent I stay. I think he's afraid of his new wife, and he should be. I'm not even sure they've had sex, Colleen. Not that I'm spying on them! But they act like brother and sister, not man and wife. He's so formal with her. And she's just so weird. I still don't trust her, but I promised him I wouldn't say another word about it, and I won't. Now that he's married the crazy Russian, I can only hope I've been wrong about her all along.

Thank God for Sullivan & Associates and their ironclad prenups, right? (I'm not literally thanking God, of course, seeing as I'm an atheist).

Elizabeth is the same. I'm starting to think she and Connor might be more than friends, but I like the kid, and if anyone deserves to be happy, it's our sweet Lizzy. But what is it with our family and Sullivans, eh?

Just don't tell Mama, or she'll never let him anywhere near the townhouse again. She still treats Lizzy like a baby, and probably will long after she spits out her own babies.

Since I know you'll take me to task if I don't mention it, classes are fine. Gonna ride out this year and see how things fare with the fam, and then, maybe, MIT.

Maybe. No lectures.

I was thinking I'd come out this summer and help you get settled. I could fly back with you after Huck's death sentence, I mean wedding. Any objections? No, I didn't think so. It's settled!

Love,

Evie

Evangeline paused as she sealed the envelope. She'd kept it all so lighthearted, never diving too far below the surface.

She couldn't say why she'd never told Colleen about Amnesty. There'd been plenty of opportunities. Maybe, she thought, it was because Colleen would have questions Evangeline couldn't answer. She couldn't answer them because she herself had no answers, and she'd promised Amnesty that having a full understanding of the situation wouldn't be a condition of their... friendship? Relationship?

Evangeline didn't know what it was, and that, too, made up the substance of the box containing her deepest secret.

Amnesty had shared one thing, though. She'd shared it only because showing up with bruises without explanation was unacceptable, so she grudgingly revealed her father was not only still alive —despite telling Evangeline he'd died when she was a child—but terribly abusive, which explained her floating from place to place. He searched all over for her whenever she'd disappear, and so she was always changing things up. He kept finding her because she had nowhere real to go, and so she slept under trees and on porches, out in the open.

Evangeline could solve this. Every problem had a solution, or multiple solutions. She couldn't very well let her stay at Magnolia Grace. Augustus would have a conniption. But Evangeline, like all Deschanels, had her property entitlement coming to her. She was twenty now, and all entitlements were available at eighteen. She'd only delayed hers because she was in no real hurry. Augustus wanted her to stay, for now, for inexplicable reasons that made no sense for a newlywed. But he wanted her there, so she stayed.

But the property on Third and Chestnut was hers.

And right now, *for* now, Amnesty's. Evangeline had picked up the keys last week and now she slept a whole lot better with the comfort of knowing Amnesty was safe from her father's sick abuse.

Evangeline opened the front door. She opened her mouth to call out for Amnesty, when a chill passed through the air. Arms came about her waist. Lips tickled the back of her neck.

"I'm so glad you're here," Amnesty purred, and Evangeline melted into her touch.

CHAPTER 3

Working Girl

Maureen pulled the completed sheet from the typewriter, blowing on the ink. She grinned. It may have taken her twelve tries to get a clean letter, but no one else had to know that. Not Mr. Blanchard, and certainly not the snickering biddies scrutinizing her every move.

For the moment, they weren't a problem. They'd taken their ugly purses and shuffled off in their too-tight dresses to the lunch counter at Maison Blanche. They'd return precisely an hour later, hands pressed to their bellies, bemoaning the poor decision to "eat so much," and vowing to nap under their desks, don't think they won't.

Not Maureen. Even had she been invited, she knew better than to spoil her figure with a noontime meal. She was strictly a grapefruit-at-breakfast and half-a-plate-of-Mama's-dinner gal, because there was a reason these women had either never married, or were left by husbands seeking something more attractive than award-winning muffin tops and the art of gossip.

They were awful, these women. From their lipstick that bled due to sour mouths full of wrinkles, to their fat feet bulging from the swell of standing on heels all day. They spent their days buried in vicious giggles like a pack of bridge trolls, forgetting they were hired to do actual work.

Most of their derision was reserved, at present, for Maureen. They seemed incapable of sharing a genuine smile and word, instead passing her with knowing sneers and under-the-breath comments about how she "wasn't special," and would "learn about Mr. Blanchard and his young girls soon enough."

Maureen, who'd been raised to respect even the most vile of elders, said nothing in return, but knew they'd die miserable and alone. Her life was only beginning.

As for Mr. Blanchard, he was an aging recluse without anything too terribly special to offer beyond his successful architectural firm. She'd pieced together a few facts and determined he was probably around forty, though he could pass for sixty or more. He was devoid of humor, or joy for that matter, but there was something in the way he lumbered around the office he'd built from the ground up—literally, as he'd designed it as well—exuding a mysterious sort of power that had been his replacement for happiness. Edouard, she'd tried to call him once, and the look he leveled upon her was so scathing she wondered if she'd miscalculated his measure and he was, in fact, the Zodiac Killer. Then, he patted her shoulder and reminded her he was Mr. Blanchard. He'd then dropped the folder in his arms and watched her pick up each sheet, one by one. When she tried to shuffle them all together, he touched the small of her back and coached, "Slowly, Miss Deschanel."

Yes, he was odd, but what of it? He'd never been married, so how could anyone expect him to know how to deal with women? She imagined him returning at night to his mansion with no natural light, staring into the dark abyss until morning.

Evangeline had taken Maureen and Elizabeth to lunch a week ago. Maureen almost told her older sister about her strict "no lunch" rule, but the idea of the three of them hitting the town, without their mother, felt so deliciously adult that she happily broke down. A salad couldn't hurt.

Both her sisters wanted to hear all about her new job, and she was excited to share. The growing look of horror on Evangeline's face made her wish she hadn't, though.

"He did *what*?" she cried. "This is your *boss*?"

"Don't be vile, Evie," Maureen protested. "Not everything has to be sexual or gross."

Evangeline's mouth hung wide, and Maureen had the urge to ask her if she was trying to catch flies.

"So," Evangeline said. "He sat there and watched you sharpen *all* one hundred pencils in the box?"

Elizabeth grinned into her grilled cheese.

"He's a perfectionist," Maureen explained. She straightened her skirt, which she'd worn to show her sisters how far she'd come. "All successful people are."

Evangeline's face played the spectrum of horror to humor. "Uh-huh. And how long did this take you?"

"Oh, about an hour or so."

"I see. So this very successful, very busy, *perfectionist* stood and watched you sharpen each pencil, one by one. Where were his hands?"

Elizabeth burst out laughing.

"Evie!" Maureen cried. "Are you trying to corrupt our little sister?"

Evangeline snickered. "This one? You realize she's a year older than you were when you were fucking that Shakespeare flunky?"

Maureen froze. "How do you know about that?"

"Don't tell me you still believe there are any secrets in this family."

Maureen said nothing. If Evangeline had really wanted to rile her, she would've mentioned the Virgins Only Club, and the absence of this only proved Evangeline wrong about secrets.

Elizabeth tapped her head. "Seer. Remember?"

Maureen groaned. "Neither of you have ever had a job. You wouldn't *understand.*"

"That's not true. Evie has helped Augustus for years."

"I just hope he pays well," Evangeline said, hiding her grin in a sip of Coke.

"You're the worst, you know that?"

"What did he do with the pencils after?"

"Sorry?"

Evangeline set her glass down and watched her from behind that wild mane of hers, looking like a feral cat. "Did he use them?"

Maureen balked. "No, Mr. Blanchard uses *pens*."

She sat alone in the quiet office. The biddies wouldn't be back for another thirty minutes, and Mr. Blanchard had a meeting across town until three.

The office was hers. Every desk, every potted plant. Every watercolor of the birds of Louisiana.

Her sisters could keep their cute little jokes. She was a woman now, and everything the world had taken from her now prepared her for something no one could claim.

COLLEEN HELD THE CARD IN ONE HAND. HER OTHER gripped the receiver of the phone on the desk.

Rory and Carolina Sullivan are pleased to announce the addition of a healthy son, Clancy Sullivan.

The enclosed picture was what gave Colleen pause. The birth announcements her mother had received over the years had the respective families standing in a yard, or under a tree, or sitting on a bench. Something light and happy. In this picture, Rory knelt at the hospital bedside, one arm around Carolina's head, the other holding the hand of his son. Carolina smiled through bleary, purple-rimmed eyes.

She set the letter on the old wooden desk and dialed.

The house phone rang and rang, so she pressed the receiver a few times and then tried Sullivan & Associates. One of the secretaries answered and said that Rory and his family were still at Charity Hospital, and gave her the number.

Colleen turned the envelope over in her hand. Post-marked two weeks ago, and Clancy had been born two weeks before that.

Her heart did flips in her chest as she dialed the hospital and asked to be transferred to the room of Mrs. Rory Sullivan.

The desk nurse explained that Mrs. Sullivan was resting, but she'd see if Mr. Sullivan was available to come out and talk.

Rory was on the other end five minutes later. His sleepy voice answered, "This is Mr. Sullivan."

"Rory?"

Pause. Followed by a strange sound. "Colleen?"

"I... got your birth announcement. Congratulations. Clancy is a beautiful boy."

The soft sound of static appeared. Hand across stubble. "Thank you, he really is. He was ready to go home the day after... but his mama..."

Colleen swallowed. Her throat was dry. She didn't know how to ask the question, so she said, "And Carolina..."

Her answer from the other end came by way of soft sobs.

"Rory, she's not..."

"She's sleeping. She's always sleeping, and three doctors have seen her now. They all say she'll get better, that it will just take time, but every time I go in, I have this fear... I check her pulse..." His words dissolved back into his grief.

"Do you want..." *me to lay hands on her?* she almost finished. Colleen chewed her thumbnail. She'd never been certain just how much Rory knew about her. Never had she ever said anything outright, though there'd been hints... she'd even healed him once, when he was sleeping. He'd gashed himself on his car, and she waited until he was soundly in dreamland before laying her hands on him. The next morning, he'd puzzled over the dramatic change in his injury, but not enough. Not nearly enough. Like he knew, but didn't want her to know he knew.

She'd be home soon for Charles' wedding, but she could amend her ticket and be home sooner...

"It's my fault," Rory cried. "I kept insisting we had to have three, four children. You know Carolina... she said yes, of course, anything you want, dear. I couldn't even wait for the first one before I was making plans for the others, and I ignored how her skin had grown sallow... how she'd lost weight, instead of gaining. I'm a goddamn fool, Colleen."

"That's simply not true," Colleen insisted. "Maybe you missed signs, but how can we see the changes in those we see every day until it's too late?" She thought of Madeline. Of Maureen. Of Evangeline. "She was pregnant before you ever knew you'd want a family together. Before you were married."

"And she lost that child, Colleen. That's my fault, too. I wasn't as careful as I should have been. I think a part of me was hoping she'd get pregnant, and we could start a family."

Were you less than careful with me, too?

"It takes two to make a child, Rory. And there was no way you could've foreseen she'd struggle to bring this one into the world, even if she did lose the first one. This is not your fault. It's not anyone's fault."

"It won't matter whose fault this is if I lose her, Colleen." Rory pulled the phone away as he cried.

Colleen played with the phone cord, her mind spinning. If she could only see Carolina, she'd know how serious this was. She'd know if she could fix this for him, because... because...

Rory loved Carolina. He really, truly loved her. Colleen could hear this in his voice, and in the words he chose to keep for himself. She wasn't a replacement for Colleen, not anymore. Colleen was the first, but Carolina was the last.

Colleen put her hand over the phone and sighed. The sound was born of relief, and a small pinprick of grief.

"I'll be home soon, Rory. I'd like to come see her, if that's okay?"

Rory blew his nose. He sniffled as he returned his mouth to the phone. "You'd do that? You'd come back, and... and lay hands on her? As you did for me?"

He knew. He'd always known.

"I think I can help her."

"Colleen." He breathed the sound out with his grief. "I'd owe you my life, if you could save hers."

Colleen didn't know where the tears came from, or who they were for. She glanced out the window, at the green hills of Arthur's Seat, covered in the light fog of a Scotland spring. Her future was here, but her past would always call to her. It hung by several gossamer threads, and she could break this one, as she'd broken others, by giving Rory this gift. A gift that, for her, would provide closure and a sense of peace as she embraced the world looking forward, instead of back.

"I'll call the airline today."

CHAPTER 4

The Cold Darkness of Russia

Charles exited the Playboy Club on Iberville just after midnight. It was early, but he'd started the day far too early as well, signing the paperwork for his prenuptial agreement down at Sullivan & Associates. There were few things more depressing, in his estimation, than signing your freedom away, so he'd started his pub crawl around ten, and now, fourteen hours later, he needed his own bed more than he needed cocaine and mollies.

He should have ordered a car to take him back to Ophélie. Not that he couldn't handle his Trans Am fully loaded, but he wasn't in the mood for more work. His hands were too tired to roll the gears, and as he paid the bartender in cash, he realized his brain wasn't working so well, either.

Charles fumbled with his keys and cursed as he dropped them into the gutter with God-knows-what-else. The French Quarter gutters were a game of guesswork and prayer. His head spun as he reached for them, and he fell back as another set of hands came upon them and pulled them out.

He blinked the stars away and stumbled back two steps. "Darwin. The fuck you doing here?"

Darwin Hendrickson made no point in returning the keys. He

crossed his arms, pushing the keys into the fold. His lips curled in disgust as two women emerged from the doors of the club, stumbling drunk. "Aren't you getting a little old for this scene, Charles?"

"Only you could be too old for fun," Charles slurred. He reached for his keys, but Darwin twisted his body sideways. "Give me my keys, nimrod."

"You're in no condition to drive," Darwin said. "Not that I care about what happens to you, but my sister does."

Charles laughed.

"Fine, we both know that's a lie." Darwin's smile was grotesque. "But your marriage is important to the family, so let's not get you killed just yet."

"Yeah? Why?"

"I'll drive to Café du Monde. We can talk over coffee."

"You lay your hands on my car, I'll rip them off."

Darwin's lips drew a tight line. "We'll take mine, then."

Charles gripped the lamppost for support. "You can do whatever the fuck you want. I'm going home."

"You won't get far as... drunk, high, or whatever you are."

"You severely underestimate my talents."

"Actually, I don't. That's why I'm here." He pulled a large manila folder from the back of his pants and waved it in the air between them. "You'll want to be sitting for this."

"Give me my fucking keys already."

"I'll give you your keys once you hear what I have to say. And we're not doing that *here,* amongst the riffraff. I can drive myself, and you can walk there, which might help sober you up, or you can get in my car and we can get this over with."

Charles didn't trust Darwin not to drive them right into the river, but he was too drunk to reason with someone who possessed their full faculties, and there was even a small part of him that was desperately curious.

What was in the envelope? What ridiculous shit was Darwin about to propose? Whatever it was, he'd enjoy turning him down. He'd absolutely revel in seeing the sniveling shit lowered to begging.

Charles crossed his arms and nodded in the direction of the river. "Why not? The night's still young, and I haven't been sufficiently entertained yet."

CHARLES SOBERED UP ON THE SHORT DRIVE. THIS WAS A shame, for having his wits would only make any conversation with Darwin that much more painful.

Darwin ordered them both a café au lait. Charles let him do it, even though he didn't drink coffee, and enjoyed the way Darwin watched him in anticipation as the drink sat untouched under the breeze of the overhead fans working the humid air around the open diner.

"Would you like beignets instead?" Darwin asked, as if he was a gracious host, eager to please.

"The only white powder I want anywhere near my face starts with the letter C and ends with *go fuck yourself, Darwin*."

Darwin gave a terse smile. "Very well. I had hoped you would've taken my admonitions at your brother's nuptials to heed."

"I thought I told you to use words from this century."

"Which one was confusing to you, Charles?"

"Not confused. Annoyed."

"I share that sentiment," Darwin said with a frown. He opened the envelope and slid a stack of photos across the table. "I thought we were on the same page about preserving the reputations of both you and my sister leading up to the wedding."

Charles glanced at one photo and realized he had no need to look at any of the others. He knew what they were. And he knew, then, finally, what Darwin's game had been all along.

"These will be great additions to my photo albums," Charles quipped.

"Those aren't the originals. I still have those."

"Why would you keep dozens of photos of me fucking women who aren't your sister, Darwin? You into that sort of thing?"

"Your repeated use of my name in conversation is rather unnerving, I must say."

"So is your choice of subjects for your photography hobby," Charles challenged. "Everyone has their kinks, I guess."

"I didn't take these. I hired someone, assuming you'd go against our promise," Darwin said with a smug twitch of his lower lip.

"Promise? I never promised anything."

"You seemed clear on the risk of compromising your reputation at this crucial period in the engagement."

Charles leaned forward. He enjoyed the slight recoil of his host. "And yet, the only risk here is from you. The only one coming forward with blackmail, is you."

"Blackmail!" Darwin declared, clutching his chest with mock offense. "I would never, especially not to a man who will be my family in such short order."

"And yet you aren't here to buy me coffee and donuts."

"I'm *here* because you are a danger to yourself, and to your family!"

"None of the tabloids have approached me with this bullshit. I haven't seen this on the news. Not a single other person has said a word about it."

"The point is, it very well could be on the news, because you've shown no discretion whatsoever!"

Charles tapped the table, grinning. "Cut the shit. You don't care about your sister, her reputation, or her happiness. These pictures have value to you. Don't they?"

"That's not why I'm here."

Charles jumped to his feet. "Great! Then you'll see that these are destroyed, and we can all go on our merry way."

Darwin rose across from him. "Don't you understand that I've done you a great favor here? I'm saving you from yourself!"

Charles smiled. "You think you're too much of a gentleman to call this blackmail, so what should we call it? Extortion?"

"I've helped you, and you can help me now. It seems fair,"

Darwin replied, with an overly exaggerated attempt at sounding reasonable.

"And if I don't help you, you'll... what, exactly?"

"I wouldn't do anything, though imagine if these fell into the wrong hands? Files are lost every day. The local gossip rags would have a field day."

"I see."

"But that doesn't have to happen. Your reputation need see no blights as a result of your foolish liaisons. Let the world believe you've matured with taking a bride, and no one has to be the wiser."

"How much and why?"

"I was hoping we could discuss this like—"

"How much and *why*, Darwin?"

Darwin sighed. He straightened his tie with a look to see if anyone was listening. The only three other couples in the café were caught up in their own discussions. "We need two hundred and fifty thousand dollars to make good on an investment, or we have to file next week. You may not think this is your problem, but your wife's name is attached to this business, and solvency will harm the name your family enjoys so effortlessly."

"Does this come naturally to you?"

"What?"

"Being a total piece of shit."

Darwin blinked, seemingly deciding whether this was a serious question.

Charles reached for his wallet, then stopped. No. This worm would pay. "I'll have the firm draw up a check tomorrow. But let's be clear, *Darwin.* This is the last check I will ever write you. I couldn't care less what happens to your father's silly little textile business, or to you or your sister. I can call this wedding off and be better for it. *You* need *me*, and for someone who thinks they know so much, you really don't know anything about me. You don't know what I'm capable of. What I've done. And what I will do if you *ever come to me asking for money again.*"

. . .

Augustus leaned against the doorway, watching his wife craft a letter at the roll top desk in the corner of the dining room. It was a decorative piece, not meant for serious work. He assumed it had been used at one point in the family's history, since according to the Sullivans it was an original piece from a bygone era, but in today's world of excess it was no more than a lovely prop. He'd encouraged Ekatherina to use the one in the office he'd set up for her. But she was drawn to this tiny desk, forgotten by time, relegated to the corner like a set piece one is aware of but rarely acknowledges.

Except Ekatherina, who sought her comfort and happiness in the familiarity and modesty of home.

It was in these subtle, but important, choices that Augustus found peace in his decision to make Ekatherina his bride. He knew what his family thought. Not just Evangeline, either. He saw it in the eyes of all of them, even his mother, who seemed as if she couldn't decide whether to be happy for him or desperately afraid.

If Ekatherina wanted Augustus' money, she could have had it far sooner. The others didn't see her hesitation had been for this very reason... this fear that all her hard work would be nothing in the shadow of the man who had everything. Even more than she desired to have her family here, she wanted it to be the result of her own hard work. She wanted to look her family in the eye, as they stepped off the plane, knowing she'd brought them here, just as she promised the day she left.

But money wasn't her problem. She'd saved every last penny after her meager expenses were paid, and she had more than enough.

"Who're you writing to?" he asked.

Ekatherina jumped in her seat. She turned her head over her shoulder with a sad smile. "My sister. Anasofiya. Mammochka's last letter has me worried."

"Is your sister unwell?" Augustus wondered if this was the right word. Anasofiya had been unwell since before Ekatherina left the Soviet Union. But he knew nothing of the illness ailing her, or the severity. He didn't know how to ask if what made his wife's sister sick would eventually take her life, or merely inconvenience it.

Ekatherina nodded. "She cannot get appointment with doctor for months. She cannot leave bed. I tell Mammochka we bring them here soon, that they be patient and all will be well."

Augustus internalized a heavy sigh. He'd been working up the courage to tell her that his letters to the embassy had gone unanswered. His calls had been lost in a sea of bureaucracy, and when he did finally reach someone, he was told that due to increased tensions between the countries, all requests for new VISAs were on hold. For how long, no one knew. In the past, they said, the holds had sometimes been days, and sometimes months. The harried office worker further explained that there were job cuts now impacting intake, and the rumor around the office was that the delays would become indefinite. "I'm sorry to tell you, you're in for a hell of a wait."

He had half a mind to fly to New York and persuade them in the way only Augustus Deschanel could. But the pall this would leave over his marriage... this deliberate tainting of something he wished to keep pure... kept him at bay. The Deschanels might see this as his value, but he wanted to start anew with his wife and new family.

Meanwhile, Ekatherina's loneliness and despondency grew more worrisome by the day. She still put in her long hours at the office, and her work hadn't suffered. But she spent her weekends resting or writing letters home, or sometimes on the porch swing, staring blankly into the distance. Although they shared a bed, it was mainly ceremonial, as they'd made love only once, the night of their wedding. Augustus was afraid to proposition her, though a part of him knew very well that's what a husband should do, but she gave no indication she would want such a thing in any case. The pit growing in his stomach was born of his fear she didn't want him, and the knowledge that he *did* want her. Desperately. More than he'd ever wanted anyone or anything in his whole life. He'd puzzled for months over what drew him to the shy young woman revolutionizing his finance team, but perhaps Charles was right for once: Love wasn't supposed to make sense.

If Madeline were here, she would know what to do. She was an expert on the matters of despair, and would have advice for how he should help his new wife through whatever she was experiencing. She would know the right things to say and coach him away from making grievous errors that would harm her psyche further.

But she wasn't here. Madeline was gone, and Ekatherina was retreating further and further into her melancholy. When he casually mentioned it to Evangeline, her reaction first disappointed, and then surprised him.

"If you're asking me to heal her, it doesn't work that way, bro. Healers mend the physical sickness in a person. If we could fix the mind? The heart? They'd call us goddamn miracle workers."

"I don't know that she needs fixing, exactly," Augustus had said, regretting opening his mouth at all. Anytime he dipped his head above the surface of life, he wished he hadn't.

"What she needs is something to get her mind off whatever's bothering her. Look, I know you're going to hate this idea, because you're you, but did you ever consider she might have enjoyed a honeymoon?"

"A honeymoon?"

"Yes, you know, it's what newlyweds—"

"I know what a honeymoon is, Evangeline." The thought had never once crossed his mind. In deciding that Ekatherina was a woman more comfortable with less means, he'd also, inadvertently, placed her in a box of his own making. One where he knew what she wanted, rather than asking.

"I'm sure you also know what a smile is, but I rarely see you use one."

"I don't waste them, is what you mean."

"Semantics, preaches the miserable man."

"I'm not miserable."

"Your wife is. According to you. You have my advice... take her on a trip. Just the two of you. Forget the business for a couple of weeks. It will run fine in your absence, much as I know that pains you to admit."

"I only hire the best," he said, both a defense and an agreement. "But Ekatherina wasn't raised with excess like vacations."

"Don't you think that's even more of a reason to give her such an incredible gift?"

Augustus would have given his wife the world, if he thought she wanted it. "Maybe," he'd said, but the idea was planted and began to take immediate root.

Another fortuitous interaction helped the idea take shape into something actionable. He'd been having lunch with one of his investors, a real estate mogul, Jeremy Anderle. Augustus mentioned casually that he'd been toying with the idea of vacation, and Jeremy had said, "Augustus, a man of your means should be investing in properties, not renting them. Second, third, fourth homes. You wanna take a vacation? Holiday at one of your own places. Costa Rica... the Maldives."

Real estate investments were a staple of the Deschanel fortune, and Augustus was abashed he'd never considered this as a way to grow and protect his own wealth. "I don't think Ekatherina would enjoy the beach much. It may be a shock to her, compared to what she's used to."

"The cold darkness of Russia? In that case, I've got just the place."

Jeremy had a packet sent over the following day, of a property off the coast of Maine, in the icy waters of the North Atlantic. The old Victorian home sat on a small island, Summer Island, with a population of under three hundred. The only way to reach the tiny crop of land was an hour by ferry from Portland mainland. The home itself was beautiful, ominous, holding court over its stretch of coastline like a novel by Daphne du Maurier come to life.

Anyone else would have sent the proposal back. A remote island in the Atlantic? But Augustus, who was still not entirely sold on the idea of a vacation, saw immediately the allure of something that felt a hell of a lot more like an escape than a retreat.

He appeared behind his wife and kissed the top of her head. "I'll take that to the post office for you."

"Thank you, husband."

"Would you like me to bring anything home? I could stop by the market."

"No. Thank you."

Augustus slipped the envelope into his inside jacket pocket. "Ekatherina... I was thinking. Maybe it would be nice if we got away for a while."

"Away? You want go away?"

"No, I mean... yes, in a manner of speaking. More of a vacation. Somewhere different... quiet. Cold, even." Augustus tensed as he awaited her reaction. The pit in his stomach blossomed.

Ekatherina looked away. She leaned back in her chair and her head fell to the side. "I do not like the heat of New Orleans."

Augustus nearly doubled over in relief. "The place I'm thinking of gets quite cold in the fall and winter. I was thinking we could leave at the start of fall, after Huck's wedding. Gives me time to get things set up at DMG before we go..."

"Where is it?"

"Summer Island, Maine. It's in the North Atlantic Ocean. I looked on a map, and it's not quite as far north as where you're from, but the weather this time of year looks to be comparable."

Ekatherina turned in her chair and smiled at him. Not the smiles he was used to, born of her desire to please him, but a real one, from somewhere new. "I would be much pleased, husband."

Augustus touched her cheek with one palm and pulled her mouth to his for a kiss. Brief. Wonderful.

When it was over, she was still smiling.

He'd do anything to see this smile for the rest of their lives.

CHAPTER 5

Just Sometimes

Elizabeth set her jaw. She was rarely this frustrated with Connor, because Connor *got it,* but Connor definitely wasn't *getting it* now.

He was afraid. His fears of the world had always been his Achilles' heel, though they were also what made him so open to believing when she showed him who she was, and what she could do. He'd never doubted, even from the beginning, because in the world Connor Sullivan lived in, bad things not only could but *did* happen, and frequently. They were predetermined. Predisposed. Perfectly terrible. Of *course* she could see the future! And of course everything she saw was a horror show. That made sense to him and fit with his image of the world.

Well, she hadn't expected this to be easy. Even with someone more open-minded, it would be a hard sell.

"I've tried everything," she countered with a heavy exhale. "If *Tante* Ophelia says there's no way, then there's no way. She's the closest thing we have to an expert about peering into the future, and when we tried to prove her wrong, remember how that worked out? I need a break from this, Connor. Just *sometimes.* You of all people know what I go through."

Connor looked appropriately shamed at the dig. "You know I'd do anything for you, Lizzy."

"Except this."

"You act like I'm a monster. I'm trying to help you!"

Elizabeth's hands gripped her hips. The anger that was in her, always, her constant companion, rippled through from neck to feet. "Tell me, Connor, how are you helping me?"

He dropped his eyes. "By trying to be your friend."

"Sorry you have to *try* to be my friend!"

"Lizzy, that's not fair!"

Elizabeth scoffed and turned away from him, pacing the room. No, it wasn't fair, but nothing was fair, and that was the whole point, wasn't it? Nothing had ever been fair for Elizabeth Deschanel, and was it so wrong that she was looking for even transient relief to that problem?

"There has to be another way." Connor made as if to approach her, but thought better of it and wrapped his arms across his chest instead. "I joined you in that harebrained scheme to try and change the future. I'm up for almost anything, you know that. Anyone else would have walked away, or told you that you were crazy, but not me."

"You think I'm crazy?"

Connor's cheeks flushed. "I've never thought that, Elizabeth."

"What did I say about calling me Elizabeth, huh?"

"It gets your attention, so I'll use it if I have to."

"If you overuse it, it will stop having the desired effect, ever think of that, *Connor*?"

Connor groaned. His arms tightened across his chest. "You're trying to change the subject. I haven't forgotten, you know. And you're my favorite person, so turning my words around just hurts me. If I didn't care about you, I'd be the first person to hand you the heroin. If you just want a friend who agrees with everything you say, then any of the girls at my school will do."

Elizabeth paused and watched her dearest, oldest friend. He kept his words direct to hide the genuine hurt behind them, which played out in his eyes and in the twitch of his mouth. She'd terrified him with her idea to try heroin to shut off her visions, and then made it worse by acting as if *he* was the villain for trying to talk her down. And he was right... any of the girls, in any of the schools she'd gone to, would have watched her in anticipation of an exciting story to spread around later. Connor loved her, and he put that above any potential thrill he might get.

This was going all wrong.

Elizabeth stepped forward. Her bare feet tangled in the shag carpet as she walked, she was so tense. With both hands, she unfolded his arms and wrapped herself in them. Connor stiffened and then relented.

"You don't think I'm afraid, too?" she asked, releasing the words into his chest, where his heart beat so fast she thought he might have a heart attack. But that wasn't the future she'd seen for him. In many ways, what lay ahead for Connor was worse. "I've never done anything bad in my life. Never partied, like Huck. Never slept around, like Maureen. I can't remember the last time I lied to my mother, unless it was about the visions, and you see, they ruin my life in so many ways. I know they won't go away, but if I can block them even sometimes, I can find peace. I've never had any interest in getting high, but if this is the only way..."

"Why does it have to be the only way?" Connor pleaded.

"Do you know of another that we haven't tried?"

His arms ran up and down her back. His chin fell atop her head, and she felt the shuddering sigh all the way from his chest to his jaw. "People die from drugs, Lizzy."

Elizabeth tried not to smile. She was getting through to him. Slowly. "They die from using too much. We don't need more than a little. We're not trying to go crazy here, just take the edge off."

"I'm sure that's what all drug addicts say in the beginning," Connor muttered.

"People use drugs recreationally all the time, without having a problem," Elizabeth defended.

"Don't use your brother as example, for the love of God."

Elizabeth laughed. "He's not a *bad* example. He knows when to stop."

"Before or after he got kicked off every college campus in New Orleans?"

"He would've been kicked out stone sober. Some would say the drugs make him more tolerable."

Connor exhaled. His grip on her loosened. "We wouldn't even know what to do. We're not professional druggies. I couldn't even tell you if you smoke heroin or snort it!"

"Most shoot it." Elizabeth left her hands looped around his back and pulled away so she could see him. "But I know someone in the neighborhood who sells marijuana cigarettes laced with heroin. They say that's a great way to get started."

"Get started," Connor scoffed. "Like we're training for a marathon."

It might be like that, if this works. "I meant, for people like us, who've never done it. They say it's better and safer."

"You keep saying 'they,' like you know them."

Elizabeth leaned up and kissed him on the mouth. She felt his surprise. They'd kissed a few times since that first one, months back, but neither of them knew what *this* was anymore, and every kiss confused the matter further.

"You're evil," he whispered.

"You love me anyway."

The look that passed across his face sent a hard flutter through her stomach. "I would have rules, Lizzy."

"Name them."

"We stay here, in your room."

"Easy. Done."

"I mean it. We don't leave."

"I know. Next?"

Connor untangled himself from Elizabeth and chewed his nails. Both hands were a mangled mess, and when he was with others, he often looked for ways to hide them, so others wouldn't see. Now, he seemed unaware of the need. "We agree it's one time only, until we're sober again and can talk about it like rational adults."

Elizabeth grinned. "Is that what we are?"

"I'm not kidding."

"Fine. Fine. Anything else?"

Connor winced at the blood prickling to the surface of his thumb. The side of his knuckle was littered with such scars. "One time. And we won't even think about doing it again unless we *both* agree. Both of us. Both. Of. Us."

"Sure, okay," Elizabeth said, impatient, exhilarated.

"I mean it!"

"Heaven's sake, Connor, I know you do!"

Connor turned away. He focused his gaze out the window, which she knew he did when he was afraid looking at her would weaken his resolve. "I can't believe I'm agreeing to this. Jesus. Okay... we need to set a date. Maybe first week of summer?"

"Tonight."

Connor spun back around, eyes popping from his head. "Tonight?"

"Tonight," she repeated firmly.

MAUREEN BENT TO WATER THE TWO FICUS TREES flanking Mr. Blanchard's office. The task warranted very little complexity or thought, but she tended to the plants with all the care of a concerned mother doting on a colicky infant.

She watched him through the open door. Mr. Blanchard tapped his fountain pen against the desk with increasing intensity as he shuffled through a stack of paperwork from the folder Maureen delivered earlier. The small sounds he made as he processed his thoughts were only a step below talking to himself.

When she noticed him look up, she made a quick point of leaning over the plant, bending neatly at the hips, to examine a browning leaf. He didn't indicate that he'd seen the display, but she knew, as she knew all men never missed her important but subtle gestures.

He'd been noticing her a lot, too. Nothing about this was surprising, and he'd never said anything even bordering on inappropriate. Sure, some of the things he asked her to do were weird. Like the stuff with the pencils. Or when he had her stand high upon a ladder, for over ten minutes, so he could gauge the proper height for a painting. She watched over her shoulder to see what he was doing to measure, but he only stood and watched her. He never did hang a painting there, either.

She could handle weird, especially from a middle-aged man who'd never been married and didn't know how to be around women.

The biddies had gone home two hours ago. They always punched their timecards at the exact moment the clock struck 5:30, not a minute later. They'd exit the building, giggling at their inside jokes that were always, always about other people. Maureen liked to wait until 5:40, when she could be sure the streetcar had swept those women back to their miserable lives. The few times she'd walked out with them, or walked out too soon, she'd deeply regretted it. In the office, Maureen could disappear into her work. She still heard them, flocked together like a gaggle of geese as they shuffled their girdled bodies around, pretending to be doing something more productive than gossiping. Outside, she had neither the shelter of the office nor the shield of her favored position with the boss to protect her from their mean-spirited targeting.

It was now past 7:30, and she'd never stayed this late. She knew better. Mr. Blanchard was a spendthrift who declared he'd never pay a cent over the thirty hours scheduled for his secretaries, and Maureen took this to heart. She never expected to be paid for the ten minutes additional she used to avoid the other women each evening—though he did pay her, and without complaint.

But tonight was different. Maureen felt a keen urge to be defiant, and to see what he did with that disobedience.

Six o'clock rolled around. Then 6:30. Then 7:00. He said nothing, and her tension mounted. What if this was a test? Would he fire her for her insolence? Did he say nothing because he was marking ticks on the sheet of grievances against her, waiting to see how far she'd go? Besides, she'd watered the plants to the point they were probably drowning to death.

Maureen's heart was a thumping mess, and she wondered if she shouldn't just go home before he *did* fire her.

She tucked the watering can under her arm and headed in the direction of the janitor's closet.

"Miss Deschanel."

Mr. Blanchard's voice stopped her. The blood in her veins hardened to ice. She turned.

"Before you head home for the night, I'd like your help."

Her tension dissipated. He wasn't mad. He had noticed her. He'd seen how useful she could be and wanted her help.

Maureen set the can down by a nearby desk and slowly approached the door to his office. He beckoned her in.

"Yes, Mr. Blanchard?"

"This blueprint on my desk is for a new bank my client wants to build in Carrollton."

Maureen leaned forward to marvel at the detailed rendering with the appropriate level of enthusiasm. "He'll love it. It's incredible."

"She. Mrs. Kerensky is a petite woman, who has, in the past, complained about the width of my blueprints, as she struggles to hold them."

This seemed a most curious thing to complain about, but Maureen nodded.

"Due to this, I tried to work within smaller boundaries, and I suspect you're about her size."

Maureen couldn't guess where this was going. "Tell me how I can help."

Mr. Blanchard stood. He turned the blueprint around, so it faced Maureen, and then spread it wide across the surface of the desk. He pulled the corners taught with paperweights.

He came around behind her. "Lean forward. Like this." He demoed the request by spreading his hands so they reached each corner. "Go ahead."

Maureen's pulse soared. There were many ways to solve problems, she knew, and this was a particularly strange way to solve this one. Was there not a measurement tool he could use? A more technical way?

She did as asked, leaning forward into the desk. The blueprint was wider than it looked, and her arms were spread so far to the sides that she was folded almost completely over. Her face pressed into the soft paper, with nowhere else to go.

"Like this?"

Mr. Blanchard backed away. "Yes, Miss Deschanel."

"Did it work? Is it the right size?"

"Be silent a moment. I'll let you know."

Moments passed and turned to minutes. She imagined he had his tools and was marking down the measurements, or whatever it was he did, but his tools were on the desk, and she'd heard him settle into the chair across the room.

Her arms ached from the unnatural position. Her calves had started to tremble as they wobbled in her high heels. A fresh heat soared through her body as blood coursed in unfamiliar directions.

She wished she could see a clock. How much time had passed? More than minutes. And how many since she heard his zipper? The soft movement of flesh moving flesh?"

Mr. Blanchard grunted. The sound was quick, clipped, like it had been scheduled ahead of time for precisely half a second. His zipper came up, and she felt the air change as he approached her.

He leaned past and over her and reached for a pencil. Jotted a quick note. As he pulled away, the pencil landed on the edge of her shoulder. He traced it down over her back, through to the seam on her skirt, and then it passed *under* her skirt and rested at the precise spot where she'd grown damp from the confusion... from the secret knowledge of what had happened.

Maureen stifled a moan. The pencil sat there, unmoving. The

urge to press herself back onto it... onto him... left a sour longing in her belly.

"Most helpful, Miss Deschanel," he said finally. He removed the pencil. "You may go home."

THE RUSH OF PLEASURE WAS IMMEDIATE AND overpowering. Elizabeth fell back against her pillow with a sigh that didn't sound like her. Wasn't her. Beside her, Connor moaned.

They didn't even finish the joint. Two hits, they each took, and that was enough. It was too much. It was exactly right. The rest smoldered in the ashtray they'd found in Charles' room.

"Touch me," she whispered.

"What?"

"I'm going to open my mind and look for your future. Touch me."

Her eyes avoided the growing lump near his groin. It happened a lot now, and she was both afraid of it, and desperately excited that she had caused it, and that it could be hers. He was hers, and always had been, and she was his, but she wasn't ready to explore what that really meant.

Connor wrapped his hand in hers, and she closed her eyes and cleared her mind. Clearing it was both hard and easy... there was nothing there, thanks to the rush of euphoria... the heaven that replaced the hell she lived in every day.

She searched, and searched, but it was pointless. There was nothing.

Nothing except the two of them.

Nothing except the bliss.

SUMMER 1974

VACHERIE, LOUISIANA
NEW ORLEANS, LOUISIANA
SUMMER ISLAND, MAINE

CHAPTER 6
Revelations

The day started with one of the Broussard kids screaming about the swamp turning red.

Charles didn't know where Cordelia was. Supposedly she was still getting ready, though Maureen had whispered to him that she'd just been lounging on the couch in the bridal suite without a care. He searched for her, then followed the buzz of the wedding party and guests rushing toward the reedy cypress bog at the back property line of Ophélie.

"Jesus wept, it *is* red!" Pansy cried. She pulled her husband, Placide, to the front of the gathered crowd, dragging her parasol across the ground behind her. "Look at that!"

Her father, Pierce, crossed himself and whispered, "With the staff that is in my hands I will strike the water of the Nile, and it will be changed into blood."

"Daddy, how many times have I told you to stop quoting the Bible when ain't no one ask you for it?"

Irish Colleen frowned in deep contemplation. "If that's not the strangest thing..."

Charles blew out a breath. "That's not really in the Bible, is it?"

"Exodus 7:14," his mother replied without pause. "But don't

you pay your superstitious cousins no mind, Charles. Today is a blessed day, not one for silly worries or end of the world scripture."

"It isn't *nothing,* Cousin Colleen," Pansy countered. "It's the first plague of Revelations!"

"Or," Evangeline said, appearing in a gap of family. "It's an excess of nutrients... iron... algae. You know, scientific explanations not involving some magical grandpa in the sky."

"You take it back, Evangeline," Pansy warned.

"Nah."

Pansy's brows rose, scandalized. "I'll pray for you."

"You think this is normal, then?" Charles asked. The morning was warming up, but not yet hot enough to explain the sweat accumulating at his brow and the nape of his neck. "Nothing to worry about?"

"It's not a Biblical prophecy foretelling the end of the world, no," Evangeline said. "As for whether you should worry..."

Colleen kissed his cheek. "Really. Everyone's imaginations are just going wild. Now, if a plague of locusts appear, or fire rains down from the sky as hail..."

"It *is* cloudy..." Augustus added helpfully.

"Nobody fucking asked you for the weather report," Charles said.

Colin broke through at his side. He tapped his watch and mopped his brow with the other hand. "We're already ten minutes off schedule, Charles. You should be saying your vows." He turned to Colleen. "I'll corral everyone back to their seats if you can go tap Franz to get Cordelia ready to walk?"

THANK GOD FOR HIS BEST MAN, BECAUSE CHARLES wouldn't have known where to show up, when, or even if he should. He'd had cold feet all night, and only Colin dragging him through the motions of waking, dressing, and aiming him in the right direction had led him to this point.

Colleen nodded. "The rest of the bridal party is all accounted for?"

"Weatherly hasn't run off with a bridesmaid. Yet," Evangeline quipped.

"No, but he's been calling himself a pallbearer rather than a groomsman," Augustus said.

"The bridesmaids are even more stuffy than the bride," Elizabeth pointed out.

"I'll make sure they're ready and in position, and that the organist is in his seat," Colin said to Colleen. "Think five minutes is enough for the bride?"

Maureen looped her arm through Colleen's. She smiled sweetly. "Oh, we'll make sure it's enough. I have an especial relationship with Franz."

Everyone but Charles gave her a funny look. He suppressed a grin.

Colin clapped his shoulder. "And you? All ready?"

Ready to live? Ready to die?

Both?

Neither?

And where is Cat?

"Yeah. All good."

NEXT CAME THE INSECTS.

They started their assault when Cordelia was already halfway down the aisle. When she first started waving her hands around her, Charles assumed it was a physical representation of the same sinking disgust he was feeling as he tried to keep his sweaty hands from reaching for the flask inside his tuxedo.

Then, the guests seated at the back followed suit, and the gestures poured forward over the crowd in a dark, grainy wave that only became clearer as it neared the bridal party standing dumbfounded at the altar.

"Are those… bees?" Colin asked, one hand at his forehead, the other shielding himself from the inevitable onslaught.

"Locusts!" Pansy cried. "I will bring locusts into your country tomorrow. They will cover the face of the ground so that it cannot be seen."

"Told ya," mumbled Dan.

"They are not locusts, and you're not impressing anyone with your Bible verses, Pansy," Irish Colleen said with her best, *you hush now* voice. But the look on her face did not sell the message quite so well.

"Do we even get locusts here?" One of Cordelia's bridesmaids made a contribution to the day. Charles didn't know her name. No point in learning it. The women here were not Cordelia's friends, but rather, daughters of her father's colleagues.

Augustus grumbled as he leaned over to Colin. "I told them not to clear the cane until next week. Damn it all."

He marched off, unbuttoning his tuxedo jacket as he pushed through the crowd of panicked onlookers and the swarm of whatever had come barreling out of the cane when it no longer had a home.

Cordelia closed her eyes. Her bouquet fell to the side and her lips moved, though she seemed now oblivious to everything around her. Was she meditating? Summoning her personal demon?

It took thirty minutes to sort out the mess of bugs and disgruntled guests. Augustus and the hired ushers eventually moved the chairs and trellis to the front of Ophélie, and out of the path of the exodus of insects.

Colin smiled tersely from his side as the music started back up. Even the faces amongst the crowd had dropped the pretense that this was a happy day.

"Grasshoppers," Augustus murmured to himself. "Not locusts. Not locusts."

The fact he felt compelled to clarify only put a finer point on this second plague of Charles' wedding day.

. . .

THE PRONUNCIATION OF THEIR UNION OF MAN AND WIFE was marked by a very sudden and powerful downfall of rain, which quickly evolved to hail and then...

"These are rocks!" one guest cried, and then others followed suit with similar proclamations of horror and wonder.

"We should tell them all to go home," Cordelia remarked. The ring on her finger, that Charles had put there moments ago, glittered in the onslaught of water from the heavens. "Did what we came here to do."

"My mother would have a conniption if she didn't get her party," Charles said as they rushed forward for cover, traipsing up the broad porch. Whoever said the hail had turned to rocks wasn't kidding... and Charles didn't know what to make of it.

"I've read about this," Evangeline said, panting. Her wild curls were soaked and flat against her face, for a change. "It's rare, but it happens."

"I'll be," Augustus said with a sigh. He tousled his soaked hair and flapped his jacket. "If that's not the damnedest thing."

"It's going to fucking dent my car!" Charles cried. Richard was leading a refurbishment of the old livery, so he'd parked his baby outside yesterday.

"Yeah, this is the end for her," Elizabeth said.

"What?"

Elizabeth shrugged.

Irish Colleen pulled her shawl tight and turned to address the tightly-packed crowd on the porch. "I suppose this is our sign to head inside for the party!" she announced, with nervous laughter.

"So the Lord rained hail on Egypt," Pansy whispered with a shake of the head.

As the thick crowd shuffled through the double doors, Charles pulled his cousin aside.

"What are you talking about? Why do you keep talking like you're Jesus?"

"God," Pansy corrected. "I'm quoting God, by way of His most holy book, the Bible."

Charles rolled his hands through the air. "Yeah, I get that. Why?"

"Cousin Charles!" Pansy exclaimed, with both bejeweled hands clutched over her heart. "You've had no less than three of the plagues of Egypt accompany your wedding day!"

Charles frowned. He'd never read the Bible, beyond the verses their mother sometimes made them read at dinner when they were younger. "Is that a bad thing?"

Pansy laughed.

Colin clapped a hand on his shoulder. "Be that as it may, all of these things come with logical explanations. Don't listen to superstition, Charles. Not today, of all days."

"Of all days! You think it's coincidence the Good Lord chose *today of all days* to rain down hell upon Charles?" Pansy asked.

"I think summer storms are common in Louisiana," Colin said, pressing his lips tight in growing consternation. Pansy was a tough one to take for anyone, but especially a pragmatic Sullivan who never liked even the hint of something supernatural to take front and center in a conversation. "And the cane was just cut. The grasshoppers had to go somewhere."

"And the swamp?"

"Evangeline explained that... where did she go?"

"Evangeline is too smart for her own damn good," Pansy answered. "And science has its purposes, but not when it lets us veer from God and His message!"

"Pansy, let's not quote too much scripture, lest you piss off your voodoo gods, yeah?" Maureen said as she passed by with a knowing look and disappeared inside the house.

Augustus ushered folks past, encouraging them not to dally at the door. With a wink at Charles, he nudged Pansy through and the crowd behind her prevented her from turning back.

When it was just Charles and his brother, Augustus said, "No one expected this marriage to be a match made in heaven, right? So who cares about God and his Biblical messages? You already knew what you were getting into. The others just want something to gossip about."

"I really have to go in there, don't I? Dance with her? Touch her?"

Augustus looped an arm around his shoulder. "Tonight, yes. But after? Charles, when has anything ever stopped you from doing what you want?"

Charles stared ahead, through the doors of the plantation that was his, and was now also Cordelia's, and if fate was kind, his son's.

"If you tell anyone I gave you this advice, I'll deny it," Augustus said. "But you only need to get and keep her pregnant, Huck. That's it. This is the beginning of your legacy, but it doesn't need to be the end of anything else, not if you don't want it to be. Yeah?"

Charles nodded, and the smile slowly reappeared. That Augustus would even suggest this belied the bigger truth, that even Augustus could not deny the horror show this marriage would become. But he said the words out of both love and practicality, and Charles had never felt closer to him. Augustus was the family fixer, but it went beyond anything supernatural. He knew what they needed, and he delivered.

Charles let his head rest on Augustus' shoulder for a brief moment and then nodded deeper this time. "Yeah. You're right, brother. You're right."

CHARLES WONDERED IF HE WAS THE ONLY BRIDEGROOM who'd ever intentionally, and successfully, avoided their own bride for the duration of the reception.

He couldn't take full credit. Cordelia had clearly masterminded some of the evasion herself, such as when she'd been on a "bathroom break" during the call for first dance, or how she'd managed to break the heel on her shoe just as toasts began. The second took forethought, and Charles admired her, however briefly.

But as the last of the guests filtered out, just past one in the morning, he feared being alone with her. Not only that night, but all nights, and he thought back to Augustus' words, *this doesn't need to be the end of anything else,* and could think of nothing else.

Irish Colleen was the last to leave, on the arm of Augustus. She looked radiant that night, and Charles had noticed it but not really seen it, not until she regarded him with sleepy, proud eyes. He sometimes forgot how young she was.

"You've made me so proud, son," she said. She craned on tiptoes to kiss him, and he leaned down to meet her. Her tiny hands patted his arms as they embraced. "You're living up to your father's greatness, and that is no small thing."

"Thank you, Mama."

Augustus smiled over their mother's head. "Father was a good man, but you're your own man, Huck. One day, someone will say to *your* son that they are living up to yours."

Charles blinked to erase the evidence of tears and closed the door behind them both.

Cordelia was nowhere to be found. She hadn't stayed to thank their guests as they departed, and he wondered, for a moment, if she'd left as well.

Charles loosened his tie and ascended the stairs.

HE FOUND HIS WIFE IN THE BEDROOM. CORDELIA SAT upon the bed, rigid, hands folded. She wore a nightgown that was so matronly that, on anyone else, he'd think it an attempt at humor. Her spine formed such a straight line that he wondered if it pained her to keep it so, and then, secretly, hoped for exactly that.

"I hope you can perform with expediency," she said. "I'm wearied, but I know my duty and will not be said to have shirked it for my own comfort."

"Sorry?"

Cordelia's head, only her head, turned in his direction. "I'm exhausted. I know we need to fuck. Can you come quickly?"

Charles laughed. He didn't know how else to respond... how else to address the horror at these words, which might actually be funny coming from someone else. But they came from his wife. His *wife.* Charles' blood raced to his head in a rush. Wife.

"Can you?"

Charles inhaled a deep breath. "I can try."

"Do that." Cordelia lay back against the bed with all the tight control of a robot. She slid down her underwear and lifted her gown as high as her stomach. "It's been a while, so I'll remind you of the rules. Clothes on. You may remove your pants, of course, out of necessity, but I'll ask you to keep a shirt on. You get five minutes. No kissing. No talking. I'll make whatever sounds you want, but if you touch me anywhere above the neck, I reserve the right to abort with no questions asked."

"Is that all?"

"I can create more."

Charles swallowed. This was wrong, all wrong. All of it. The way she lay, crudely sprawled but without any of the sexuality that would normally accompany such an image, made him feel like a predator, not a man. The thick swatch of dark hair between her legs did not beckon him, it repulsed him. It went beyond the physical and attached a deep disgust directly to his soul, like a passenger.

But he did not come this far to punk out at the moment of truth.

Charles dropped his pants and underwear to the floor. He started to unbutton his shirt, and almost heard the *tsk* from his wife, and remembered himself.

He approached the bed. Cordelia wore a bored, but impatient look. He couldn't do this. He had to do this.

Charles climbed up and fell over her. Her face curled in annoyance at their closeness, and he wanted to bark at her that there was nothing he could do.

She reached her hand forward and grabbed him so suddenly that he gasped. "Limp. Clock is ticking."

"This isn't helping."

"I'm not here to help," she said. "I'm here to be the vessel by which your children come into the world. Nothing more."

"Right." Charles closed his eyes and tried to think of something that might stir him, but there was no image strong enough to erase the reality waiting underneath him.

But he was a man, and her hand against his organ, no matter how unwelcome, gave it the tiniest spark of life, and that was enough.

Charles pushed against Cordelia's thatch of hair and entered her. Her expression didn't change. She may as well have been enjoying an afternoon nap.

He thrust against her, at first slowly, afraid of angering or annoying her, but then faster and harder. He worked to convince himself he was enjoying the act, when he had never in all his life been so averse to sex as he was with his wife, in this moment, on their wedding night.

"This is going nowhere," Cordelia remarked. Judge. Jury.

"Give me a minute," he replied, through gritted teeth.

"That's about all you have left."

Charles blocked her out. He tried to clear his mind, but there was no use in it. He knew where he was, and only one thing could take him away from here.

Catherine. He saw her in those red stilettos he'd bought her. She lay on her back with one heeled foot pressed into his chest. Her sex glistened for him. Called to him. *Huck. I want it dirty the first time.*

Charles cried out in shock as the orgasm rocked through him.

Cordelia smiled tightly, pulled her nightgown back into place, and rolled to her side.

CHAPTER 7

We All Have Our Paths

Clancy Sullivan was a tiny little thing. Although close to three months old, he could have passed for a child born that very day. But while he was small, his little limbs jabbed to and fro, and his smile lit up his whole cherubic face, and Colleen suspected his traumatic birth would not stop him from having a long and wonderful life.

"He's beautiful, Rory," Colleen said as she played with Clancy's baby toes. He was soft and warm in her arms. She realized how rarely she'd been around babies by how wondrous she found this child's feet. They were hardly anything at all, just whips of digits with the teensiest sliver of nails. She pinched them softly with her fingers and the chubbiness of the silken, unmarred skin was almost too much. Even more, the scent, which must be unique to babies, she thought, had the strange effect of stirring her womb.

She would look this up later, in one of her medical books. Surely there was a biological, if not evolutionary, connection to how strangely appealing babies were to women.

Clancy ripped out a peal of laughter. Rory squealed back in delight and went in with both hands to tickle his belly, probably hoping to elicit more of what Colleen thought had to be the purest joy she'd ever seen.

No, she thought. Rory's was the purest.

"He just started that a couple days ago," Rory said proudly. His face again dissolved into that of a bona fide tickle monster for the next few moments, before his mother, Josephine, emerged from the other room with a rag over her shoulder and a look of intense purpose.

This was Josephine Sullivan's first grandchild, and she took her new charge of grandmother very seriously.

"Time for a feeding, little lamb," Josephine said and lifted the infant into her arms to the soft protests of Rory. She smiled at Colleen. "It's so nice to see you again, Colleen. Please give your mother our warm regards."

"I will, Mrs. Sullivan."

"If we left it to Rory, he'd do nothing but play with the wee one," she added, though her consternation had a touch of admiration at the end.

"The temptation would be too much for me as well, I'm afraid."

"I guess she's the expert," Rory said when they were gone, with just the hint of an eye roll. They both laughed.

"You are lucky to have a mother who's here to help and knows just what to do."

"I am," he agreed, with a look toward the door they'd disappeared through. "Carolina couldn't even feed him for weeks. She'd try, God knows she wanted to so badly, and it just took so much from her. The doctor finally forbade it. It broke her heart and her spirit." He shook his head and sighed into his lap. "I can't thank you enough for what you did for her, Colleen. I wasn't sure..."

"No use in fussing over what might have been," she chided. She reached forward and tried to pat his leg, but the gesture, what remained of whatever had been between them, was so awkward she decided to keep her arms folded.

"You wish I didn't know this about you," Rory said.

"What?" Colleen asked and then laughed. No use in playing

coy. "What can be said about it? Some are born with the voice of an angel. Some can lay hands on another and heal."

He smiled. "There's not much to equate the two."

"No?" Colleen smiled back. "Still. I don't understand it myself. All I know is, it works, and as long as it does, I'll use it to help others."

"This is why you wanted to become a doctor."

Colleen looked to the side, thinking. He might not understand her desire to study who she was, and even dissect it. "Partly. It might seem like cheating, to know whatever science can't mend I can assist with... but I see it another way. That when God has given us a gift, we'd be foolish to waste it on principle."

"I don't think it's cheating. I think you have something no one else has, and you have an opportunity to use it for good. You *have* used it for good."

"Not no one else."

Rory's eyes widened. "You know someone else who can do this? Heal?"

"Evangeline," she said and wholly enjoyed his scandalized expression.

"How did I... so this must be a Deschanel thing. What about Charles? Augustus? The others?"

"I've already said too much," Colleen said with a wink.

"*You're* too much," he said.

"Besides," Colleen said, returning to the point. "I believe wholeheartedly in the purity of science. I intend to take whatever I learn in my studies, and whatever science and technology has allowed me to do, and push it to the fullest extent. When I hit a wall... that's where the other can come in."

Rory watched her. "You really are the most unusual person I've ever known."

"I won't ask 'how so,'" Colleen said with a guarded chuckle.

"Good, because I wasn't going to tell you!"

"When will the three of you leave for Boston?"

"Thanks to you, we should be able to leave by the end of

summer, in time for fall term. Carolina hated that her illness might have kept me from starting on time, but I don't think she realizes that none of this... law school, the future, none of it would be... without her..." Rory trailed off and checked the clock on the wall. "Carolina will be waking soon. I know your plane leaves in a few hours, but are you sure you won't stay and say hello? Or, goodbye, I suppose, since next time you're home, we'll be in another state."

Colleen rose. She looked around the room, one she'd seen many times growing up, as it was where Rory had grown up. It was different now... everything was different now. Rory was married to their mutual childhood friend, she was married to her future, and the world around them had already proven that none of this would ever come easy.

"Give her a kiss for me." She took Rory's hands in hers. "And you'll call me, if anything else happens? If anything comes up that you... need me for?"

Rory nodded. He kissed her cheek and then dropped her hands as he reached for the door. "You've already done so much, but I'd be lying if I said it wasn't a relief knowing my wife and child will always be safe as long as you're in our lives."

"I'll always be in your lives," Colleen said and immediately worried about the implication of such intimate words.

Rory smiled. "One day, I hope to be holding *your* little one, Colleen."

She laughed; stopped short of telling him that, on top of all these lovely abilities, the Deschanels were plagued by an ancient curse that she wasn't about to pass on to anyone else. "Doubtful."

"Maybe our children will play together. Hell, maybe they'll even date one day! Wouldn't that be something? My son, marrying your daughter?"

Colleen couldn't help but imagine such a future, caught up in his silliness, but she wouldn't lie, either. "Children aren't in my future."

He tapped the door and sighed. "What a shame that would be, if the best, most natural caregiver I know chose to forego an experience I can only describe as the best thing that's ever happened to me."

"We all have our paths, Rory."

Mine takes me far, far from here.

MAUREEN'S CALVES WERE ON FIRE. HER FEET TREMBLED in her heels, wobbling her balance. She'd lost track of time well over an hour ago, and from her unnatural angle, bent over Mr. Blanchard's desk, she had no view of a clock.

She'd wonder if he was still there, still paying attention, but a slight shift in her stance, an attempt to get comfortable, had him chiding her in an instant. Contrite, she'd grit her jaw and bite through the pain of the position.

A week ago, he'd ordered her to stop wearing panties to the office. He said it so casually, in passing, as she took the stack of folders from his arms. "Looks like it may rain," he remarked. "Miss Deschanel, I'll ask that you not wear underwear in my office again."

And then he walked off, and she replayed that conversation in her head at least a hundred times, looking for any other possible interpretation of his words.

The next day, trembling and naked under her skirt, she'd taken the streetcar and imagined every last businessman and woman seated knew her secret. Knew, and were judging, as God was likely judging.

She'd been so nervous as she stepped through the office. Had she heard him wrong? Maybe he'd ordered her never to bring glassware? Or neckwear? That seemed far more likely than hearing him *right,* though her peculiar boss had asked other things of her that were unorthodox.

But then he'd asked her to order Italian for him, and then followed the request with, "You did as I asked?"

"Yes... yes, sir."

"Good. Extra sauce on the meatballs, Miss Deschanel. Don't let them forget the parmesan this time. They always look for ways to cut costs at my expense, but damn if their meatballs aren't the best in town."

And now, spread wide for his perusal, Maureen understood this was an escalation of their previous late evening encounter in his office. She could pretend she hadn't heard him pleasuring himself—that familiar crisp zip of his pants—but pretending was the work of little girls, and Maureen was a woman. She knew she was a woman, for her boss was a man with exquisite tastes. He was no Peter Evers, seeking below his maturity to cover for the lack of his own.

Her sex throbbed. The air in the office had a light chill, and the exposure, combined with the occasional rumble and passing of air of the air conditioner across her flesh, teased her in a way she had never been able to tease herself. No man had made her this wet... had ever made her long to be entered like a wild animal, rutting away their primal instincts.

It was torture. Knowing he could see this, that he could see her desire laid so bare, made it all the more worse.

At last, she heard his clothing shift as he stood. His steps were the only sound in the room, the light presses and depresses, one after another, against the shag carpet.

Mr. Blanchard's hand cupped her right buttock. Squeezed, released, and then did it again, marveling in a light whisper at the supple responsiveness of her young flesh.

His fingers moved inward, toward the throb, which now sent the blood coursing toward her head in such a rush she saw stars. His fingers splayed along the outside of her vagina, in a fan. Then, the middle one dipped inside of her, and Maureen's moan emerged all the way from her belly.

He left it there, unmoving, as her groans devolved to whimpers. She was an animal on the inside, an animal she fought to contain from turning around and mounting him, bucking like a wild animal as she took her most basest desire. *Now, now, now, take me, take me, take me.*

When she pressed herself back onto his hand, a move she couldn't have stopped herself from making with all her willpower, he tsked her, and as punishment, slowly removed it. The sound of her own juices following him aroused her more than anything that had come before.

She heard, but did not see, the light sucking sound as he slid his finger into his mouth and tasted her.

"If you leave now, you can catch the 7:55 streetcar," he said.

CHAPTER 8

Summer Island, Maine

When Augustus was young, his father made them travel. In his own youth, August had spent a summer on a Grand Tour, a now antiquated coming-of-age ritual for young men of standing and wealth. He wanted the same for his own sons and daughters, he said, and so they spent their summers and break periods on road trips, with the looming promise that, when they were all old enough to enjoy it, he'd take them around the world.

They traveled mostly around the South, sometimes dipping up as high as Virginia or Kentucky. Once, he took them to Boston. August Deschanel didn't say this, but everyone knew he'd met his first wife, Eliza, in Boston, when they were in college. She was a Yankee, which was an oddly backward word their family still used, even today, to describe her.

When August died, the traveling ceased, but Augustus never forgot his father's words to him, on the day they'd stopped the car at Plymouth Rock for a family photo. *Son, the only way to truly know and appreciate the world we have is to see the world beyond.*

Summer Island felt more like the end of the world, but it definitely had a sense of *beyond.* It was an hour by ferry from Portland, at the mainland. The ferry station was clouded in dense, blinding fog, and when they were greeted by two men, Anderson Edgewater and Bill Whitman, the first thing out of their mouths was to question whether they had all they needed, as the next ferry was two days hence.

I suppose so, Augustus had thought, but any of his own doubts were stifled by his wife's wide-eyed wonder at the remote island, which even in the dead of summer felt cool and damp, the way he imagined the moors in *Wuthering Heights.* A lighthouse at the top of the nearby hill shined its beacon through the fog, landing over the high tide of the choppy Atlantic.

The men took turns reciting the things they thought Augustus and his wife ought to know on the short drive that took them first past a wildlife refuge, and then down Heron Hollow Road, which Whitman explained was the road the Deschanels lived on. Augustus had never seen a heron in his life.

The island, they said, was just 2.2 square miles, with a population of around two-fifty, now in the summer, though just under a fifth of those would drop off in the fall. *Summer birds,* they called them, and Augustus understood because they had something similar in their snow birds who came down from the North in the winter.

"Everyone knows everyone here, and I 'spect you will soon, too," Whitman said. "That is, if you intend to stay?"

"The summer, perhaps," Augustus answered, though his mind was already twisting around the business he'd left behind.

"Ayuh. Well, I 'spect you'll want to know Mayor George Cairne, in any case. He sees after the town year round... we used to have one of those city boys in here overseeing things. Didn't know a thing about a thing. We voted him out and put one of our own in the job. He's born and raised here, like many of us. The Cairnes, Farnsworths, McElroys, Shepards, Aldridges... all good folks, and you'll wanna get to know them. Summer is the best time to know your neighbors, though the winter brings us together in a most unique way."

"We don't have much here, but we have what we need," Edgewater added. "We of course have a town hall, and we have law, same as anyone. We even have a library, should you be needing that."

"I love to read," Ekatherina said, and Augustus learned this fact along with the men.

"There's Flanders Grocery, our only one on the island. Flanders, he gets regular shipments, so you shouldn't find yourself lacking anything."

"Unless you need something fancy pants," Whitman said with a light sneer.

"Yeah, unless that," Edgewater said. "There's a True Value, and a good four or five restaurants, including the one my wife and I run, Edgewater's, which is nice if you're looking to take the missus for a date night. But The Clam Shack will do for a quick bite, and I'll never turn one of Jack's burgers away. If you need a drink, most of us end up at Fisherman's Wife. Some more'n others." He cast a glance at his friend.

"Do you fish, Mr. Deschanel?" Whitman asked.

"No," Augustus said.

"Shame," Whitman replied. "Deep Sea Tackle is here, in any case, should you be wanting to take up the hobby. The boys there'll take care of you. Teach you, even."

Edgewater went on, as they rounded a tight bend. "You didn't come with children, but our schools are good, or as good as they can be out here. We've got three churches. One Catholic, one Methodist, and one of those new non-denominational types who welcome everyone. You'll find nearly everything the town has to offer smack-dab in the center of the island, along Androscoggin Avenue. The rest is no more'n a block or two off the main path. I left a map on your dining room table, not that you'll need it after a day or so. Aldridge Beach is nice for a picnic this time of year, but your house has its own stretch that's just as nice, and with less folks running around."

"Don't forget the Maritime Museum and the military fort!" Whitman cried. He laughed, to a joke apparently only he understood.

Edgewater rolled his hands over the wheel with a strange look. "The military fort is a point of strong opinion among the locals. You'll find them divided between those who agree with all our tax dollars going to its continued restoration, and those who'd just as soon see her broken down into boards and tossed into the Atlantic." He flipped his turn signal and eased down the start of a long driveway, flanked by tall emerald trees very different than the ones Augustus was used to in Louisiana. Tires crunched on gravel. "In any case, you can't miss it. It's an eyesore."

Edgewater parked the car at the back of the looming, gabled Victorian. From the back, it had an eerie, foreboding presence, one that beckoned to Augustus in a way that made him feel as if his imagination had run wild.

"One last thing," he said. "Your neighbors. To the east, the Auslanders are a middle-aged German couple. They don't speak much English and won't give you any trouble. If you see 'em, give 'em a wave, and that's enough. To the west, you'll find Andrew and Claire St. Andrews. They've been here, oh some years now, but they're from Scotland and you'll hear it when you speak to them. They have a young son, Jonathan. He's about two, I reckon. He'll be in my Carla's class, when the time comes, I think." Edgewater ran his hands over his face. Whitman watched him in anticipation.

"But, ah, what I really want to tell you about Mr. St. Andrews is that he's actually *Doctor* St. Andrews. And I hesitate to tell you this, because it's one of the island's secrets, and we keep our secrets better than anybody, but if you find yourself or your wife in need of medical care, Dr. St. Andrews can help."

"Off the record," Whitman said with emphasis.

"What does that mean?" Augustus pressed. "Off the record? Is he not really a doctor?"

"Oh, he's a doctor," Edgewater said with a short laugh. "Best one I ever saw. But he couldn't get the business license to open shop officially on the island, so he runs his own out of his house."

"Off the record," Whitman repeated.

"And this is illegal, I take it," Augustus said.

"We do what we have to do out here, Mr. Deschanel," Edgewater said. "We take care of our own. We don't take too well to outsiders telling us what's good and what's not."

Augustus didn't know what to say to this.

"But you're not an outsider now, are you, Mr. Deschanel?" Edgewater added with a laugh. "Even if you and your missus *are* just summer birds."

SUMMER ISLAND LOVED THEIR PARADES. THEY HAD ONE every Sunday, and if there wasn't a reason, they made one up. They had the Heron Hollow Parade one day, and the Fort Summer Island Parade another. Then there was the Summer Island Lighthouse Anniversary parade, followed by the Farnsworth Fellowship parade. The latter, he was told by their new friend, Mayor George Cairne, was a celebration of community fellowship, marked by their town food supply that was available to anyone in need. Their harvest came earlier, so far north, so they celebrated this in the summer instead of fall.

Yes, the Summer Islanders loved their parades.

This was one of the first things Augustus learned about the small community, shut off from the world.

The second thing was that everyone was nice to the point that Augustus was constantly in suspicion of their motives. From the saccharine smiles of Mrs. McElroy as she whisked Ekatherina away to meet the other women, to the overzealous back claps and laughter from Mr. Aldridge and the men when they bought Augustus beer after beer, he could not help but feel as if he'd dropped not into an *actual* town, but instead a play *about* one. One where all the actors were in on it, but the audience was not.

The outward appearance of every single person they met on the island was one of amity and brotherhood. He saw no fights or disagreements, not even among the men who had been drinking all day, only to take their friends' wives for a spin at the evening dance.

No one said anything that would betray whatever lay behind the town's veneer.

No one was this more true of than George Cairne. Augustus didn't know what he'd been expecting, hearing the men describe him in the car that first day, but it wasn't what he saw when they were introduced.

George was a beguilingly handsome man who couldn't be older than thirty. Augustus thought he looked far younger, in fact, but couldn't imagine a town as clannish and careful as Summer Island electing a child to manage their affairs. He insisted Augustus and his wife join him for dinner almost every evening, and, though he was married, his eyes were for Ekatherina alone on those nights as he practically begged her to tell him stories of her homeland.

Augustus bristled at the attention to his wife—and didn't miss Mrs. Cairne's similar disapproval in her tight expressions—but learned more from this handsome stranger's inquisitive asks than he had on his own. While he spent his days on calls to the office, worried about what he'd left behind, Ekatherina had found company among people who did for her what he *should* have been doing. He was ashamed that it took this man to help him know his own wife, and he went to bed most nights frustrated.

Meanwhile, Ekatherina blossomed.

She loved the parades. Loved the over-sweet women and their false friendships. Adored George Cairne's bright smiles and deep focus as he hung upon her every word.

On the evening of the Farnsworth Fellowship Celebration, after they'd been on Summer Island four weeks to the day, Ekatherina started drinking early and forgot to pace herself. She'd enjoyed the cabernet Farnsworth produced from his small vineyard and continued to drink it as she laughed with Sheila McElroy and danced with George Cairne, not once, but three times, to the light of the bonfire. Andrew St. Andrews, a man Augustus was happy to discover shared his love of pragmatism, raised his glass of Scottish whisky and said, "Blessings come in verra odd packages a'times."

That night, Augustus watched her as she let her dress fall to the floor of their bedroom. She'd forgotten her modesty in her drunkenness and turned to him with a sparkle in her eye.

"You do for me," she whispered, half-slurring, half-deadly serious. "You do for me, husband. You know what I need and you do. You love me."

Augustus swallowed back his hurt at his own inequities, laid bare by the dashing George Cairne almost every night since they'd arrived, and nodded. "I love you very much, Ekatherina. I only want you to be happy."

"I am happy. Thanks to you, I am very happy. For once I think not of what worry me."

Ekatherina didn't reach for her nightgown. She made her way to him and settled herself over his lap. "I love you, husband. Can you forgive me, for not showing so much?"

Augustus blinked. His hands hovered awkwardly at his sides, and then he lifted them to touch her nude, hot flesh. Ah, she was beautiful. So beautiful she caused all his fears to evaporate away as if they'd never been. "There's nothing to forgive."

"I show you now," she whispered against his ear, and Augustus melted in her arms, in a mix of love and relief.

CHAPTER 9

Show Them Who You Are

Amnesty nibbled on Evangeline's earlobe. Evangeline cringed, afraid to tell her she hated her ears, hated when they were touched. Really hated being touched anywhere, always had, but not by Amnesty. She was afraid Amnesty would *stop* touching her.

This guy called the Fonz made jokes on the small black and white television Evangeline had trucked over to the house. She didn't know about this show, but Amnesty roared with laughter at the anachronistic friendship of Arthur Fonzarelli and Richie Cunningham. Evangeline had always felt the laugh tracks on a sitcom were insulting... pandering, to the lowest common viewing denominator, telling them when it was appropriate to laugh. Often, the laugh tracks on these shows appeared at the least funny times, and yet people laughed, because they were told to.

Evangeline ran her friend's baby fine blond strands through her fingers. She loved Amnesty's hair, which was so unlike her own wild mane. She loved to marvel at it; to touch it. To imagine her own hair so silky and smooth, and without the need for constant attention to keep it from running free. What must that be like?

And then she felt guilty for the thought, for Amnesty's hair was the least of her priorities, and always would be as long as her abusive father was in the picture.

She still refused, or perhaps simply neglected, to talk about him, not beyond that first moment of vulnerability where she'd given Evangeline a problem to solve. Amnesty, over time in staying at this safe and well-protected house, became less jumpy at loud sounds and stopped sleeping with one eye open. Sometimes, Evangeline would watch her as she slept and think how much more beautiful Amnesty was when she was at peace and not forced to look over her shoulder.

Evangeline propped herself up on an elbow. "Hey, I have an idea."

"You have a lot of ideas," Amnesty said, smiling.

"Yeah, but this one might surprise you."

"Oh?"

"Up for an adventure?"

"With you, always."

EVANGELINE CHANGED HER MIND SIX OR SEVEN TIMES ON the walk deeper into Uptown. The tree had always been *her* place, first, for the many years she'd grown up in Oak Haven, and later, when she needed to get away and Magnolia Grace felt oppressive. Evangeline had always been the most in tune with herself when she was alone and unfettered by the oddities and needs of others. It wasn't enough simply to hide... she had to transcend, to move beyond where others could touch her, could reach her, and just be.

Amnesty had always been good about not asking too many questions. This seemed fair, given how unwilling she was to part with her own answers, and Evangeline liked to think this was a sign that her friend possessed a high emotional intelligence. In any case, she appreciated it now, as they entered Audubon Park, and made their way back toward the zoo, and the place Evangeline was only partly sure she was ready to share with another.

Because, really, who was Amnesty? A complete stranger whose affections depended entirely on Evangeline's acquiescence to her unwillingness to share anything about herself. Amnesty probably wasn't even her name. And everything else? Was that true?

Amnesty slipped her fingers through Evangeline's, and the inner sigh that followed chided her about her overactive brain and trust issues.

The park was alive with activity on a Saturday. Joggers navigated the path, parents and children fed the birds down at the water. But this wasn't where Evangeline wanted to take her, and she hoped it would be quieter when they reached the destination.

Evangeline started to sweat. She could blame the sweltering humidity, but she'd never been affected by extreme temperatures, not like most. She didn't know why. Assumed it might be something to do with being a healer, because Colleen was the same. She didn't think she'd ever seen her older sister break a sweat unless she was stressing about her studies.

"I would've worn my tennis shoes if I'd known we were going for the long haul!" Amnesty declared. Evangeline wondered if she even owned a pair of tennis shoes. She'd never seen her wear anything except the brown boots currently on her feet.

"Almost there," Evangeline replied. They'd just crossed over Magazine Street, which divided the majority of the park from what lay beyond: the zoo, and this other place, that Evangeline prayed would be empty.

Amnesty squeezed her hand tighter and moved closer so their shoulders were touching. Evangeline felt a chill cut through the hot day.

And then they were there. Evangeline's soul eased even being in the presence of the low, bowing arms of the giant oak. There were many live oaks in the park that held court with their drooping limbs, welcoming you, but none like the Tree of Life. It was not the first tree to take this name, and it would not be the last, but it was hers, and that was all she cared about.

"Wow." Amnesty whistled. "I had no idea this was here."

"It's kind of tucked away," Evangeline said, though it was no longer such a secret, and she'd come, more than once, and had to turn back when she'd come upon lovers making out, or a family having a picnic under the canopy of leaves.

"Well, what are we waiting for?" Amnesty asked, and she scrambled up the nearest branch, skittering her way up like a spider monkey.

Evangeline loved her in that moment, the moment where she feared she'd opened herself up too much and, somehow, her friend had known just what to do.

She laughed and followed her. She pretended not to know the best route upward. It was best to let Amnesty discover the maze of branches herself, and the reward when she reached the center, where they could sit and watch the world.

Amnesty found it with ease... as if she was born to climb, to explore, to seek beyond. She nestled back into a tangle of branches and waited for Evangeline to get there.

Evangeline's heart soared at the giggle of glee that came next.

"Look at all the animals!" she cried. "Evangeline, you have to see this!"

"I'm almost there!" she called back, though she'd seen it, she'd seen it all, so many times.

She started to settle in across from Amnesty, but Amnesty moved to the left to allow her into the small alcove she'd found. The small spot was so intimate; more, somehow, than cuddling on the couch, or holding hands.

When Amnesty's face started to fall at the hesitation, Evangeline bounded over and into the spot. Amnesty's arm came around her, and Evangeline let herself fall into the embrace, heart open, soul happy.

"This is your place, isn't it?" Amnesty said. Before Evangeline could answer, she nodded, and added, "Yes, this is definitely an Evangeline place. I can feel it. And you wanted... me here? I'll bet you've never taken anyone else."

"Yes to the first question... no to the second."

"Why not?" Amnesty threw her hands up moments after the question. "I'm sorry. You don't have to answer that if you don't want to."

Just because you won't, doesn't mean I won't. I want to know you so badly, and maybe the way to do that, for now, is to let you see through the windows I keep shuttered.

"I don't know," Evangeline said after a sharp consideration of the answer... one she wasn't even entirely sure about. "I've never had a friend I wanted this near to me. As for my family, well, we're close, but not in *that* way."

"I get what you mean."

Evangeline doubted that, seeing as Amnesty was an only child, but it wasn't her place to disabuse her of the thought. "If there were any siblings I'd take here, it would be Augustus or Colleen, and neither one of them would find this excursion much more than a waste of their time."

"A waste!" Amnesty clutched her chest in mock, but slightly serious, offense. "How could time with nature be a waste?"

"They're both so focused on their future."

"Couldn't the future involve a beautiful tree and a few moments with someone you love?"

Evangeline blinked. Her mouth went dry. "Yeah, I suppose, but just not for them."

Amnesty leaned her head against a nearby branch. "I find that really sad."

"Happiness is pursuing what we need and want, though," Evangeline replied. "I don't think either of them would be happy up here in a tree, because what they want is down there."

"And you? What do you want?"

Evangeline hadn't spent much time considering this question, because within that answer lay all the myriad reasons and horrors that had tied her to New Orleans. She had aspirations, too, but to pursue them meant first addressing why she could not, and even she —the sister everyone thought possessed no emotional intelligence of her own—was self-aware enough to recognize she was still, even now, bottling away the things she could not ever talk about.

"I just want to be here, in this moment," Evangeline said, and that was about as close to the truth as she could step.

Amnesty reached over and touched Evangeline's springy curls. They responded to her touch, bouncing and reassembling in even more fantastical patterns. Her hair, of all things, made her feel so ugly and unwanted, but Amnesty's touch, full of wonder and affection, softened that about as much as it could be softened.

"This moment," Amnesty repeated. She wound Evangeline's hair into a tight fist, pulling it back from her face, and she watched her with such honest scrutiny that Evangeline almost willed herself to fall out of the tree to avoid the assessment.

Amnesty pressed her forehead to Evangeline's. Then, head to the side, she pressed her lips to Evangeline's, parting them with her tongue. Gentle, but leaving no room for interpretation of her intentions.

Evangeline wound her arms around Amnesty and surrendered herself to the kiss.

ANYTIME MAUREEN THOUGHT IT WAS A GOOD IDEA TO have lunch with her sometimes friend, sometimes enemy, Chelsea Sullivan, she regretted that idea about half the time.

Chelsea was different than the other Sullivans. She wasn't a goody-goody like her three older brothers, or the numerous attorneys lumbering around the family law office. She'd been squirreling a flask into her private school skirts since she was thirteen, and had been using the slumber party excuse to sneak out just as long. She cursed like a sailor, but could morph back into the angel her parents believed her to be with no more than a blink of an eye. She was equal parts rebel and sweetheart, but the trouble, for Maureen, was that she preferred Chelsea when she was the former and couldn't stand her when she was the latter. Predicting which side of her friend would show up was about as accurate and fickle as predicting the weather in New Orleans.

But Maureen could never miss an opportunity to show Chelsea she was doing well. She didn't exactly think poorly of Chelsea for her blood being slightly less blue than Maureen's. The Sullivans were established in their own right, and few could remember a time that they *weren't* a prominent New Orleans family. Only the oldest families would even have the clout or daring to point out that the Sullivans started with nothing; came from nothing. Maureen would defend Chelsea and the Sullivans to anyone… but at the same time, privately, she needed girls like Chelsea to remember who they were when they were standing next to a Deschanel.

So she invited her for lunch at Galatoire's, which she knew would immediately send the message that Maureen's professional endeavors were more than paying off. She didn't just come from money. She was capable of making it on her own.

Chelsea had just turned eighteen, and, to the horror of her parents, was both enrolled in community college—her grades hadn't been enough for university—and dating a young man named Mason Landry, who had no money, no family prestige, and nothing to bring to the table. His family were laborers from the Irish Channel. Not even Lace Curtain Irish, as Mama would say.

And Chelsea was positively *delighted* at all the pearl-clutching this produced at home. Maureen, who often couldn't decide whether she was mildly put off by Chelsea's anachronistic leather-and-lace act or in awe of it, was excited by Chelsea's lack of fear.

"And you don't worry they'll write you out of the will for this?" Maureen asked. She sipped her martini, as if she wasn't a few weeks shy of legal consumption. The waiter had carded Chelsea first and assumed Maureen was also legal, and served them both, to Maureen's great relief.

Chelsea shrugged. She tugged at the shoulders of her frilly blouse. "And so what if they do? I was never going to law school. Even if my grades had been better, there was no way."

A Sullivan opting out of the family law firm was like an angel disavowing heaven. Maureen had the good sense to look scandalized, though she loved this as much as she loved her own acts of rebellion over the years. "And you're engaged now?"

Chelsea wiggled her fingers, as if she was wearing a four-carat diamond and not a tiny little gold band.

Maureen finished off her drink and rolled the olive around over her tongue. "Does anyone else know?"

"They all know I'm dating him, but my parents and Colin, and even Rory, think I'll grow out of it." She rolled her eyes and popped a mint in her mouth. "Patrick is also dating a nobody. You know Isabella Livingston?"

Maureen shook her head.

"Might as well be a Landry, for all my parents are concerned. But she's smarter. He met her in college. She's on a full scholarship to Tulane. You know how few of those they give out?"

"Yeah, nuts," Maureen said, though she knew nothing about scholarships, or any handouts.

"So he knows, but I'm keeping his secret and he's keeping mine. I think he knows he'll never be a Colin, or a Rory, even if he is toeing the family line and heading to law school next year."

"He's marrying her, too?"

Chelsea leaned back in her seat, nodding. "Yeah, but he cares more about the fam than I do. He'll wait until after law school and hide behind that good news to keep them off his back. As for us... we'll probably elope next week."

Maureen's eyes widened. "No way!"

Chelsea tilted her head to the side with a light nod, as if bored. "Don't look so scandalized, Maureen. Not all of us want to marry a prince."

"But what will people say, do you think?"

Chelsea leaned in with a gleam in her eyes. "After what you told me about your *boss,* I don't know if anything I can do would ever top *that.*"

Maureen waved her hand, to lower her voice. "I didn't tell you that so you could shame me! Besides... he's clearly interested in me. He's playing a game."

Chelsea blinked hard. "He wants to fuck you, Maureen. As all men do."

As many men have. "Maybe I'll let him."

Chelsea chewed the rest of her mint and swallowed with a face full of amusement. "You let him do that, and it's done. He wants the chase, is all. Old men need excitement in their lives, and it's not exciting once the cow gives up the milk for nothing."

"What do you know about it?"

Her friend grinned. "Don't give it to him, Maureen. Keep him wanting it." She checked her watch. "Oh, and those bitches at the office? Time to show them who *you* are. You've let them jerk you around for too long, but you could've had them for breakfast and still made it to Galatoire's for lunch."

CHELSEA'S WORDS ABOUT THE WOMEN FOLLOWED Maureen all the way back to the office. She'd let the office biddies deride her for months, and they had to know who she was. They were nobodies, probably from Gentilly or something, and she was a princess of the Garden District. She didn't even have to work at all! And when she was married, her husband would surely insist she focus on more important things, such as raising his children and hosting charity events. Events these women would never be able to buy themselves into.

Even this short, but careful, consideration of the audacity of these women sent Maureen into a simmering rage.

As luck would have it, they were all smoking in a huddle outside the office when she returned. Normally, she'd panic and hide around the corner until they were finished, but today, she felt emboldened, and she marched right past them.

"How much you wanna bet he's done the measurement trick on her by now?" one of them muttered to the others, and Maureen's confidence melted right back into anger.

"What did you say about me?"

The woman blew her smoke out through her laugh. Her free hand pressed to her belly, as if that would help. "We're just taking bets on how far along you are compared to the girls who came before."

"And why should I care about the girls who came before?"

The women exchanged cruel looks. Another said, "Here's a different way of looking at it. We're just wondering how much longer you'll be around."

"As long as I feel like it."

"More like, once Mr. Blanchard is done playing his games with you."

"Is it my fault if the other girls couldn't handle themselves appropriately with their boss?" Maureen challenged.

"He handled them all *quite* nicely. And don't think we haven't seen your timecards."

Maureen clutched her purse tight to her body. She had many things on her side, but somehow none of them fazed *any* of these shrill busybodies. They weren't intimated by her money, her looks, her youth. They seemed past all such considerations, in a way that should have been maddening but was to Maureen, at least for a brief moment, freeing.

"Mr. Blanchard appreciates the work I do. He likes when I work late hours, because he can see how dedicated I am to making his business successful," Maureen defended and realized she'd walked right into the next comment to follow.

"I'll just bet." They all laughed and stubbed out their cigarettes in perfect unison.

"I don't know who these other girls were, or why you seem to think them leaving was any of your business, but I am *not* them. I'm Maureen Amelia Deschanel, and I don't need this job the way they did." She leaned in and narrowed her eyes. "The way y'all do, seeing as you don't have husbands or businesses of your own, aside from picking on younger, prettier girls who work twice as hard. So pick your jowls up off the concrete and mind your own damn business, and I'll mind mine."

The women ignored her the rest of the day. She thought, maybe, she caught them whispering about her, but either she'd scared them earlier, which didn't seem too likely, or they had the good sense to understand she wasn't going to trifle with their nonsense any longer. Maureen couldn't fathom why Edouard kept them around at all, for how little work they actually did each day. Were they his spinster aunts or something?

They clocked out in silence and disappeared at 5:30 on the dot. Maureen, tired from both her whirlwind lunch with an old friend and her confrontation with the women earlier, decided to leave at a decent hour and waited ten minutes before packing her purse together and heading after them.

She was also tired because she hadn't had an early night since before that first time, when she'd stayed so late she thought for sure Mr. Blanchard would fire her. Each night he'd pulled her into the office, with much of the same. For an architect, he wasn't terribly creative, and most nights he just watched her. He was ugly and old, but it didn't stop the whole thing from being maddening, and most nights she went home and pleasured herself until she passed out, only mildly relieved of the tension from the hours of doing his odd bidding.

Maureen made it halfway to the exit before Mr. Blanchard appeared at his office door. "Miss Deschanel."

She turned. "Yes?"

"It's early yet."

"Oh... well, I... is it?"

Mr. Blanchard pressed his lips tight, and he looked terribly cross. So much so that she was certain she'd fudged one of his briefs, or something equally horrifying. "I need your help with something."

Maureen dropped her purse to her side. "Of course, I'm happy to help with anything you need, Mr. Blanchard. Do I need to fix something?"

His mouth twitched, and then he disappeared inside his office, which she assumed meant she was expected to do the same.

Maureen dropped her purse just outside the door and stepped inside. He reached around her and closed, then locked, the door.

He'd never done that before. She assumed there was no need, seeing as this was his business, and by the time they were alone together each night everyone else had already gone home to their families. The strangeness of this new choice launched a pit of curious fear deep in her belly.

Mr. Blanchard's hands landed on her shoulders and pressed down. She didn't understand at first, until he increased the pressure and forced her onto her knees. She complied without further resistance and looked up.

His hands mechanically moved to his belt, which he swiftly loosened and tossed behind him. Next came the button, the zipper, and then his pants were pooled at his ankles.

His erection pressed against the inside of his briefs, trapped.

"Take it out," he commanded.

The thrill that passed through Maureen was comprised of many nights, over many months, of awaiting a moment that she would have never sought had this man not groomed her for this very thing. She swallowed hard and reached forward, but he swatted her hand away and said, "With your mouth."

The throb between her legs started with a vengeance. She almost laughed at the absurdity of the request, but she showed only acquiescence as she used her teeth to peel aside the small fold of fabric. His cock sprang forward and almost hit her in the face, but she caught it deftly between her lips and took him all the way into her mouth.

Edouard groaned. He was Edouard now, even if he'd never let her call him such a thing. But she remembered the night Mr. Evers told her he wasn't her teacher anymore, and so she should call him Peter... and was tonight any different, with Edouard?

Maureen had less experience in this particular act of sex, but she had seen some of the movies Huck thought he'd hid well in his room, and knew that to really draw out the pleasure, you needed to take long strokes and look up, so he could see the pleasure in your eyes as you pleasured him. At one point he *did* look down, and the sight of her made his knees buckle.

He said something to her, but she couldn't hear him, so he said it again, more forcefully, almost angry, "Get up. Get up, get up!"

Maureen stumbled back to her feet. He was cross with her again, and she had no idea why. Was she no good at this? Had she misstepped?

In a frenzy, he spun her around and pressed her so hard against the desk that her cheek felt bruised. With one hand he pinned her down at the neck, and with the other he parted her panties to the side and shoved his cock inside of her. His thrusts were so forceful and furious in speed and intensity that she saw brilliant flashes of light appear before his eyes every time he made internal contact, and she wondered if it was possible to die this way.

Maureen tried to hold back her anguish. His pace quickened, and he slammed harder into her. Her face slid over the stack of paperwork he'd pressed it to, and she reached wildly for purchase, for something to brace herself from what no longer felt like the thing she'd ached for all these months, but instead a violent assault born of a rage she hadn't earned and never asked for.

He cried out, like a lion addressing his pride, as he came inside of her. He didn't extricate himself immediately, and then, moments later, he shuddered and spasmed, releasing a second orgasm into her. She didn't know what had happened. She couldn't ask.

A wet pop sounded as he removed himself. The hand choking her from behind disappeared and Maureen gasped into the stack of papers. She wanted to move, but she couldn't. She could barely breathe.

The familiar sound of fabric told her his pants were again on. The metal buckle snapping back together completed the task. She heard him turn, and then, pause, and turn back. He reached forward and ran one thumb over her ass.

Then he left.

His departure didn't release her from her paralysis. Maureen breathed hard into the desk and the thick paper. The cool air from the swamp cooler passed over her exposed skin, reminding her to *get up, get up, get up,* but that wasn't what she wanted to hear, not those words, not ever again.

Where did he go? He couldn't have left altogether. He was always the last to leave, as he was the only one with a key to lock up. Perhaps he'd gone to the bathroom, to give her a chance to clean up?

No, she thought. If he'd gone to the bathroom it was because he was not a man who enjoyed facing the women he chose to sample. In all their encounters, he'd always had her faced anywhere but toward him. Maureen understood very little about very much, but she knew this was a way of dehumanizing her; or genericizing her. She was not special to him. She was like all the others, just as those horrible women had said she was.

A terrible sob rose up within her. It was so powerful she found her courage and peeled herself up off the desk. Remnants of his violence trickled down her leg, and she realized she couldn't look, because she didn't know if what she'd find would be come, or blood, and she couldn't handle the answer.

She searched his desk for a box of tissues and, pulling two, she wiped down the inside of her legs without looking. She'd never know, and that was better.

Maureen peeked out his office door and scanned the office. He was nowhere to be found, but she suspected he was hiding from her. Or hiding from himself. It didn't matter.

She couldn't come back here, and that tore her heart. This job was her one and only escape from the things that had tormented her all her life and now this, too, was a torment.

Not that it mattered. She expected the call would come soon that her services here were no longer welcome.

Maureen pressed down the swelling sob. She wouldn't cry. There weren't tears anymore, and what good were they anyway? Tears amplified and gave confirmation to the pain. They did nothing to relieve it.

She disappeared out the door of the office that had promised her freedom and instead given her exactly what she'd been running from.

CHAPTER 10
What Are We?

Elizabeth rushed from one side of her room to the other, searching for any signs of drug paraphernalia. She'd been as careful with her secret as she thought possible, but sometimes the drugs took her even further away, and when that happened, she couldn't be certain she'd taken the same care. But she was still learning, how much was too little, how much was too much. Once she found the sweet spot, the experimentation would be over, and so would the risk of leaving a pill bottle or singed tinfoil in the wrong place.

Elizabeth took her promise to Connor seriously, even if she'd clearly broken it. She had no more desire to become a drug addict than he to see her become one. But this experimentation would allow her to find the safe amount needed to get her through the worst of her visions. She could quit at any time and start again whenever the visions were particularly bad. She thought of them as flare-ups, and the visions were especially potent when she was in the middle of one.

She reacted to everything differently. Her mother's opioid prescription she'd had for years, for her back, was an especially convenient test. One pill was enough in the beginning, though it made Elizabeth's stomach turn, and her body itch all over. Eventually, one did nothing, so she switched to two, but the agony of the relentless itching was almost worse than the visions, so she squandered some of the pills away, just in case.

The heroin in the marijuana was also great at the start, but by the time she'd been at it a few weeks, the effects were lessened, and she eventually went back to the kid who'd given her that and asked what else he might have. Only a couple years older than her, he'd shot her that annoying older brother look and shaken his head as he dug into the inside of his jacket. *Look, you don't want to be one of those junkies with track marks. I'll show you how to smoke it, and you need to stick with that. Anything more, and you're crossing a line you can't come back from.*

Yeah, yeah, she'd said. This kid was a junkie himself, and acting like a concerned parent didn't change that. They all had their demons that brought them to such points.

Besides, she was just testing. That was all.

And then... and then, once she was sure she had the right amount, the safest drug—or as safe as any drug can be—she'd come up with a plan for how and when to use it in order to keep the visions at bay forever.

Because, they *were* at bay. She hadn't had anything more than weak, fuzzy outlooks since she'd started that day with Connor.

Connor. He'd be there soon. Elizabeth checked her eyes in the mirror. She'd allowed herself to come all the way down for his visit today, but in doing so, she had a nasty case of the shakes, like she sometimes did in the dead of winter when she was silly enough to jump into the pool. She hoped that didn't mean she was coming down with an addiction.

Her bedroom door opened. Elizabeth nearly jumped back, startled, but he didn't notice. He'd rolled his body forward and then, affecting an oddly good British accent, said, "My lady, would you accompany me on a walk in the park? Unchaperoned, I'm afraid, but let's give the aristocracy something to talk about, eh?"

Elizabeth's heart swelled. The shakes stopped, for now.

"Good sir!" she declared with a laugh, and for a moment she'd forgotten the months of drug use, and she wasn't that girl anymore, but his girl.

His lady.

Connor offered a stiffly bent arm and she took it.

THEY WALKED THROUGH ARMSTRONG PARK, ARM IN ARM. Despite the sweltering humidity of the late summer, Elizabeth alternated between bouts of shivering cold and sweating bullets.

They wound down through the path, and Connor chattered on about some trouble his twin brother, Thomas, had gotten himself into. She listened at the surface, while focusing as hard as she could on forcing herself to stop reacting to these rude shifts in body temperature. If she could will herself to be okay, then she would be.

When they came upon Congo Square, a new chill, unrelated, ripped through her. A vision seized her, though this wasn't a new one, but a very old one. One she'd never shared with anyone, because once she realized Madeline was the one who would die, she couldn't do that to the others. It was hard, deciding whether knowing or not knowing was worse, but knowing was nearly killing her, so she opted for not.

Madeline had been here. For a protest, it seemed, from the police and National Guard in riot gear and all the signs. Madeline didn't have a sign. While everyone else swayed to the chants and songs of the protests, she was lost to her own agony. She never outright said that these rallies helped heal her fractured soul, but it was clear that the closer she came to being part of solving the world's problems, the less tortured she was.

And then Madeline had lifted her arms to the sky and rained down fire upon all of it.

No one knew she could do that. Not one of them.

Elizabeth knew. But then what good was that knowledge when Madeline was dead?

"Lizzy?"

"Sorry. I was remembering how I saw Maddy here once." Elizabeth let the truth roll off her tongue. She'd never liked deception, but the amount of it pouring off of her these past months made her almost leap for opportunities to be honest.

He pulled her close in a half-hug. "Was it a good vision?"

Elizabeth shook her head. "It was the beginning of the end."

"Those last months, you mean?"

"No one knew why Augustus got cold on her for a while. This was why." Elizabeth gestured around at the branches still scorched black. "She set the park on fire, and Augustus used his persuasion to keep her out of jail. He'd never had to do that for her, and she'd never asked, but this situation was impossible. He would have done anything for her, but then when tested, he was..."

"Tainted," Connor finished. "He thought his relationship with Madeline was protected from the things he had to do that made him hate himself."

Elizabeth turned to him. "I suppose that's probably the truth." Her blood cooled again, and she had to clench her jaw to stop the teeth chattering.

He shrugged. "I like Augustus. He loves pretty hard, but he also holds grudges just as hard."

"I don't think he holds grudges so much," she said thoughtfully. "He just doesn't forget. He never forgets."

Connor stopped walking. "I know you'd like to forget."

She turned her head toward him. "Not everything."

He kissed her. When he pulled back, she saw in his eyes how serious he felt in that moment, and the next kiss was something else entirely.

"I don't know what we are, Lizzy, and I guess that was okay before, but I don't know if that's still true."

"You're my best friend," she said.

"I am, but isn't it more than that?"

She paused before nodding. "Yeah, it's more than that."

He pivoted and took both her hands in his. He rolled them over, and she felt the light tremor in them and realized he'd been practicing this for some time. This wasn't as spontaneous as she initially thought.

"I love you, Elizabeth," Connor said. His hair fell over his brow and he blew it away. His dark eyes had trouble meeting hers, but he found the courage and locked their gaze. "I just want to be able to say that to you sometimes."

Elizabeth initiated the kiss this time. "I love you, too," she said, when she eased herself back. And how, how she did love him. How she'd loved him from the very first.

But she was afraid of letting him in even closer than he'd already been. She had secrets, ones that would break his heart more than her standing here and rejecting him. If he ever found out... no, she couldn't think it.

"I was thinking that, I don't know, maybe we could be more. If you want that, too."

"More?"

Connor wound his arms around her and pressed his forehead to hers. "Yeah, you know. More."

"Sex?"

He laughed and dropped his eyes. "Felt weird to say it."

Elizabeth had often wondered if she was even more messed up than she'd always thought, for she was not a normal girl when it came to hormones and sex drive. She rarely fantasized and didn't notice cute boys when they walked by.

But then, maybe it was because her heart had been Connor's since long before she'd cared about these things, and so she couldn't possibly imagine herself doing anything intimate with another boy.

"I want it, too," Elizabeth said, and she had the fear she was playing with even more fire than tangling with the drugs. "With you."

She'd seen this future. Connor, grieving over the tomb holding his wife and child. Elizabeth had long avoided putting these puzzle pieces together too tightly, but it was almost impossible to do so now that he'd laid out a future that involved so much more than what they'd had all these years.

But if the future could not be changed, then what was the point of fighting any of it? Even the horrible parts.

Maybe all the good years would make the end worth it.

She had to find a way to bring him into what she was doing with the drugs, instead of hiding it. If she could make him see that moderation was everything, and that they could do this, together, as he said he wanted to do something just as intimate.

"So, we're dating," Connor said, and a broad, boyish smile spread across his soft face.

"We're dating," Elizabeth agreed and kissed him once more.

Six weeks and two days. Augustus tried not to count, but he couldn't fathom leaving his business alone that long. He had competent employees, and he trusted Evangeline to sniff out any issues, but he knew now, had always known, that the only way to do something the way you want it done is to do it yourself.

He was only twenty-three, and already he'd taken on the habits of an old man.

And now there was a problem with not one, but both of the printing presses. Evangeline insisted she was all over it, and his office manager had been in regular communication with the technicians, but they had the fall issue due in two weeks, and he wouldn't risk the reputation of the company or the magazine on the hope his office manager both appreciated and was capable of conveying the severity of the situation.

Still, he'd put off the news to Ekatherina for days. How could he tell her they were returning, when she'd been glowing for weeks? Every day, she moved about their provincial life on the small island like a nymph, full of joy and hope. Augustus found his own joy in hers, and he even stopped minding the flirting between his wife and the mayor. They hadn't signed up for a marriage where they put unreasonable expectations on one another. As long as it never went further, Augustus could abide it.

And besides, she'd come to his bed every single night since that first. He was embarrassed, that he didn't know more, have more experience, but they learned the motions together, and some nights they went well into the morning with such experiments. Most days, he had trouble rising before ten.

For a man who had never had much in the way of sexual desires, he simply could not get enough of his wife.

Wife. Sometimes he struggled to accept that he'd married this beautiful, strange creature sharing a bed with him. He was the least likely to want such a thing, but was the first of the seven to make it happen, and that wasn't ever lost on him.

He'd told her, both when he asked her to marry him, and later, after their vows: *I won't ever ask anything of you that I can't give back. You're safe with me, Ekatherina. I don't ever want you to live in fear.*

And now they had to leave, and his deepest fear was that she might never be this free and loving with him again. That the very thing he'd told her she didn't have to do was now what he wished for most in the world.

Ekatherina's fingers traced symbols on his bare chest. The chill this produced filled him with fresh desire, but he'd already had her twice that night, and he always felt better when it was her who initiated the lovemaking. It helped him to know she was choosing the act, not performing it from duty.

"Something is troubling your mind, husband," she said. "Is it me?"

Augustus brushed his lips against her soft forehead. "Never you."

"What, then?"

"There are problems back in the office," he said with a long sigh. He hoped she couldn't see there was a deeper truth behind it... that he was almost *relieved* they had problems, so he had a legitimate reason to return to a place where he was most himself.

"What kind of problem?"

"Problems plural, I'm afraid. Both printing presses took a dive. We're at risk of not meeting the fall deadline."

"Oh, no!" she cried. "It is good, this edition. It must not be delayed."

"No, it mustn't," he agreed. His face rested against the top of her head. "But I worry it might, if I'm not there to solve it."

"Patricia cannot?"

"Patricia works very hard, but she's too nice."

"And Evangeline?"

"She's the opposite, too aggressive. This issue requires a certain level of finesse, a balance."

"I see."

"I know you're happy here..."

Ekatherina buried her face in his chest and said nothing.

"But we have to go back."

She was quiet.

"I'm happy here, too," Augustus went on. "I don't think I've ever been happier in my life than I have these weeks here with you, Ekatherina. And you know, we can come back. We *should* come back. The house is ours."

"Come back when?"

"Maybe for the winter." He laughed. "Most people probably try to *leave* here in the winter, but I would guess... I mean, I would think... that the winter here would feel really familiar to you."

"Yes."

"So, we'll come back. And we can keep coming back, if you want. But right now, we have to go home."

"I stay," Ekatherina said. "And wait for you to come in winter."

"What?"

"I stay," she said, more firmly. She pulled herself up onto an elbow, the sheet draped modestly over her breasts. "I stay until winter when you come back."

"Ekatherina..."

Tears glistened in her eyes. "I stay."

Augustus' stomach was a pit of hard stones. What could he say? He had questions he was afraid to ask... and answers he only thought he wanted. That she was happy here was clear, but did this happiness truly not include him? Was he only an accidental passenger on this journey of hers?

He tried not to imagine her sitting on top of him, swaying to the rhythm of their lovemaking. Tried not to think that it meant so much more to him than to her, or that it was, worse, just something she felt it her duty to do.

"I love you," she said quickly. "I love you, husband, but I stay. You go and come back to me in winter."

It was ludicrous, leaving her here. It was absolutely out of the question! It was...

Not his decision, he realized. It was hers, and she'd already made it, long before he'd ever told her the news about going back.

But what was here?

This strange island.

Their strange parades.

The strange people.

The... mayor.

No... *stop this, stop it right now.* His suspicions did not change who his wife was, and that was a loyal, moral woman who would never do such a thing. Never. She might enjoy his attentions, but never that.

"Please do not be angry with me, husband," she said, just before she erupted in sobs.

Augustus held her close to him and insisted he wasn't angry, he could never be angry with her.

For what else could he do?

FALL 1974

VACHERIE, LOUISIANA
NEW ORLEANS, LOUISIANA
EDINBURGH, SCOTLAND

CHAPTER 11

Celebrate and Protect

Maureen had chewed her thumbnails right down to the quick.

She'd left the doctor's office an hour ago, and mercifully, she found the house empty when she got home. At least for the time being. Mama had left a note to say she was out shopping with Elizabeth, and to expect her back in time to make dinner.

If she could find even a single miracle to celebrate in this horrifying situation, it was that her eighteenth birthday a couple weeks ago meant she could visit the doctor on her own. She could *not* bring Irish Colleen into this. The trauma from the last time was still so fresh and sharp, and no matter how this would change her life, she would never, ever go through that again.

Not that she had a choice, if she wanted children in the future, her doctor said. He tried to be gentle during the exam and tests, but it was mortifying and painful anyway. But she was shocked when he passed no judgment, only concern.

Whoever did this to you last time, Miss Deschanel, did not do it well. I know this is a hard time for a young woman who finds herself in an impossible situation, and that there aren't many options available. Hopefully with the passing of Roe vs. Wade, we will see less examples of young women butchered by inexperienced surgeons.

I never wanted the procedure, Doctor. My mother made me, and now that she has no legal authority over me, I'll never make that decision again.

I see. Well, I'm glad to hear you say that, because if you should choose to have another abortion, I fear the damage done from the first time, combined with a second procedure, would render your future chances of carrying a child to term close to nil.

Maureen had touched her stomach as the tears fell. *And when will she be here?*

We don't know whether you've having a girl or a boy, yet, but April.

Oh, she's a girl. I just know it.

Being firm in having her child this time didn't mean Maureen was any less conflicted about it. She would be shunned, as an unwed mother. Her family would disown her. She'd never be welcomed into polite society again. There was no future that did not involve disgrace.

What she needed was someone on her side.

She couldn't turn to Edouard. A day after the encounter in his office, his office manager had called and let her know her services would no longer be required. Not that she'd needed a call to confirm what she'd known the moment she fled his office. The whole room stank with his desire to see her gone; the feeling that whatever he'd gotten from having her around was at an end.

Maureen thought Charles would understand. He probably had little bastards running around all over New Orleans, and he'd been her one and only real ally in the family. But when she called him, his awful wife, Cordelia said he was indisposed and, no, she would not leave a message, not after that bullshit Maureen and Charles pulled with her father.

If Cordelia hadn't hung up the phone so swiftly, Maureen might have added, *get pregnant already so my brother doesn't have to debase himself in your bed.*

Well, thought Maureen, Cordelia's father would off himself

soon, and maybe she wouldn't be so damn smug about everything then.

Augustus was out of the question. He'd want to fix the situation, the same way he fixed everything for the family, and she wasn't looking for a fix. She needed moral support, and that also eliminated Evangeline. Elizabeth was too young, and wasn't it Maureen's job to be a good role model for her?

That left Colleen. Maureen's mind, as she rolled through her siblings, kept hitching back to Colleen, despite the deep burn in her belly at the thought of telling her anything at all. Colleen was the picture next to "sanctimonious" in the dictionary. Maureen was so wiped out from the last six weeks, starting with that horrible night at Mr. Blanchard's office, that she couldn't even fathom listening to a lecture about it, especially not from someone as good at it as Colleen.

But Maureen remembered something Evangeline told her one night, as she helped Maureen pack her things at Ophélie in preparation for the move back to New Orleans. Maureen couldn't even recall how they'd come upon the subject of their oldest sister, but she never forgot what Evangeline said. *I know you think Colleen is impossible, but it comes from a good, if really twisted, place. When I really needed her, and she wasn't there... well, I don't think Colleen will ever get over that. I think it changed her. And where I think she used to believe she had to be our mom, I think now she understands better how she can be there for us.*

How's that?

Our sister, of course.

Maureen never asked how Colleen had failed Evangeline, because she knew. The whole family knew, save Mama, and this, like so many other things in their family, was an unspoken rule. Never talk about the worst of it, and never, ever let Mama in on the news.

Her black address book sat unopened on the desk. Maureen, proud of all the organization skills she'd learned as a secretary, had everyone's information in the little book, including date of birth, place of birth, and all other important dates. For Charles, she had his wedding date, and once he had a son, that would be in there, too.

But Charles wouldn't have a child before Maureen. She, the second to youngest, would be the first.

She flipped to the tab with the D and scrolled her finger until she found Colleen. Colleen had written them all letters with how to dial Scotland, which she'd said was a bit tricky, and Maureen copied those instruction directly into the listing titled, *Deschanel, Colleen Amelia.*

The instructions worked perfectly, not that Maureen was surprised. They *had* come from Colleen, after all.

Her sister answered on the second ring. "Hello, Colleen Deschanel speaking."

"Colleen. It's Maureen."

Pause. "Maureen? Everything okay?"

Maureen grimaced. She didn't know if Colleen's concerned voice was what grated at her most, or the fact she'd called out, without saying it, that Maureen would never call unless something *was* wrong.

"You don't have school today?"

"Not for another couple weeks," Colleen said. "The anticipation is killing me. I've already met all my professors, though, and my books are ready to go."

You would. "I'm sure it's beautiful there."

"Absolutely breathtaking. You should come out when Evangeline comes to visit."

"Evangeline is coming to visit?"

"Well, nothing's planned yet, but she's talked about coming out, sure. Was supposed to be summer, but you know how time gets away."

"Yeah, okay. Maybe I will."

"It's not like you to call."

Maureen settled into the chaise lounge. She didn't know how much time she had before Mama and Elizabeth got home, and she needed to get the words out, or more time would pass without help. And the last thing she wanted was to take all her advice from the ghosts in her life. "I'm calling because..." The phone cord was tangled on something and she yanked it, causing a vase to fall to the ground and shatter. One of Mama's favorites. Great.

"What was that?"

"Nothing. So, you know I was working for Edouard Blanchard at his architecting firm?"

"Was? I didn't know you stopped. Everyone said you were really enjoying it there."

"I was," Maureen said, and then felt a sick pang. She really *had* enjoyed her job. What started as an escape from home had turned into a feeling of usefulness, and then she'd gone and let her hormones lead her down the exact path those old biddies knew she'd go down.

"And you quit?"

"Not exactly."

"You were fired?"

"I was let go, because my services were no longer needed."

"I see," Colleen said, and Maureen could almost hear her searching for how to be supportive, instead of a nagging bitch. "I'm really sorry, Maureen. There will be other jobs, though, if you want them."

"Yeah, but, that's not why I'm calling."

"Oh?"

Maureen didn't feel the tears coming, so when they erupted in a storm of sobs, she clutched her chest in fear of the onslaught.

"Maureen? Sweetheart, what is it? What's wrong?"

"It's... Mr. Blanchard... Edouard..." And then Maureen let the whole sordid story spill out. She didn't edit it, as she might have at another time, when she was feeling less vulnerable, but it all rolled forward, and she couldn't stop it if she'd tried.

Maureen almost heard the air sucked out of the room across the ocean.

"That bastard," Colleen hissed. "That no good bastard! He has no business hiring young women if he can't keep his hands off them, and what happened that night..."

"What?" Maureen sniffled.

"Was *not* your fault, Maureen. I know this must be all very confusing for you. What, after... well, after another man your senior decided to use you as his play toy."

Maureen didn't bother defending her own part in the affair with Mr. Evers. It was easier for her if they believed she was a victim.

"You can't tell Mama," Maureen cried. "Please, she can't know."

"I won't. I promise," Colleen said. "But, sweetie, she's going to know. You won't have more than a couple months at best before she'll figure it out."

"I could run away."

"To where?"

Maureen whimpered through her tears. "What am I going to do, Colleen? I have another year before I get my estate entitlement, but even if I have a house, I'll be... I'll be shunned. My name won't even matter!"

"Don't you even think about worrying about money right now," Colleen said. "I have my estate entitlement, and you'll get whatever you need. And you're due for your house now, not in a year, so you'll have that. Money won't be a problem for you, Maureen, I'll make sure of that."

Maureen sniffled. The sobs rocking through her upper body had subsided. "I don't know if I can raise a baby by myself, Colleen."

"You'll never be alone, not when you have three sisters who can help. And Mama."

"Mama!" Maureen laughed.

"I know, I know, but... I think you underestimate her a bit, Maureen. She'll hem and haw for a while, but she'll love this baby as her own, once she comes around to the idea."

"I don't understand. You're acting so normal. You're not upset?"

Colleen sighed. "What's done is done. You're having a child, and that child will be a Deschanel. One of us. We're past the point of prevention, so now, we make plans."

"I didn't expect you to be like this."

"You must have called me for a reason. You have four other siblings right there in New Orleans."

Maureen didn't mention she'd tried Charles first. But Colleen was right. Maureen might loathe her older sister much of the time, but somewhere, she'd known Colleen would jump in with both arms and help her with whatever came next.

"What do I do now?"

Colleen's heels clicked across the floor on the other end. "Well... you're not the only parent in this situation. Edouard Blanchard needs to own up to his part."

"Leena, I do *not* want to see him ever again!"

"I don't blame you at all, and we can find a way to keep him away from you. But he owes you support. Of the financial kind."

"I thought you said not to worry about money?"

"You'll never have to worry about money," Colleen insisted. "But he shouldn't just walk away from this without any consequence. He's *going* to support this child financially, whether he likes it or not."

"But what if he wants to see her?"

"Her? Isn't it a bit early to find out?"

"I just know," Maureen said.

"Okay, well, if he wants to see her... we'll cross that bridge when it comes. I don't think he will, though. He's unmarried, has no other children, and a child born out of wedlock hurts his situation, not helps. I think he'll be content to send checks and be done with it."

"What if you're wrong?" Maureen's free hand rubbed across her belly. Her daughter was nothing much of anything yet, but the slight swell, reminiscent of having eaten a very large dinner, helped remind her she was real.

"If it comes down to it, we pull in Augustus."

"He *hates* doing that, Colleen."

"Life isn't always comprised of the things we love."

"What are you going to do? Call him?"

"Edouard?"

Even hearing his name aloud was painful. "Yeah."

"I need to think about it a bit..." Colleen said, thoughtful. "But you did the right thing in calling me, Maureen. I'll make sure this is handled in a way that doesn't add any more stress to your life. Right now, you need to focus on your daughter and your own health, because she will be here before you know it. Let me handle Edouard."

"I don't know what to say." Maureen was choked up again.

"You don't have to say anything. You're going to be mother to the very first little baby of the new generation of Deschanels. That's something to celebrate!" Colleen lowered her voice. "And protect."

Augustus never actually expected Ekatherina to stay in Summer Island through to winter. He suspected she'd follow him within the week, and they'd return to their life in New Orleans with a similar ease, or disease, depending on how you saw it, as they'd had before. They might or might not return to that beautiful investment Victorian off the coast of Maine.

But she didn't come home. And as summer turned to fall, there was nothing in her voice, or her words, that suggested her stay was anything but permanent.

"Ekatherina," he pleaded one night, over the phone. She giggled on the other end, and he didn't hear another voice, but he imagined one. Not that he believed George Cairne was foolish enough to visit a woman in her house alone. But would she see him later that evening?

"Husband," she replied, using that husky, placating tone he'd come to see as at least mildly manipulative. "It still too hot for me in Louisiana. I stay. You come in winter."

"I might not be able to come in winter," he said.

"Oh." He heard a click of some makeup container and then, "Then you come in spring."

"Ekatherina, we live here, in New Orleans."

"I like Maine."

"I like it, too, but I never intended for us to stay long-term there. Our life is here. Our company is here."

"My work," she said with a sudden gasp. "I take too much time off?"

"You know you only have to work if you want to," he said, sounding more short and frustrated than he intended. He discovered he wasn't only hurt, but angry. She didn't belong across the country, she belonged with him, and she showed no inclination that she felt the same. All her pretty seductions were long forgotten now that he was out of the picture.

He also had more news for her. Bad news. He'd been shut down permanently in his attempts to secure a visa for Ekatherina's family. All requests were on hold, as tensions increased along with the testing of nuclear warfare on both sides.

If he told her that now, she'd never come home.

"What is it about Maine that you'd rather be there?"

"I do not know."

I think you do. Two days ago, the call had come in from Edgewater. He called to give him an assessment of some damage done by a fall storm. He'd taken care of the repairs, he said, but would send the bill for Augustus to pay at his leisure.

"Have you seen my wife around much?"

"Oh, ah, yes, yes, I see her quite a bit in town."

"How is she occupying her time?"

"She's made some friends. The ladies have taken to her, for the most part."

"For the most part?"

"A couple... well, pay it no mind. You know how women get, telling takes out of school. It's nothing to get yourself concerned about, not when you've got a business to run."

But Augustus *was* concerned, and he was starting to think his instincts were not so far awry.

"Please, husband. Do not be mad with me."

"I'm not mad."

"When you come in winter, we have special time together. Remember?"

It was all he could do to forget. When he thought of those summer nights wrapped in his wife's arms, he'd wondered if it was all some dream.

"I don't know if I can come," he said again. The front door opened and closed. Evangeline. "I have to go. I'll call you tomorrow."

"I know you'll come for me."

I'd do anything for you. "I'll try, but, Ekatherina... I really need you to think about when you'll be coming home. We can try to return in the winter, but if we do, we'll go back together."

A horn sounded in the background of her call. "Oh! I must go. I love you, husband."

The line went dead, and Augustus held the crowing phone in his hand.

"That the wife?" Evangeline asked. She reached into the fridge and rifled around with all the ease of a stray dog.

"Yes," he said. He could hardly get the word out through his tense jaw.

"Not like you to be home before eleven."

"I did some work from home tonight."

"Ahh." She crunched into an apple and tossed it into the air, catching it again.

"Ahh? Something on your mind?"

"On mine? Nothing." *Crunch.*

"You're never one to miss an opportunity to have your opinion known."

"Last I checked, you didn't want my opinion where Miss Soviet Union was involved." She pointed at the phone. "But, uh, that sound is annoying."

Augustus cradled the phone. "I don't want your opinion."

"But since *you* brought it up, when *is* she coming home?" *Crunch.*

"The coming and going of my wife isn't your business."

"It's yours, though, I would think," Evangeline said. "Look, brother, she's growing on me. She makes you happy. That's enough for me. But what's she planning to do, just live separately?"

Augustus knocked his fist against the wooden desk. "It's best we don't talk about this."

"Are you talking about it with her?"

"Evangeline!"

She threw her hands up, one holding the half-eaten apple. "You can ask me not to be a bitch about your wife, but you can't ask me to stop caring about my brother!"

Augustus shot to his feet. "Since when does caring about me involve making me feel worse about something that's completely out of my control?"

Evangeline's face softened. "Does she know how this is hurting you?"

"You don't know when to stop!"

"Because I *love you,* Augustus. Jesus."

He crossed his arms. "You've never liked her, Evangeline. You've been nicer about it, but I know your opinion hasn't changed at all."

"Hey now." Evangeline tossed the apple core in a perfect arc, and it landed in the trash in the corner. "That's not fair at all. I've been nothing but nice to her, and I've made a conscious effort to stop being so suspicious of her. And it worked, for a while! But you wouldn't be looking like this, or acting like this, if you weren't suspicious right now, too."

Augustus stepped closer to her. "What did I say to you? That day in the office?"

"What day?"

"Don't play dumb. You know what I mean."

Evangeline sighed. "You said you needed me in your court. And I *am.*"

"You're out of bounds," he corrected. "I don't know what's going on with my wife, or how to fix it, but talking about it with you, or anyone, makes it real, and I can't handle that right now! Do you understand? Do you, finally, understand, that even I have limits? Even I have feelings and fears and, yes, suspicions?"

Evangeline dropped her eyes. "Aggie, it's because I know you have those things that I worry so, so much."

His voice shook. His eyes blurred. "Please, Evangeline. If you love me, just pretend this is all normal. For me. For now."

CHAPTER 12

Uptown Girl

Dearest Evangeline,

Pray for me, dear sister, for my future begins tomorrow!

Ahh, Edinburgh. If there was ever a city where Deschanels truly belonged (aside from New Orleans, of course), this lovely Scottish haven of gothic and romance is it. I thought I'd be homesick. Instead, I feel as if I've arrived home after a long absence.

I walked the Royal Mile this evening. I think I told you that my flat sits at the end, only two blocks from Edinburgh Castle, a monstrous thing resting atop a prehistoric volcanic rise. Beautiful, although the strategic high ground and improbability of enemy breach was more than likely the top concern of the original architects.

Sorry. You know I can't turn off the scholar, even when I want to. It's a sickness, I tell you. And one I know you understand all too well, little sister.

Only to you, could I ever confess how nervous I am to start at the university tomorrow. While Mama brags to complete strangers at the grocer about how her eldest daughter was one of only a handful selected from the United States for the University of Edinburgh's Neuroscience program, the thoughts running through my head are more along the lines of how disappointed she'll be should I fail.

My mind is running so many different directions that I can't focus on anything except my hopes and fears. They whirl to the brim as I fear collapse. Will I become the next successful Deschanel or a complete embarrassment to my bloodline? Stay tuned.

Hugs to Mama, Charles, Aggie, Maureen, and dear Elizabeth.

Love,

Colleen

Dear Leena,

I'll keep this short.

Mama goes to church now not one, but three days per week. For her sins.

Charles is a miserable sack of shit these days.

Augustus has been abandoned by his wife. Yes, you read that right. Poor man is in D-E-N-I-A-L.

Maureen is a miserable cow. In other news, Pope remains Catholic.

Lizzy and Connor are probably shagging, and I don't have a care to stop it.

I'm fine. Moving my visit to the spring, but I'm sure you're too busy for my meddling anyway.

Write soon.

Yours,

Evie

Dearest Evie,

Would you like to know what I've learned here, above all else? Never be the first to turn in assignments or raise your hand. Already, I've developed a reputation I'll be spending the next four years working to repeal.

I got your letter and am jumping for joy. You'll be here in the spring for a visit. I have so much to show you, although I haven't had as much time as I'd like to explore. Now, don't remind me this is nearly six months away. I'll summon the patience, somehow.

You have your heart set on MIT, I know, but once you visit, I have a feeling you'll reconsider. Sister's intuition.

As for your notes about our siblings. I know Charles is miserable, but what can we do? He was determined to marry her, for reasons we'll never understand. Aggie, too. I understand why you don't trust Ekatherina, but Augustus must make his choices, and his mistakes, or he'll never learn. Lizzy and Connor... can't say I'm surprised. But if there was ever a boy for our Lizzy, it's him.

As for Maureen... please be kind to her. She's going through something I can't share, but when you know, you'll understand the reason for my plea.

You failed to mention how you're doing. Meet anyone worth talking about? Sister's intuition, but I feel like you're intentionally leaving out your own news.

Did I mention in any of my other letters that there's a local boy here? I believe he's the only other one from New Orleans in the neuroscience program. Fourth year. He's an aide, and at least halfway responsible for the terrible reputation I've earned for being an overachiever. He reserves his eyebrow raises just for me, but I don't believe he intends them with any degree of playfulness. The guy hasn't said a single word to me even though he's plenty amiable with the other first years. Leads me to wonder if he had some past dealings with our family that didn't go well. Noah Jameson is his name. I'm guessing Charles knew him from his public school days. Remember those? When he was kicked out of Brother Martin? Lord help me if he was the target of Charles' merciless bullying. It will be a long year.

On the other end of the male spectrum, no, I haven't met anyone, you goose. We both know I'm not here for that, and even if I was, "he" would have to work around my insane schedule, which will only get worse in a few years if I get into the doctorate program, and then beyond that, clinicals, internship, residency. I'll be lucky if I ever have a family. Thank goodness we have two brothers, so I'm not counted on to carry on our "beloved" name. Ha.

As for your last question about quitting the pointless endeavor of college and traveling the world: I think we both know the answer. You and I may both be natural healers (as natural as any supernatural gift can be), but our pursuit of medicine isn't about healing. We both agreed we'd go into this field to learn more about the mind, about genetics, and anything else that might explain how and why we are this way. When we were girls, we promised Aunt Ophelia we would take the cross, so to speak. That way, if we were destined to serve the Deschanel Magi Collective one day, we'd have to have something to offer. And as it turned out, she seems to think I'm the one for the job.

Not that traveling the world for a living wouldn't be tempting.

Alas. No rest for the wicked. Early class. Tomorrow.

Hugs to all.

Love,

Colleen

"Look, Lizzy, I've never asked you to do this before, but I'm worried about Augustus, and I'm afraid of overstepping. But I'm afraid if I don't..."

Elizabeth tapped her pencil against the desk. "I've already seen his future where his wife is concerned."

Evangeline leaned over her, hands open. "And?"

"What I've seen isn't about the stuff happening now." Elizabeth frowned and looked off, across the room. "I don't know what's going on with her there in Maine. I don't know if you should be worried, or if he should. But I would, if it was me. Visions aside. Does that help?"

"No, but thanks anyway."

Elizabeth stopped her before she left the room. "Look, Evie... whatever does happen, and however stuff turns out, you know, it's not about what's happening now. I know that's really vague—"

"Yeah, super vague."

"I guess all I'm saying is, if Augustus is worried, worry with him, but if he's not, then just take it easy."

"Thanks, Confucius," Evangeline said, but as an afterthought, she leaned in and kissed her sister on the head. "Sorry for asking. I know it's not easy for you."

Elizabeth grinned. "It's okay. I know you're just trying to help Aggie. And, Evie?"

"Yeah?"

"If I thought my visions could've helped you help him... I would've broken my rule and told you."

Evangeline smiled back. "Remember that, if something does pop into that head of yours, okay?"

Evangeline left her youngest sister's room feeling no less concerned for her brother, and no more equipped to deal with it.

But she felt somewhat better. Whatever his future held, it didn't seem to involve Evangeline's current concerns.

That is, unless Elizabeth just hadn't seen it, yet.

She grabbed her keys from the bowl by the front door and yelled, "Bye, Mama!"

Irish Colleen rushed out of the kitchen, rag in hand. She always had a rag in hand. "What? Leaving so soon?"

Evangeline could be there a week and her mother would have said the same thing. "Only stopped by for a minute, Mama."

"Do you have somewhere to be?" Irish Colleen's face grew serious, as she stepped closer to her daughter. She wiped one hand off and ran the back of it across Evangeline's forehead. "You don't look well. You're flushed. Do you have a cold?"

"I feel fine, Mama."

"You should eat! I have a casserole I can pop in the oven and have it out right quick. You know what they say, 'feed a cold, starve a fever.'"

Evangeline smiled. "That doesn't even make sense. Your body needs nutrients when you're sick, even the flu."

Irish Colleen patted her cheek. "Well, when you're a mama, Evangeline, you'll know best."

Evangeline felt the anxiousness all the way down to her toes. She had another matter to deal with, another one that required answers she hoped would satisfy her but wasn't at all sure they would. "I'll come back later."

Irish Colleen kissed both cheeks. "You do that. And I'll feed whatever ails you."

When Evangeline was back at Magnolia Grace, she double-checked both the spot she knew she'd been keeping the money, as well as anywhere else she *might* have hidden it. It was no use pretending it could be anywhere else. Evangeline was methodical in such matters, and she knew she'd never moved the money.

She wouldn't have full access to her Deschanel Trust money until the following year, but she had partial access, being in college, and she'd carefully kept her costs down so she'd have money to spare. Not for herself, but to help Amnesty. She'd been able to squirrel away over a thousand dollars, only extricating funds when Amnesty needed groceries, or other living expenses. Only Evangeline knew where the money was hidden, because only Evangeline was ever in her bedroom.

But now it was gone.

Augustus was out of the question. A thousand dollars was nothing to him, but even if he'd needed it, he would never go through her things. Never take from her. She wouldn't put it above that Russian bride, but the money went missing when Ekatherina was in Maine, so she wasn't responsible for this.

What made it all worse was that Amnesty herself seemed to be missing. Evangeline had been over there almost every day for the past week, hoping to sneak some time in with her, but each time the house had been empty. And as the week went on, it seemed the house was *truly* empty, because the milk left on the counter had begun to spoil, and nothing that had been pulled out had ever been put away.

Evangeline was terrified that Amnesty's father had found her, after all those blissful months of security and warmth. She didn't like to admit this, because she did truly wish Amnesty could live a life out in the open, but she liked the secret boundaries of their relationship... of hiding away from the world, wrapped in each other's arms, a love without a label. Amnesty had shown her that intimacy could come wrapped in many bows.

Evangeline liked not being able to define what was between them, because she wasn't sure anymore if she was made for things that could be so easily defined.

But now Amnesty was gone, and the money was gone, and she refused to believe the two things could be related.

She left her keys at Magnolia Grace and walked to the house. Walking to clear her head was how she'd met Amnesty, and it still helped give her a strength over whatever she was preparing to face.

Evangeline intended only to clean up the mess that was growing more pungent by the day, but as she mounted the porch, a harried Amnesty flew from the front door. Her eyes pooled with panic when she saw Evangeline.

"Amnesty..." Evangeline approached, and her friend cowered back. She stopped. "Are you okay? Where have you been?"

"It doesn't matter, Evangeline. I can't see you anymore."

"You can't what?" She wanted to ask if Amnesty was breaking up with her, but that would imply there was more to this than either were willing to admit.

Amnesty clutched her purse tight to her chest, as if for dear life. "I left the keys inside. Thanks for everything, but this is over."

"You're acting so weird."

"Says the weird girl."

Evangeline took a risk and stepped toward her. She didn't want her to feel cornered, but she couldn't stay away. Not when she was here to help, and had already proved that. "You're not yourself. Did something happen? Is it your father?"

"You know *nothing* about my father! And you don't know me!" Amnesty took advantage of the surprise in Evangeline's face and bolted past her, shuffling down the path and out the gate. She turned back and what was in her eyes then was most certainly fear. "Stay away from me, Evangeline. It's best for both of us."

Her heels clicked down the street as she ran away, and out of Evangeline's life, as strangely and swiftly as she'd entered it.

CHAPTER 13

A Red Mark

Charles showered off the lasting effects of the horrible sex he'd had with Cordelia that morning. The act had gotten no more bearable than their wedding night, though, to her credit, whenever he asked, she was ready. As ready as a dead fish.

The news that had come that day had sent a knife right to his heart. Colin and Catherine were expecting their first child next year. A child. A child made things permanent. It removed the sense that perhaps all of these decisions could be reversed, and the parties could go on to live their real lives, the ones intended for them.

He'd found the announcement on the top of the mail pile, already opened. So, Cordelia had seen it first. That explained her knowing grin when he came in and told her it was time for them to increase things a bit. *You get pregnant, we both get a break. Capisce?*

We'll move from three times a week to five, she agreed. *I still need weekends off.*

Why? You don't do anything.

Off from you.

Charles wished he could have all days off from Cordelia. They'd settled into their strange routine at Ophélie, one where she did her thing and he searched for what his should be. But she was no less cold toward him, and though sometimes, for the fun of it, he tried to make her laugh, or even angry, she was unruffled by anything. He toyed with the idea that he'd married a psychopath. He remembered Evangeline said that psychopaths didn't feel the same human emotions as most, like empathy, or anxiety. They only pretended to, when it suited them. He considered asking Evangeline to evaluate Cordelia, but decided it was sometimes better not to know.

Especially not now, when the woman he loved was growing a child inside of her that wasn't Charles'. He had to have his own son, and then he could stop touching Cordelia altogether. One son. That was it. He'd always wanted more children, but could give that up for his own sanity.

It was so tempting to go back to Colin and re-open the wound Charles had let close so soundly. The one protecting him from the knowledge he already *had* a child out there somewhere. A little girl.

A knock sounded on the bathroom door. Richard called out, "Your brother is here. He said you had an appointment together?"

"Shit," Charles whispered. He pushed his hands over the remaining soap on his body and hurriedly rinsed. "Tell him..." This wasn't a conversation he wanted Cordelia to overhear. He didn't need her to have anything she could use against his family. "Tell him to meet me in the heir's office. Have another chair put in there for him."

"I'll do that."

Augustus gaped at him. "Again? You're not serious."

Charles tossed his towel over the back of the chair. "There are things I find funny, and things I do not."

Augustus looked away. "How could this happen? Again? What did we miss?"

"We didn't miss anything," Charles said. "Maureen is legally a woman now, but she's been acting like she's one since she was a kid.

Short of locking her in a chastity belt, I don't know that anyone could have stopped her."

"And she's determined to have it."

Charles didn't share what Maureen had told him, how she believed the last child she'd aborted still haunted her. He had the feeling he'd be the only one advocating for her, and he had the unique access to her darkest secrets to do it.

That came with a certain responsibility, one that Charles took seriously.

"Not all our problems can just be erased with abortion, or that mind trickery you do, or murder," Charles said.

Augustus shot him a look. "I'm not suggesting anything, Huck, just trying to piece this all together. Get the whole picture."

Charles put his palms up. "I don't know much more than this. I'm not an information factory."

"The father..." Augustus winced. "Edouard Blanchard. I know him."

"And?"

Augustus blew out a long breath. "Well, nothing bad, really. He's a peculiar fellow. Something of an eccentric, and there's been talk about why he's never married, but other than that..."

"He likes the cock?"

"How should I know?" Augustus shook his head. "No, I don't think that's it. I think he's just a touch odd, is all. A recluse, perhaps. Are we sure? That he's the father?"

"Yes, Augustus, we're sure. This Blanchard fellow is fathering the very first child of this generation of Deschanels. He fucked our little sister when she was working for him, and she insists she wasn't having sex with anyone else at the time. Not like when she was leading that Virgins Only bullshit. Thus, he is the father."

"Virgins Only? What?"

"Nothing. Never mind. Can we focus?"

"Rich, coming from you," Augustus quipped. "And you learned this not from Maureen, but Colleen?"

"Maureen called Colleen, who called me."

"That doesn't seem odd to you?"

"What?"

"I don't know, Huck, all of it? Colleen is the most judgmental of all of us, and that's who she calls? And Colleen calls... you?"

"If there's an insult in there, Aggie, I'm failing to identify it."

Augustus stood. He started to pace the small office. "But what do you think Maureen wants? She's an adult now, and doesn't need anyone's permission, at least not in a legal sense. She'll have other battles, but no one can exactly *tell* her what to do. So what does she want?"

Charles almost laughed. Augustus had more heart than he'd ever realize, but he was severely lacking, at times, in the department of emotional insight. "I thought it was obvious. She wants her family. She wants our support. And we're her older brothers, and we're going to do just that."

Augustus stopped his frantic steps. He scrunched his face. "That doesn't *sound* like Maureen, but if you really believe that—"

"I do—"

"Then we do that. We support her."

Charles stood and clapped his brother on the back. "Great! So... how?"

Augustus laughed. "I thought you had the answer!"

"Me?" Charles cackled. "When do I ever have the answer? I called you here because I know, between the two of us, we can help her."

"I suppose we need to talk to Mama."

"*Hell* no! That was an absolute requirement to our being sworn into this insanity."

"You might have mentioned that first," Augustus replied, frowning. "Anyway, as I was saying it, I realized it wasn't such a swell idea. Mama, I'm afraid to say, is the last one who should know about this."

"Amen to that."

"All right. Let me think."

"I did have one idea."

"Never mind," Augustus muttered.

"One that would put the fear of God into this flim-flam peculiar motherfucker." Charles turned his left hand into a fist and pounded it into his right palm.

"Don't think that hasn't been rolling around in my head as well," Augustus said, in an offhand manner. He paced again, and when he turned back, his cheeks had reddened. "But that won't help our sister. She's never been the same after what happened to Evers. And no, Huck, I do *not* want to talk about it, not now or ever, but we can't do that to Maureen. I don't care what happens to Blanchard, but we have to protect our own. The only solution to this problem is one where Maureen comes out of this in one piece, and she and her baby are protected."

Charles smiled. "I like this side of you. All fired up. It's sexy."

"Stop." But Augustus smiled a little, too.

"He needs to pay, though. In some way."

"Yes, but... maybe not in the way you're thinking." Augustus' anger faded to something more thoughtful. He wrung his hands over his suit jacket. "I think Blanchard needs to marry Maureen."

"Oh, she'll love that!"

"Hear me out, Charles. What's the recurring challenge with Maureen?" He didn't wait for an answer. "Only she can say why she's chosen sex as her... escape, or whatever she would call it. This is now the third time we've had a situation as a result of it, but it's not the third time period. And it won't be the last."

"I'm listening," Charles said.

"But it has presented an opportunity that would not have been possible with Evers, or whatever high school kid was the father of her first child. Blanchard isn't only self-made, he comes from money, as you know. The Blanchards are long established in New Orleans, and, if we take this pregnancy out of the equation for a moment, this would make a good marriage for Maureen."

"He's an old fogey!"

"He's not that old. He's maybe in his forties. And he's an only son, Huck. His sisters have been trying to match him up for years, because their line is going to die out if he doesn't have a son. A marriage between two prominent families wouldn't raise eyebrows, even with the age gap between Maureen and Edouard. You know what else wouldn't raise eyebrows? Maureen's little child."

"People can do math, Aggie."

"So? Even if they do the math, it won't matter, because Maureen and Edouard will be happily married, and the talk will die down quickly. Everyone loves a scandal, but they move on to the next one in a minute."

"Happily?" Charles fixated on this word. It troubled him. He couldn't counter Augustus with logic, because what his brother suggested *was* logical. It was the most logical of all the solutions. If Maureen had this child unwed, it would dramatically harm her future prospects. She might never marry. She would struggle to find her place in society, which had come a long way, but still had a harsh eye to single mothers.

Charles didn't know very much about Maureen, even after the bond they'd developed that night by the river, but he did know this: Her vision of happiness included being the mistress of her own home, with a husband who came home to kiss her each night and children underfoot. He'd tried to tell her that this scenario didn't always come with happiness. Who knew that better than him? But if he knew one thing, especially after the debacle with Catherine, it was that women couldn't be dissuaded from a notion once it was stuck in their head. If Maureen was convinced this was the future she most needed, that was the only future she'd settle for.

Still... he felt agreeing to this was a betrayal of their trust, which mattered to him.

"Maybe not at first," Augustus agreed. "You and I both know Edouard wouldn't have played with this fire if he'd expected to be burned. He'll be even less happy, I assume. But he won't want a scandal."

"She's just barely eighteen," Charles said. His chest hurt. This couldn't be the only way, but yet he had no better one to propose. "We're damning her to a hard marriage."

"Huck." Augustus clapped a hand over his shoulder. "Come on. Who knows better than us that marriage isn't like television?"

"Still."

"Yeah." Augustus sighed and dropped his hand. "I know. But what else is there?"

Charles shook his head. He hated this. "You're right. We have to protect her future."

"And think of it this way. Maybe we can help her with another problem."

"What's that?"

"The first two incidents were really hard on Maureen. Really hard. And in both cases, she came out feeling like she'd been victimized. Maybe this time, by turning this into a positive path for her future, she can feel like she had a choice."

Charles smiled sadly. "Yeah. I hope you're right."

"And when we brute force things, to try and fix them, we both know that comes at a cost."

Charles said nothing. He didn't need to.

COLLEEN'S WHOLE BODY WAS ON FIRE AS SHE SCANNED the leather notebook at the head of the lecture room. Her scores had been impeccable since the first day, but now there was a red mark where her attendance should be.

A red mark.

The rest of the students filed out for the week, laughing and chatting with one another. That was nice, that so many of them were friends, but she was here for an education and *someone* had made a grave error in this book.

The heavy doors pounded closed. She looked around for her professor, but instead, she saw only that impudent aide from New Orleans. Jameson. Noah Jameson. He milled through the aisles, picking up the last of the discarded textbooks and forgotten pencils.

Colleen had an urge to pull the large leather tome from the desk and carry it off to make her point, but the thing was probably a hundred years old, not to mention heavy as a boulder.

"Hey!" she called out. Noah paused briefly, then continued on his menial task. "Noah, right?"

"That's my name," he replied without turning. In his arms was a precarious stack of books so tall she secretly hoped they'd topple out of his arms.

"There's a problem in this ledger."

"Ahh."

Colleen raised her voice. "This ledger? Who's responsible for updating it?"

Noah didn't respond at first. He edged his body carefully down the steps, and somehow managed to make it all the way to the shelf, where he stacked the books. She was too mesmerized by waiting for him to spill them all to kingdom come that her annoyance at his effrontery tempered.

He slapped his hands together to remove the dust, and, finally, looked at her. "Me. I update it."

Colleen smirked. "Well, you need to check your work."

"Pardon?"

Colleen shook her finger at the red entry. "You've marked me absent for the last two classes. I was here."

Noah shook his head. "I don't arbitrarily make decisions about who is and isn't here, Miss..."

"Oh, cut it. You know who I am."

Noah's tongue ran across his bottom lip, which curled out in amusement. "I know *of* you, and that's different. Be that as it may, I didn't mark you absent. You did."

"How's that?" Colleen's hands shot to her hips.

Noah made swirling motions with his finger. "Turn to page four hundred and seventy."

She did. "Okay."

"You see what you're looking at?"

"I'm not *blind*, Mr. Jameson."

"Noah is fine. I'm not my father." He peered from afar as if inspecting the page with her, but made no move to step closer. "You'll see that's the official attendance log. I'm sure it's familiar to you."

"Of course it is."

"Maybe not *too* familiar, as you failed to sign into class twice." He grinned. "All I do is copy the sign-in to the grading sheet."

"What? No, that's impossible." Colleen ran her finger down to her name in a fury, and when she slid it to the right, she was aghast. Two entries missing her initials. "Someone must have erased these days."

"They're in pen for a reason."

Colleen snapped her head up. "This isn't right. I was here!"

Noah nodded at the book. "Then fix it."

"What, you're not going to argue with me?"

"I didn't make it to graduate school by arguing," Noah replied. "Besides, I graded a paper you submitted on at least one of those days, and the other I remember you asking a thousand questions."

"So, why didn't you fix it, if you knew I was here?"

"I also didn't get this far by shirking personal accountability," Noah replied with an even wider grin, and now she knew he was toying with her.

Colleen opened her mouth to retort and then closed it in a huff. She marked her initials on the missed days and slapped the pen back to the desk. "There."

"Great. Problem solved." Noah turned back to the shelf, where he started to re-stack the textbooks.

"You don't like me," Colleen ventured.

"I don't know you."

Colleen took a few steps closer. "You sure act like you do. You act like I stole your cat or something."

Noah snickered. "I don't have a cat."

"Or something."

Noah turned, with a smaller stack of books in his hands. "Look, I'm sure you're really proud you got into this program, but we both know *how* it happened."

"Excuse me?"

"Your own brother gets thrown out of every college in town, and yet, somehow, the Deschanels *still* have the kind of clout that can get one of their debutantes into a coveted neuroscience program across the world!"

"No," Colleen said. She was fuming now. This was not happening, not when she'd left New Orleans to escape it. "You can think what you want about my brother, or my family, but I got into this program on my own merits. I've worked hard my whole life to get here."

"Sure." He stacked one book after another.

"I came here for an education, Noah. Not to be ridiculed about something I have no control over. I know what you and others think of my family, and that's *why* I came to Scotland! I don't want anyone opening a door for me I didn't earn."

"That's very big of you," Noah said, so coolly she had the urge to march across the room and smack him.

"I don't expect you to understand."

"Good," Noah replied. "Because I don't." He nodded over his shoulder. "Look, get out of here. Enjoy your evening doing whatever it is rich girls do with their evenings. I'll go in and fix your grade before I leave tonight."

"So, that's it?"

"Did you want a cookie?"

Colleen spun on her heels and stormed out of the lecture hall, leaving Noah and his smug assumptions to stack books, hopefully for the rest of the damn evening.

CHAPTER 14

The Price

Elizabeth waited until she heard the front door close and lock before she let Connor touch her. She still couldn't quite believe, even after all these years, that Irish Colleen let them be alone together in the house. In her *room.* Their mother had never let any of the others do this before they turned eighteen, not even prudish rule-abider Colleen. She didn't know if she'd dodged a bullet with this trust, or if she should be slighted by her mother's clear lack of fear in Elizabeth doing anything interesting.

Connor made a funny, anticipating face as they'd listened first to her mother's heels haphazardly move back and forth as she seemingly remembered things she needed to take with her on her short voyage to the grocer. Connor would feign going in for a feverish neck kiss, and then, foiled, his face would fold back in defeat.

Elizabeth giggled, half underneath him. He was still the only one who would bring her to the unguarded act.

When at last they heard the joyous sound confirming her mother's departure, Connor went in on her with comical energy, and the giggles continued until she could hardly breathe, and he, too, couldn't stay in character as her ardent assailant.

Connor flopped to the side, still laughing. "How long do you think she'll be gone?"

"It's Two Cart Tuesday," Elizabeth remarked, and Connor's whole face lit up. "And who knows, she might even stop in at the fabric store first. Could be a whole event."

"We can live in hope." He reached a hand over and laid it on her belly, letting his finger swirl mindlessly.

Ever since they'd cleared up the nature of their relationship, an invisible shackle had come loose. Now, it was all they could do to keep their hands off each other, which was both exhilaratingly wonderful, and also mortifying in the worst way. Elizabeth had finally fallen in love, and found her safe place, but it was never safe as long as her visions were allowed to play.

The first time he slipped his hand in her underwear, she saw a flash of anguish from his future; of a fight with his future wife laced with pain and torment. Of anger that can only be born from unparalleled love.

Later, she cried herself to sleep. She wanted this with Connor. She wanted it all so badly! Elizabeth, who had never really wanted anything except peace, now saw the opportunity for a feeling she could run toward, instead of away from, and the curse of her birth reminded her she would never have that life.

Except… there was a way. She'd been better about the drugs, at least as she saw it. She still used them just as much, but she was judicious in when and how much. She tried to reserve them for family dinners, or when she knew close contact with anyone she loved was imminent. When she was alone, she took her chances.

But now Connor was making a confession, and it snapped her back to the present, stone cold sober.

"You what?"

"Oh, God." Connor covered his eyes with his arms. "You're mad."

"No, I just… need you to repeat what you said."

"So you can be mad!"

"No, so I can fully appreciate it."

Connor peered from under his makeshift blindfold. "It was hard enough to say it the first time."

"If you said what I *think* you might have said, then the implications are far more serious than a few silly words, Connor."

He sighed. Groaned. Legs twitched. "I'm a fool. I'm so dumb!"

Elizabeth winced as she kissed him. Prayed her affection for her love wouldn't be rewarded with more pain. "I love you. Say it."

"I bought condoms." His lower jaw spread in horror of anticipating her response. He dropped his arms. "For, you know, us."

"Of course for us," she teased. "Who else would you buy them for? Mama?"

"Oh, God!"

Elizabeth laughed. "Don't be so embarrassed. How do you know I haven't been thinking about it, too?"

Connor stopped wiggling. "Have you?"

She shrugged. "Yeah. I have."

He jumped up on one elbow. "Yeah?"

"I said it, didn't I?"

"There's that anger." He grinned.

Elizabeth chucked him one good in the arm. "You know what my anger looks like. It isn't this."

"So... um..."

"This is the weirdest conversation we've ever had."

"Should I have just jumped you and asked questions later?"

Elizabeth considered this. "Hard to say how that might have turned out. Depends on my mood, I guess."

"Which is as unpredictable as Louisiana weather."

"Amen, brother."

Connor brushed a strand of hair off her face. "Lizzy, I don't want to make this even weirder than it is, but how do you want to, uh, proceed? Should I surprise you one day? Should we do it now? Do you have another idea?"

"I definitely didn't see it going like this," she murmured and kissed his frown. She didn't know how to say what she needed to say next. That to take this next step would require something he said he'd never, ever wanted to do again. Something he had no idea she was *still* doing, had never *stopped* doing. Every time she touched him, she awaited the inevitable agony that her visions never let her have reprieve from for long, and she couldn't bear to have their first time be awash in grief.

"What are you thinking?" he asked. He always knew when her mind had drifted beyond the immediate conversation.

"I'm afraid, is all," Elizabeth said. She searched for the truth, knowing it could never be the full truth. He'd never understand. "I still see… stuff, when we touch. And if we do *that,* I don't know what I'll see, but I couldn't handle it being horrible. Not with you."

Connor was silent as he considered this. She had never read his mind, and never wanted to, but sometimes she was curious at the process that rolled through his head. She adored this about him; that he never made decisions lightly, and was so deeply considerate of how his words affected others.

"I know we said we wouldn't do it again, but… would it help if we tried that stuff we did before?"

"Oh, um, I hadn't really considered this," Elizabeth lied. "But, yes, I think it would."

"We'd have to buy some more, and I'm not exactly the hippest dude on the block. I still don't know how you scored it."

"I told you, the guy is my neighbor," Elizabeth said. "But we don't need to buy more."

"No?"

"I still have more left from that first time," she lied. She had some, but that original stash was long gone. She worried it wouldn't work anymore with her resistance what it was, but she would just take harder hits, and she also had more of her mother's pills she could throw on top to really dull the blade.

Connor laughed to hide his discomfort. "I guess that's good, right? Would really kill the mood to have to go track down a drug dealer for a score."

"Want me to go get it?"

"Right now?"

"You don't want to?"

Connor's eyes widened. "I'm a guy. And I love you. I always want to, Lizzy."

"Okay, then." She tried not to laugh. Tried not to cry. She was so conflicted at what she was about to do. What she'd been doing for months, deceiving him, in order to love him.

She scrambled from the bed and did her best to keep her back blocking her work in the corner. She dug three pills from the baggie and choked them down. Her throat gagged, and she had to fight it back, because to grab the water near the bed would be to give herself away.

"What are you doing over there?"

"Trying to find it."

Elizabeth made enough sounds to seem like she was searching, and then lifted the heroin-laced joint and lighter with a light, "here it is!" sound and brought it back to the bed.

Connor looked at it with the same horror she should feel. He was doing this for her. He didn't want to touch the stuff. "Should I, you think, put the condom on first? In case my judgment is compromised when I'm high?"

"Now, probably," Elizabeth said, because it sounded responsible and she needed him to think she was. Especially now, when her heart raced so fast against her chest that she was sure everything she'd been up to was written across her flesh.

Connor nodded. He puffed out his cheeks and blew out a breath as he fumbled with the wrapper. Neither of them had done this, but his face flushed at his lack of finesse. Elizabeth laid her hand over his and smiled. This eased him, and he was able to successfully fish the contraception out.

She figured the next part would give him even more performance anxiety, so Elizabeth turned to the side to light the joint. While he was preoccupied, she took two deep, strong hits, praying for the head start she'd need to get enough of the heroin coursing through her to lift the shield.

"I think I've got it," he said, and she took one more hit before handing it to him.

Connor wrinkled his mouth, and with a hesitant look, drew the cigarette to his lips and inhaled. He coughed, shot her an apologetic look, and tried again.

She immediately took another, and offered it back. He shook his head. "Last time, one was enough."

Elizabeth secretly stole one more hit as she turned to place it in the glass bowl at her bedside. Yes, this would be enough.

She turned and wrapped Connor in her arms and opened the rest of herself to whatever came next.

Maureen willed the phone to ring. She'd talked to Colleen twice after the first time she'd spilled her news, and each time, Colleen said she was working on it. To trust her to help.

"Colleen is a pain, but I would trust her," Madeline said.

Maureen realized she really was in dire straits if she found comfort in the dead.

"I do trust her, but look at me!" Maureen pressed her sweater tight and turned in the mirror. "You can tell!"

"Only if you're paying close attention."

"Have you met Mama?"

"Colleen knows you're racing a clock here. She'll come through."

"What if she doesn't?"

Madeline reached forward and squeezed her hand. Maureen felt nothing, because there *was* nothing. "Then I'll help you."

"I wish you could. I wish we could rewind the clock. To before you died... before Charles married that wench... before I foolishly let my boss use and discard me. I'm such an idiot! I never, ever want to see him again, Maddy. Colleen said he should pay up, or something, but I don't want a damn thing from him. Nothing. If I even see his face, I'll hurl myself off a bridge."

"He can send checks in the mail."

Maureen laughed. "I'll rip them up and toss them in the fire. Then piss on it as it burns."

"That's dramatic, even for you, silly girl."

August had been oddly quiet since she found she was pregnant. She hoped he was off in some peaceful place, having a good time, or whatever it was he did when he wasn't haunting her. But she suspected it was worse than that: His judgment and disappointment kept him away.

"Why, Maureen?" Peter, as always, reminded her that nothing could keep *him* away.

What was she going to do? The life growing within her now *felt* real. It was more than the results of a test. It was now a she, and Maureen had never wanted anything more in her life than her daughter. Her extrinsic worries, about what people would think, how she'd show her face, seemed so petty and vapid in the face of the love she bore for a child she'd not yet met.

She still had the money she'd earned from the Virgins Only Club. She could still run away and start a new life, where she could tell everyone her husband had died saving orphans or something. By the time the money ran out, she'd have her trust, and she'd be the eccentric Widow Deschanel, who pined for her nonexistent dead husband, when she wasn't knitting blankets for the destitute.

Yes, there was that. And if Colleen didn't come through for her, she would leave in the middle of the night and never come back. Starting over would be the only option. She couldn't dare face her family as a disgraced woman.

But that was not the life Maureen was born for.

It was the life choice that had killed sweet Madeline.

Give it to God, Mama would say, but Mama was not someone Maureen looked up to. She loved her, but she did not respect her.

Colleen would know what to do, and Maureen was placing everything on the line in the hopes her wise older sister would come through with a solution that allowed Maureen to move forward without shame.

She glared at the phone and *begged* it to ring.

. . .

When Elizabeth awoke, it was dark. She rolled her head to the side, in a panic. Downstairs, the sound of her mother rustling around in the kitchen sent her heartrate skyrocketing.

Connor was awake. He stared at the ceiling, with a look that chilled her heart.

"What happened?" she whispered. Her voice was hoarse from the hits. "Connor?"

"I don't know."

"Did we have sex?"

Connor's eyes glistened. "Don't you see the problem, Lizzy? That you even have to ask that?"

"Yeah, but..." Elizabeth winced. "Did we?"

"We must have. The condom was full," Connor replied. He turned away from her. "I remember some stuff, but..."

Elizabeth remembered nothing. Nothing at all, after rolling over him and deciding to give herself to him. Nothing. Not even a flash, like she had with her visions. There was only a void.

She'd given her virginity to the only person in her life she loved with her whole heart, and the memory was lost to her haze of drugs.

"We shouldn't have done the heroin," Connor was saying. "It was a bad idea the first time, it was a bad idea this time, and... oh, God..."

The sob started in her throat and rolled forward, pitching her body up and off the bed as it made its way out of her. Elizabeth grabbed a pillow and buried her face in it and screamed and screamed and screamed.

Because this wasn't the first thing she'd missed.

She'd been high through Charles' wedding.

She'd been high at Maureen's eighteenth birthday party.

She'd been high when they had the going-away dinner for Augustus and Ekatherina in the summer, and later forgotten they'd ever left.

She'd been high when they sent Colleen back to Scotland.

And she'd been high for what should have been the biggest moment of her life so far.

If she didn't have a problem, how could she explain all these losses? Did they outweigh the gift of losing her visions? Did any of it matter, if nothing mattered?

Elizabeth sobbed into her pillow.

CHAPTER 15

You Can't Always Get What You Want

The whole evening had been an exercise in uncomfortable choreography.

Of all people, Cordelia the Ice Queen was the one who insisted that, once a month, they entertain guests. Charles shouldn't have been so surprised, really, seeing as the only thing his wife cared about more than her own personal space was her sense of duty.

This desire to remain relevant in society did not, unfortunately, transform into a super hostess, however. She was cordial, asked most of the right questions, and sipped her wine at the right times. Knew how to arrange silverware for place settings, and the right timing to direct the kitchen staff on when to bring which course. She was a walking textbook on proper etiquette and form for bluebloods.

But anyone who had ever interacted with an actual human being could see the ruse.

When she suggested the party, Charles had only paid half a mind to the idea and told her to do whatever she pleased. They rarely existed in a manner that dared allow either of their spheres to overlap at any point in orbit, and so when they did speak—usually about things of a matter-of-fact nature—he was happy to have it done.

He didn't think what they had could be considered a marriage at all, unless, as Evangeline said one night with a beer in her hand and four in her belly, you considered marriage in a much more old-fashioned lens: a business arrangement.

That seemed right to Charles. Cordelia exacted her transactions in the bedroom like a janitor clocking in and out, right on time, to a job he loathed but required to survive. She retreated to her own room after, and he'd never awoken or fallen asleep with his wife at his side. They had no memories together, no inside jokes. No shared stories of how one of them had done a silly thing, and the other still found it funny. He dreamed of a day when Cordelia was pregnant and he could slip away into the night and find his own prurient pleasures, as he once had.

In the beginning, this was some terrible fresh horror he believed would turn out to be a nightmare, but as their marriage entered its second quarter, Charles wondered if it wasn't, instead, a blessing.

If he couldn't marry for love, then maybe the best alternative was to marry purely for the benefit of fulfilling his sacred duty as heir.

Because Charles paid no mind to the party Cordelia wanted to throw, he hadn't had an eye to the guest list. Later, he wondered, had she known? Was that why she'd done it?

Colin. Catherine. Dan Weatherly and his new wife, Mary. That hack, Darwin. Some other names that didn't matter, not behind the ones previously listed.

There was little to no chance Cordelia cared about keeping the fires of friendship burning between her husband and his pals, so she *must* have known. That prick of cruelty that ran through her veins must have required entertainment, the kind that could only be produced by seeing her husband squirm in heartbreaking discomfort.

They'd sat around the table. Cordelia, who did not care a whit for things like seating charts, had created one and placed Catherine at Charles' left. Cordelia sat directly across, the best seat in the house.

"You look well," Catherine had said, and Charles smiled and pretended the conversation was as congenial as it might have been if it was anyone else in the world, because Cordelia's eyes were glued to him, completely ignoring Mary Weatherly's attempts at conversation at her side.

"I am," he said. He sniffled, wishing he'd had the foresight for a bump or four of cocaine. "And you do, too."

Catherine's cheeks flushed with the early days of pregnancy. She kept one hand protectively over her belly at all times. He'd heard men wax about their wives never being more beautiful than when they were carrying a child and figured it for bullshit, but she was as radiant and lovely as she'd ever been, and he fell in and out of love with her twelve times in the span between their silences.

It had been so much easier when they kept their distance. All his hard work came undone in her presence, and he was a mess.

For one, secret, hopeful flash, Charles wondered if the child could be his, but he hadn't been with her in close to a year.

"How've you been, Huck?"

"You know me," he said. He flexed his fist under the table to snap him back to the moment, to keep him from drifting into the past. "I always have something to occupy me."

"You always did," she said and smiled into her apple cider. There'd be no wine for Catherine that night, or any night until her child was born. "And Augustus? How is married life treating him?"

"You never know with him, but he seems happy."

"Are you?" Catherine asked. A leading question, if there ever was one, and she was clearly unaware of the devious Cordelia eagerly awaiting his answer.

"I'm always content. You know that."

"Yes," she replied, and this time looked away. Good. He was past the point in his grief where he wanted her to feel pain, but it was nice to know he wasn't the only one still suffering. "You've never needed anyone else to make you happy."

"Nope," he said, then added, quietly, "But, once upon a time, it didn't hurt."

"Charles will be *much* happier soon, I should think," Cordelia said, her words rising with her lanky frame. "I have an announcement to make."

"You do?" Charles asked. Catherine shot him a curious look. He shrugged, but his heart ricocheted around like a fresh high. He couldn't guess what she had up her sleeve, but it couldn't be good.

"We do, darling." Cordelia's smile was black ice; the venom invisible at the surface, unless you knew.

Charles sucked in a breath. "By all means, go on."

She reached her hand across the table. It took him a minute to realize she was looking for him to *hold* it. *Maybe she can act.* He frowned and reached for it. Her skin was cool and rigid, like a body in the opening act of rigor mortis. "Charles and I are having a child!"

Charles swallowed the remainder of the wine in his glass.

Catherine's smile died on her face. Not for long, but long enough. She recovered and was the first to congratulate them. "You'll make such a wonderful father," she said, raising her glass.

Colin beamed with pride and wiped at the corner of his eye. "Charles, I'm speechless. I've always hoped this day would come for you. Just think of how much has changed in a year."

Chancing a glance in his peripheral, Charles said, "Yes. A year can make a world of difference."

THE REST OF THE EVENING PASSED BY IN A BLUR OF inebriation and dim lighting. He lost track of his drinks, the number surpassing his humor and good nature somewhere between watching Catherine sip her non-alcoholic drink like a perfect mother-in-waiting, and hearing Dan make repeated arcane jokes about how he'd enjoyed slipping it to his wife four times a day so they could be the next to make an announcement of their own.

Everyone's eyes occasionally turned to Charles; for once, not to judge his behavior but to gauge his reception of the news his wife had chosen to share with not only their close friends but also *him.* Did they pity him? He could take a lot, but they could fuck off with their sympathy.

As they said goodbye to the guests, one by one, Cordelia turned on a level of charm that was both uncomfortable and entertaining to watch. Uncomfortable, because it was not the least bit authentic or natural, and entertaining for the same reason. She curtsied when a kiss on the cheek would do and laughed at things that weren't funny. Charles almost felt a stab of affection for the young woman who'd never had a mother to guide her and was now floundering.

A stab only, though, as he remembered she'd intentionally put him in a position to be humiliated that night, if not with his pairing of Catherine, then for certain catching him unawares of the news of his impending fatherhood.

He'd done it. He'd fucking *done* it, and now he didn't have to touch her at all, ever again. Or at least until he felt it prudent to produce a spare.

Cordelia stood at his side and waved at the last of the guests. She closed the door as the engines roared outside, and headlights flooded the night.

"Couldn't have told me *before* dinner, dearest?"

"What would have been the fun in that, darling?"

He reached for her arm as she turned toward the stairs. "Cordelia. Seriously, you're really pregnant? Finally?"

"It would seem so." She grunted. "May."

"That's the due date?"

"I wrote it down somewhere," she said, dismissive. "I'll find it later. Right now, I'm exhausted, and I have an early day."

"Why? Tomorrow is Sunday. Don't tell me you've found the Lord all of a sudden."

Cordelia sighed and brushed his hand off her arm, like swatting off an annoying insect. "Now that the unpleasant task of procreation is checked off our list, I'll be moving to my townhouse on Esplanade for the winter, and into the spring."

Charles laughed. "Ophélie isn't big enough for you?"

She pinched her face even tighter than usual. "It will never be big enough for the two of us, Charles. Don't look so grim. I'll be back when our child is born, and we'll resume our duties another thirty days after that." She took his chin in her bony fingers. "In the meantime, darling, feel free to whore your way through New Orleans a hundred times over. These are the glory days, husband. When we have a passel of brats running through these ancient halls, we'll no longer have the time or the energy for anything that brings us the remotest bit of joy."

Cordelia turned and ascended the stairs without another word.

Charles moved into the parlor. He had other business to attend to that night, but he needed a drink, and also something else, and he always had his secret stash of coke in the trap drawer of the bar table.

"Charles."

Charles jumped at the sound of his name. He spun, bringing the room in and out of focus, before landing on the only face he'd deem as unpleasant and unwelcome as his wife's.

Darwin.

"Why the fuck are you still here?"

Darwin spread his arms over the back of the sofa, one hand dangling a whiskey on ice. Charles bristled at the thought of this vile man partaking of his booze. "Have you never mastered the art of small talk, or do you find it offensive?"

"I find your face offensive."

"Insults don't become a man."

"Your face doesn't become you."

"Then again, perhaps you're not capable of more," Darwin quipped. He drew a sip from his tumbler and leaned back into the couch, making himself right at home.

This will never be your home. It's hardly hers.

"You really don't want to know what I'm capable of, Darwin." He checked his watch. "But you're right, I don't deal in small talk. So tell me what you want and leave."

"I need money."

Charles laughed. "Obviously."

"Would you like to hear why?"

Charles pointed at his watch. "Not hardly, unless you can do it in thirty seconds."

"Costs are rising. We need to move some of our operations to China, but this requires an investment. I need an investor. How's that for a brief summary of my needs?"

"Efficient as that was," Charles replied. "You can well and truly go fuck yourself. I gave you money once, and I told you that you'd never get another goddamn penny."

Darwin grinned, and Charles saw Cordelia in him. "I think you're forgetting what's at stake."

Charles laughed. He laughed and laughed. "Maybe you should have showed up yesterday, then, brother. Because *today,* I'm officially going to be a father, and *today,* I have the upper hand. You wanna release those photos and turn your sister into a laughing stock?" He spread his arms wide. "Be my fucking guest, Darwin. Post them in triplicate, and on every telephone pole. Because it's Cordelia you'll be hurting, not me."

Charles slipped an unopened bottle of cognac in his jacket and left.

Augustus awaited outside the St. Charles mansion for his brother to arrive. The world outside was still, except the passing cars. It was late, and many of the homes here had turned down for the night.

He'd never enjoyed, or sought out, the quiet spaces in life. These were times where thoughts threatened to take over and turn into assumptions or fears. Augustus had opened his business almost exactly a week after Madeline had died, because he was terrified of falling into the quiet place. He thought it possible for a man to go there and never emerge whole again.

But he'd been waiting going on an hour and there wasn't anything else to do now *except* think. And all he could think about was his wife, and the call he'd received earlier that evening from Andrew St. Andrews in Summer Island.

I dinnae want to fuss ye, he'd started, and then the rest unfolded in a series of apologetic starts and re-starts. Augustus didn't hang up the call with a full picture, but it was enough, and suddenly Ekatherina's strange turn toward the melancholy on their calls started to make sense.

Her friends in town had grown cold on her, and the reason, according to St. Andrews, who did all but the tango around the point, was Ekatherina's close association with George Cairne.

He'd told Augustus not to pay too much heed to the rumors, because small towns didn't know any better and would stop gossiping the day they stopped breathing. But that rumors were enough to change the entire temperature of a person's welcome, and Ekatherina had been holed up in the house for days, while the rest of the women in town rallied around the scorned Mrs. Cairne.

Ekatherina had breathed not a word of this on the phone calls home. But he'd heard it, somewhere, underscoring everything she didn't say.

Augustus couldn't ask the lingering question of his neighbor in Maine. It was too much, and even a hesitation on the other man's part would send his imagination to a dark and dangerous place.

Light flooded the car as Charles' face appeared in the door. "We ready to get this show on the road?"

"I was ready an hour ago," Augustus muttered.

"Get the twist out of your panties, Aggie. I found out tonight I'm going to be a father!"

Augustus paused midway through extracting the keys from the ignition. "Seriously?"

"I did my fucking duty," Charles went on. He tapped the roof of the car, hard. "And now I don't have to *touch* the bitch for another... well, however the fuck long it takes for her to grow and expel the baby. And then heal, or whatever."

Augustus slid out of the car. He regarded his brother over the top of it, in the dark. The family needed some good news. They needed it bad. "That's really great news, Charles. I'm so happy for you."

"Thanks, man. Thanks." Charles slammed his door and grinned under the streetlight. "Now, let's go secure the future of Maureen's baby."

Edouard Blanchard wasn't expecting them. Augustus almost—almost—felt bad for the guy. Whatever his extracurricular activities, he was a self-selected hermit, who'd let fun with the wrong young woman become the unintended path to what remained of his future.

But Augustus couldn't forget Maureen had been underage when the affair started. And he could never, ever forget the last time she'd gotten caught up with an older man. Charles taking care of that problem had been the tippy top of the pendulum swing now cutting a swash through the family. Happiness, quickly replaced by agony. Over and over.

"Catherine was at our party tonight," Charles said as they crossed one side of St. Charles and paused in the neutral ground, between the east and west streetcar tracks. They waited for the light to change and oncoming traffic to stop.

"I didn't know you were having a party tonight."

"Oh, don't be cross. I figured Cordelia was half-kidding when she said she was throwing one, and then I wasn't consulted on the invite list. Not that you would've come anyway."

"You mean your wife invited Catherine?" Augustus frowned.

"Let's try not to call that hellbeast my wife, when it's just us chickens," Charles said. "And yes, she did, and no, I don't think it was a fucking accident."

Augustus started across the second half of the avenue. Blanchard's mansion was just ahead, protected only semi-well by high shrubbery and thick trees. "How did it go?"

"How do you think it went? I fell in love with her again in front of everyone, and Cordelia ate it right up. Oh, and then broke the news about her being knocked up, in front of all our guests. Including me."

Augustus stopped on the other side and gaped at him. "She didn't tell you before she told everyone?"

"Hellbeast," Charles muttered.

"As you said," Augustus replied. "This means you've done your duty, both to the family and to her. Enjoy the break."

EDOUARD WAS STILL AWAKE AND LET THEM IN, WITH A thousand questions and half as many reservations painted across his face. He knew who they were, of course. Everyone did. But he didn't know why they were there, and at the late hour.

"Our sister is why," Charles said.

"Your sister?" Edouard asked from across the room as he mixed the drinks. "Augustus, you're sure I can't make you something?"

"Quite sure."

Edouard handed Charles his drink and settled into the armchair across from the brothers. His tired face creased with his lack of sleep and anticipation of what might come next.

"Maureen," Charles said. "You might know her. Petite brunette, just turned eighteen. You might know her better from behind, though."

"Charles," Augustus hissed.

"Maureen..." Edouard's eyes wandered and then snapped wide. "Maureen! I didn't... I didn't quite place, or piece, that together, that she was one of *those* Deschanels..."

"There's only one Deschanel family in New Orleans," Charles said. He emptied his drink and slammed it on the table to his left. Augustus tried to shoot him a look, but couldn't catch his eye. They hadn't discussed this "good cop, bad cop" routine Charles seemed to be heading down. "Only one that matters."

"You fired her," Augustus said. He watched the older man. Studied him. They'd been at events together. Had some casual conversation, the kind that brought the loquaciousness out of a man in the moment, but later unable to recall what was said. But Augustus had never taken the measure of the man. Was he weak, or merely odd? Would he have to employ a skill he'd hoped to keep away from this night?

Not if Edouard was a true man.

"Not exactly," Edouard said. "Maureen was a wonderful worker. A harder one than the secretaries who have been there for years, and I can't seem to be rid of them. Unions." He swallowed a drink, and it was then Augustus realized his hand was shaking. "But work slows in my profession in the fall and winter. The role Maureen occupied was always meant to be seasonal. I could have hired her back in the spring."

"Did you tell her that when you hired or, or just after you'd fucked her?"

Edouard's mouth dropped open. "I don't know what she's told you..."

"We know what went on between you in the office, late at night," Augustus said. His voice was firm, hoping to cut off the inevitable stream of bullshit coming from Blanchard, and at the same time, discourage the Clint Eastwood act from his brother. "Maybe not all the details, but the salient ones. We also know she was underage when it happened, but we're not here to debate the legalities of what passed between you. I'm sure you're already well aware of them."

Augustus, in his head, heard Charles remind him the age of consent was seventeen, as only Charles would know.

Edouard's jaw flapped. He set his drink aside. "If you're not, as you say, concerned with the legalities, gentlemen then... I'm almost afraid to ask, why *are* you here?"

"It's late, and a lesser man reminded me tonight that I'm shit at small talk," Charles said. He stretched his arms over his head. Cracked his knuckles. "Maureen is pregnant. She's keeping it. And before you go on and insult my baby sister by asking whether you're the father, *you're the fucking father.*"

The air in the room tightened. None of them made a sound. Augustus was painfully aware of even his own heartbeat, which pounded in his ear like a deadly reminder from a Poe story.

"Wow," Edouard said at last. "Forgive me, I was not expecting that."

"Man, I just found out tonight that I'm going to be a father, too, so I'll give you a minute to let that sink in," Charles said.

"Congratulations," Edouard muttered. He wiped his palm across his mouth and his eyes closed. "Jesus."

"Let's leave the Lord out of it," Augustus said. "As Charles said, it's late, and the gift of small talk missed me as well. If you're thinking of reaching for your checkbook, don't. Maureen has no need of money. She'll never have need of money."

Edouard nodded. "What, then, can I give?"

"The only thing she needs," Augustus replied. "Your name."

"My name?"

Charles slid his lower jaw back and forth. "Edouard, I know you're not this fucking slow. Maureen Deschanel *will* be Maureen Blanchard, because you're going to marry her. Soon. Maybe tomorrow."

"No," Edouard said. He inched physically back and away from both brothers, trying to disappear into the chair. "I have no desire to marry anyone."

"Your desires are how we got into this situation," Augustus said.

"You're going to marry her because it's the right fucking thing to do," Charles said. "And because if you can do the crime, you can do the goddamn time. In case you need that translated, you fucked my little sister, got her pregnant, and you do not just get to walk away from this. Her whole life is on the line. Her future. Do you get that? Did you think of that at all, when you had her bent over your desk?"

"Charles," Augustus said again.

"I assumed a girl like that would have taken the proper precautions."

Augustus' blood pressure rose so fast he didn't have time to stop himself from jumping forward and reaching for the man. Charles was faster and shot his arm out, pinning him back.

"Don't you ever talk about Maureen that way. Ever," Augustus warned. “She’s our sister, and she’ll be your wife, and you *will* respect her.”

“Are you sure I can’t just kill him?” Charles asked.

“Thinking about it.”

Edouard worked his gaze between the brothers, as if deciding whether they were seriously contemplating this option.

“I don’t think you appreciate how fortunate you are right now,” Augustus continued. He tried to steady his anger. It wouldn’t serve him here, and he knew it started earlier in the evening, after that phone call. “This isn’t a punishment. Everyone in this city wishes they could marry a Deschanel. Her trust alone is measured in the multi-millions, but we’ll send her with a dowry of five, because it’s nothing to us, but it’s something to you. Having her name attached to you will skyrocket your business far beyond any successes you *think* you’ve had today. Instead of going to jail, we just gave you the meal ticket for your future.”

“And if I decline this offer?” Edouard asked.

The brothers exchanged a look. “That would not be in your best interest.”

THE BROTHERS WALKED BACK TO THE CAR IN SHARED silence, each contemplating the victory that was really no victory at all, but instead a hollow triumph. Maureen would marry Edouard, and she would do it at the expense of her joy.

But her future was protected now.

“You driving back into Vacherie, or staying somewhere in New Orleans?”

Charles took a deep breath of the cool night air. “I should go home. Ophélie *is my* home. Not hers. I won’t have her chasing me away, when I can’t stand to be under the same roof.”

“She’ll leave you alone for a while, in any case.”

“Yeah.” Charles flipped his keys around in his hands. “What about Ekatherina? She home now?”

Augustus looked away. “No, and I think I was a fool to leave her there. I think something has... is happening. Something I could have stopped, if I'd been a better husband. A better ma—"

Charles appeared before him and took his face between his hands. "There is no better man, Augustus. The better man is you. Now, go to Maine, and go save your goddamn marriage, because at least one of us has to be happy."

WINTER 1974

VACHERIE, LOUISIANA
NEW ORLEANS, LOUISIANA
EDINBURGH, SCOTLAND
SKYE, SCOTLAND

CHAPTER 16

The Winter of our Discontent

The cold spell wasn't forecasted. They didn't have many of them in South Louisiana, even in the winter, which was now officially underway, as of that morning. Augustus had phoned the night before from Maine to tell Charles he was being dragged to a "Winter Solstice Festival, whatever the hell that means. There's already a foot of snow on the ground, and I don't understand how people are leaving their houses."

Charles awoke to a winter wonderland himself. The slight chill in his room prompted a groggy-eyed glance out the window, and a strange feeling came over him as he observed the grounds of Ophélie, as far as the eye could see, blanketed in white.

He felt like a kid. He wanted to run outside and flail his arms around, face to the sky to catch even a drop of whatever had caused this. He searched around for his pants and shoes, and then dug around in his closet for his once-a-year jacket, reserved for days just like these.

"Cordelia! You're not gonna believe this!" he called out into the hall, to her suite across. He frowned. She wasn't here. Hadn't been for almost two months. He'd only seen her at her regularly scheduled obstetrics appointments, and only because he'd forced himself into the process.

The appointments were tedious, but a visit from Evangeline after had brought news that nothing could overshadow. News only a Deschanel could know this early. He was having a son. A boy.

Charles zipped up his jacket and raced down the stairs, like he used to on Christmas, when he still believed in Santa. Legs a blur, excitement outpacing ability. On the way down, Richard saw him and chuckled.

"Charles, you'll break both your legs, you keep carrying on like that!"

Charles smiled and clapped Richard on the back. Richard, who had been like an uncle to him, even though his role was relegated mainly to the backdrop of his life. Richard, who was probably his *actual* uncle, if the rumors about Charles' grandfather were to be believed. "Have you looked outside, old man?"

"I'm not that old yet. Don't rush me."

"Have you?"

"Yeah, I've taken a gander, and I *think* I know what's got y'all in a fuss."

"When's the last time it actually snowed here?" Charles stared at the awaiting door. He rubbed his hands together, in anticipation of the cold just beyond.

"Been years, I 'spose," Richard mused. "But, I hate to break it to you when you're as giddy as I've ever seen ya, but that's not snow outside."

"Then what the fuck is it?"

"Frost," Richard said. He made his way toward the back of the house, to one of the kitchens. "Dropped below freezing last night, if you can believe it."

Charles flung the door wide and marched out to confirm for himself. He trotted down the steps and knelt in the grass, running the frosted blades through his fingers. His smile died.

It was beautiful, but it was not snow. Just an illusion, like so many things.

The hard crunch of gravel sounded in the distance. A car ambled down the frozen path. The approach to Ophélie was somewhere between a quarter and a half mile, Charles estimated, so it was always a slog waiting for the identity of a visitor to appear.

The Mercedes logo beamed through the cold fog. Cordelia.

Charles forgot how excited he'd been only minutes ago to share the enthusiasm with his wife. Suspicion permeated, taking over the happiness that had been so wonderful, and so fleeting.

Cordelia slammed the door and marched over to him. Tears cut a hard line down her bony cheeks. Her eyes were red, too red.

"You unfathomable devil," she whispered through a hoarse throat. "You... you."

Charles pulled himself off the grass. He didn't approach her, instead holding out a hand that was both welcome and caution. "What's the matter? Is it our son?"

"Our son. You and your family, and their devilry. Son." She spat the words, expelling then more than saying them. "Our *son* is a game to you, just like everything is a game to you. Everything, including that rotten sister of yours and her rotten, horrible words."

"We'll come back to what you said about our son," Charles said. His breath unfurled in the air, teasing him of what might have been. Everything had shifted so quickly. "But don't talk about my sisters like that, Cordelia. I'll put up with a lot, but leave my family out of your bitterness."

"Leave them out? How convenient, when they pulled mine in," she returned. She made no move to come closer. One hand held the car door. "Your precious sister, Elizabeth. Why did you tell me about her, Charles? Why?"

Charles rooted around in his brain, desperate to get ahead of whatever came next. Cordelia's tears were not incidental. Nothing about that woman was. And what did this have to do with Lizzy? "I'd hoped you'd be smart enough to call off the wedding when I couldn't."

She licked at a batch of tears that had come to rest at the corner of her mouth. "Hindsight is a cunt, isn't she?"

"Why are you bringing this up now? Why now?"

"Because your *sister* said things to my father that he couldn't forget. And then your *other sister* said even more terrible words." Cordelia stepped away from the safety of her car. She side-stepped through the gravel, instead of approaching. "It wasn't that I didn't believe your bullshit stories about their parlor tricks, Charles. It was that I *didn't fucking care.* What is it about every Deschanel that makes them believe they are so goddamn special? What is it that makes you all believe you can do whatever you want, without consequence?"

"Cordelia—"

"My father is *dead,* Charles, and while those insipid little cunts are surely culpable, *I blame you!*"

Charles sucked in a sharp, cold breath. And there it was. The moment they'd dreamed about, laughed about. Even thinking of Maureen turning into Daisy Mae gave him a thrill; the look of pure terror creeping into old Franz's eyes as his chickens finally returned to roost.

But he felt no joy now. Cordelia's hatred was only a mask for her grief. Real grief, not the sociopath searching for the emotion they believe their audience needed. The man was a monster, but that monster was her father, and the victory of his death was hollow and Charles struggled to find the meaning he believed it would once give him.

"I am so sorry, Cordelia." He did take a step forward then. She cringed. "I mean that. I really am."

"How?" Cordelia demanded. She rolled her gloved hands into fists at her side. "How can you mean that? You orchestrated this! You told Elizabeth to plant the idea, and then you let Maureen torture him with it!"

Now was not the time to remind her that her father was a murderer and a rapist. Charles had wondered, once upon a time, what it was like to see a mother witness her son's execution for violent crimes. To others, that son was a monster, but to the mother, he was only her son, and she grieved twice; for the man he was, and for the man he could've been.

"Elizabeth's visions are what they are. It wasn't a good idea to corner her and demand her to give them, because you never know what she'll see. She can't control her visions. But they always come true. Always. And I told you that in the beginning."

"You told me what you thought would lead me down exactly a path like this."

"I'm not capable of that kind of foresight, Cordelia! I'm just not!" Charles took another few steps. "I told you about Elizabeth and the others because I wanted you to run away screaming, not run *toward* us, and use her to your advantage. I am so, so sorry you're hurting right now. There's no love lost between us, but you're the mother of my child and that binds us for life, in a way marriage never will. But you cannot put on my shoulders your decision to kidnap and exploit my sister's ability, and I won't be blamed for it backfiring."

Cordelia shook with rage. Her jaw hung wide, a halo of cold breath surrounding her reddened cheeks. "You are anathema to me, Charles."

"I don't know what that word means, but I get the drift."

"Don't you even want to know how he did it?"

"Sorry?"

"My father. Aren't you going to ask how he did it?"

Charles set his mouth tight. This line of conversation had nowhere good to go, but he saw no choice. "How? How did he do it?"

"He hung himself from the same bridge Daisy Mae jumped from."

Charles swallowed. This tidbit erased any last lingering doubt that the prophecy and subsequent information was the cause. But was it really? Franz Hendrickson had committed the atrocious crimes. All they did was remind him.

Cordelia reached into her jacket pocket and withdrew a knife. She held it to her belly. "I should cut this demon from my womb and let you watch him hang like my father."

Charles held his hands out and began a slow approach. "Jesus Christ, Cordelia, put that down. Now."

"Why? Why should I give you what you want most when you've taken everything from me?" she cried.

"Cordelia, I didn't take anything from you! Your father killed his best friend after raping his daughter, and then sold you into marriage so he could avoid consequence. Why am I the villain in this story?" He took another step, and then another.

"Your father should have turned him in when he had the chance," Cordelia said. Her knife-holding hand trembled, and he feared she'd slice herself by accident. "He should have stopped this when he had the chance!"

"I wish he had," Charles agreed. He was close now... close enough to take the knife, but in her current state, it was risky. "I wish none of this had happened. But it did. You and I, Cordelia, we're the victims in this. Your father and my father, they decided our futures years ago by the river, and now here we are. But it doesn't have to be this horrible all the time."

Cordelia's tears rolled down her cheeks, dripping off her jaw and into the gravel.

Charles leapt forward and wrapped his arms around her from the side. The knife dropped to the ground and he gently eased her to the side, pinning her to the car. He didn't realize he was crying, too, until the horror of the past few moments caught up. "I'm sorry about your dad. I mean that." He whispered the words in her ear. He prayed they calmed her. "But we can end the suffering. With us."

Cordelia struggled, but her protestations were weak. She was exhausted by her grief. "Charles, our suffering has only just begun."

An hour later, Charles had finally calmed enough to break the seal on his cognac bottle. He had only just stopped shaking.

He would always wonder if it was wrong to let her leave like that, after she'd threatened to harm his son. But he called in a favor with some old friends, and she'd be followed from here on out, until their son was born. Tomorrow, when she was at the funeral parlor arranging her father's service, he'd have cameras installed in the townhouse. Knives removed.

Charles had always thought of his future children in an abstract way. The completion of a puzzle only he could solve. He never considered what it might be like to hold them, or hear them laugh, or grasp their life in his hands. And now that he'd seen his son on the ultrasound image, tangible proof that part of Charles had taken root and found new life, and would grow into a real, full person, he was changed. Everything he did, from here on out, would be in service to that life growing within the monster he'd married. And even she was not fully a monster as long as she could nurture and develop the son of Charles Deschanel.

His thoughts stopped there, for too much rumination on children would be a reminder he already had one, somewhere. A daughter, who would now be running around, and using words, and...

He lifted the empty bottle to the light and admired his handiwork. Drunk, but not drunk enough. Never drunk enough.

This time of year made him think of the two women who'd left his life too abruptly. Madeline and Catherine. He could never venture too far into the memories of his sister, because many of them only exacerbated his grief and regret at how he'd treated her. Not only in those end days, but always. He'd taken what gave her life and turned it into a point in which to shame her. For that, he'd always pay.

Catherine was easier to think of, for she'd wronged him far more than he ever wronged her. Her ultimate betrayal made conjuring up images of her almost fun, like playing a sport he couldn't lose. It was easy to hate her, and it felt good.

Would their children be friends, he wondered? Would they encourage it? Raise their boys together, under the guise of a friendship that was now based wholeheartedly in a lie? Colin would never be the wiser, but Charles and Catherine would know. And would, later, their daughters and sons, dip their toes into the same forbidden dance?

"Now is the winter of our discontent," Charles muttered. He launched the bottle into the flames of the parlor fireplace.

Richard, walking by, remarked, "Ahh. Shakespeare."

AUGUSTUS NEVER INTENDED TO STAY UNTIL WINTER.

In the summer, when he'd talked about returning to Summer Island in the winter, that felt like such a faraway point in time. Some distant etch in the future that he needn't worry about. Then, when summer turned to fall, and Ekatherina refused to come home with him, it seemed a lifetime away. By winter, she would have spent more of their marriage in Maine than in the home intended for Augustus and his family.

But after their successful sorting of the Maureen situation, Augustus came to the realization that he'd known all along he must return, and that, when he came home again, his wife must be on the plane with him.

When he flew up in late fall, he didn't tell Ekatherina ahead of time that he was coming. He wasn't trying to deceive her, or catch her in some salacious act. But he did need to know what her initial, and therefore most authentic, reaction to seeing him would be. That would tell him, for better or worse, what he needed to know.

He called St. Andrews and let him know. Asked if he might be willing to meet him with a car at the ferry station, to which his neighbor eagerly agreed.

The man's two-year-old son was strapped into a car seat in the back. Johnathan, he said his name was, and he was the spitting image of his father, with dark hair and wide, inquisitive eyes. He was quiet, for such a little one, and seemed to be more interested in the conversation in the front seat than the one between his two panda bears.

"You're doing right, coming here," St. Andrews said. Augustus noted how hard the man worked to cover his accent. He wanted to tell him the pretense was unnecessary. Augustus liked hearing him talk. It reminded him of the bigger world out there.

"I shouldn't have left," Augustus said. He looked away, out the window, remembering his first drive down Heron Hollow Road. "But it's hard, being the head of your own company. I can't abandon my business."

"No, I don't expect any man could for long."

"You're a doctor, so I know you understand."

"I know where I'm needed, for sure."

Augustus tried not to read any double meaning into the man's words. There was no accusation in his tone, and St. Andrews had never been anything but neighborly.

The first snow fell just as they eased into the gravel driveway of the gothic Victorian that reminded him of Manderley. Snow. How many winters had he and Charles played pretend, throwing around sand from the river bank, or tearing up old cotton? How badly they'd wanted to see the earth blanketed in that elusive white coat.

Ekatherina appeared on the wraparound porch at the sound of the noise. Her hand created a shield from the last of the afternoon sun as she strained to see who'd come to visit.

This is the moment of truth, thought Augustus. *When I know whether I'm married to a woman who loves me, or who has fallen instead for a world I can't give her.*

Ekatherina's whole body came alive at the spark of recognition. She raced down the steps, forgetting her shoes, and flew through the gravel.

Augustus stepped out of the car and caught her in his arms.

"You're here," she purred, and he forgot everything else.

A MONTH HAD PASSED, AND AUGUSTUS WATCHED HIS wife busy herself to get ready for the Winter Solstice Festival while he thought of his business back in New Orleans. He didn't know where she'd bought such a beautiful dress, and wondered, if he peered in her closet, would he find others he didn't recognize? And should he, when they'd cohabitated such a short period of their marriage?

"You look beautiful," he said. He should say it more. It didn't matter that he'd warned her, that he didn't have the pretty words of other men. That didn't stop him from saying what he meant.

Ekatherina beamed back at him from the mirror. Her fingers played with the emeralds on her necklace. Her strapless blue gown came only as high as her bust, and her soft, milky skin looked so pale against the blue. "Really? You think so?"

Augustus went to her. Frowning at her bare shoulders, he hoped this particular gala, unlike their innumerable summer festivals, was indoors. There was over a foot of snow outside, and a fresh storm started about an hour earlier. St. Andrews warned him they could lose power, and to make sure the generator was ready and gassed.

He kissed the tops of both shoulders. It seemed so unlike him, but it felt right. She felt right. "You're always beautiful, Ekatherina. You always have been, to me."

"You are good to me, Augustus."

A chill ran through his whole body. She never said his name. He'd never realized how badly he wanted to hear it on her voice.

"Where's this thing at again?"

"The grange hall," Ekatherina replied. "They're having it indoors for obvious reasons." Her annunciation had improved in her short stay on the island. He supposed she'd had more interactions with others here than ever before.

He held out his arm. "We ready?"

Ekatherina smiled with her whole face and slipped her hand through his elbow.

For most of the month they'd been reunited, Ekatherina had, somewhat surprisingly, insisted they stay at the house. She squelched his skepticism with the reviving of the ardent affections that had him believing, back in the summer, that he finally understood the meaning of happy. After days and days in bed, learning each other, Augustus didn't much care why she'd pulled herself out of society in Summer Island. She was his again, and he was hers, and she had a way of making this the only thing that mattered.

When Andrew St. Andrews invited the Deschanels to join him and his wife, Claire, at the Winter Solstice Festival, Augustus almost turned him down outright, for Ekatherina's sake. She'd found excuse after excuse not to go into town, or socialize with anyone other than their neighbors. He buried the reason why somewhere deep and inaccessible. She was his again, and he was hers.

But when he mentioned it to her, Ekatherina brightened and insisted they go. Maybe she'd grown tired of her self-imposed exile, or maybe she had other reasons. Augustus would do anything for an appearance of that smile.

When they opened the barn doors and entered the soiree, he practically heard the record scratching to an end. Everyone turned. Few smiled. Ekatherina cowered into him, and he slipped his arm around her waist to show he was with her.

The men nodded at him and then shook their heads with a sad smile as they passed. The women made no attempt at pleasantries with Ekatherina, drawing into tight packs to whisper and assess.

Ignore it. Sure, you know why they're doing it. It doesn't matter. She is yours, and you are hers again.

George Cairne and his wife passed. The small, pitiful sound his wife made at his side was almost the thing that finally *did* send Augustus over the edge. George made a sidelong glance but otherwise addressed neither of them. His wife held his arm with an indignant, shoulders-back pride that she dared others to challenge.

"Come on, let's get a drink," Augustus said.

White bulbs lit the inside of the old grange hall. He imagined it hadn't changed much since the days of the barnyard dances. What little paint once existed peeled to form a patina that belied another era, where choices, and people, were simpler. Or so it seemed.

Augustus scooped punch out of the bowl and handed Ekatherina a glass. She accepted it with a nervous, grateful smile and cupped it with both hands as she sipped, as if she could disappear behind the red Solo.

"Did you wanna dance?" he asked.

"Dance? Oh. No, no," Ekatherina said, and he remembered her dancing with the brightest smile as George Cairne led her across the floor.

"You sure? I'm terrible, but that could be fun, too."

His wife's smile was courteous, but her eyes darted around the party, at all the people who had labeled her persona non grata. They wondered, as he did, why she was here. What kept her on the island. *Why didn't you call me sooner? I would have come. I didn't think you wanted me.*

His stomach seized. None of this was right. He could pretend, but that had never been his strength. You addressed, or you moved on, but you didn't dwell and you didn't paint a picture that didn't exist.

"Do you wanna go home, Ekatherina?"

"We just got here."

"But do you?"

She dropped her eyes into her punch. Nodded.

"Not just home on the island. I mean home to New Orleans. It's time, don't you think?"

Augustus scanned the room with his own challenging stare. These close-knit islanders didn't scare him. They didn't intimidate him, and their sympathy wasn't only unwelcome, it was inhospitable.

He removed the cup from her hands and kissed her in front of everyone.

She was his, and he was hers again.

He wanted them all to know.

For the last time.

CHAPTER 17

Over the Hills and Far Away

A light snow blanketed Arthur's Seat, the volcanic hill overlooking Holyrood Park and the whole of Edinburgh. Colleen's eyes glazed, and her heart sagged, heavy with homesickness. The campus was a ghost town two days prior to Christmas, but outside the thatched windows and gothic spires, the city bustled with holiday activity. This was the Christmas of Dickens and other novelists who sought to bring the magic to life on the page.

News from home chipped away at her sleep and focus until there was little left. Charles and Augustus had solved Maureen's problem, but in a way she might never forgive any of them for. She was married to the man now, quietly, in a hushed reception at the City Hall that happened so fast Colleen hadn't even had time to fly in. All her calls to Maureen went unanswered, and she knew why. But even as she struggled with the choice her brothers made, she understood it. Was that not, maybe, why she'd asked Charles to take the lead? So he could do what she could not?

And now Charles was going to be a father. News that should radiate a fresh, much-needed happiness through the family, but was marred by the woman bearing the child.

Augustus and his wife struggled through the silence between

them, asking for no help from anyone, and offering no word of whether they'd make it through whatever ailed them.

Evangeline... something was amiss with her, but she wouldn't say what, and Colleen feared she'd let her down again, in some way she couldn't foresee. If anything tempted her to return home for Christmas, it was Evangeline, but her sister insisted she was just busy with school, and not to stress so much.

Mama implied she was worried about Lizzy, too, but didn't know why, or wouldn't say.

Keeping busy was the goal. Colleen considered taking a stroll down Prince Street, or the Royal Mile, where she'd be surrounded by crowds of shoppers and people-watchers. The lives of others had a way of helping numb the need to obsess over your own. But as she deliberated the possibility, overthinking future situations as she often did, it occurred to Colleen that rather than consoling her, this activity would serve as further reminder of her own loneliness. Grateful as she was, she'd chosen it. Bemoaning the current situation would not only be pointless, but selfish.

Funds were not now, nor would they ever be, a factor in any of her decisions, both a gift and a curse. A curse, now, because her family refused to accept her reasons for staying in Scotland during the Christmas holidays, though every single one of them was feeling the same acute, cutting ache, the same loss. They expected her to share it. Well, she was sharing it, but she would do so alone. For four Christmases, she'd mourned her sister alongside the family. This Christmas was hers. She refused to drown.

But drown she would, if she chose to mire herself in the dismally silent apartment. Her new roommate—another move that was unnecessary financially but completely necessary for her emotional well-being—had gone home to Aberdeen days ago. Colleen had an entire university at her disposal, and she intended to use it.

. . .

The heavy, oaken doors creaked open as she leaned into them, a sound that would be muffled in the busyness of a term in full-swing, but now resonated and bounced across every book, every shelf.

Colleen scanned the massive library, wide-eyed. She'd never considered what it might look like with the students scattered to their homes. How the musty, welcoming smell of hundreds of thousands of tomes would fill her with the warmth of her own.

She wasn't alone, though. That fourth-year who had given her a hard time as if it were his job, Noah, had taken up residence at a table normally suited for two dozen students or more during the term. A guilty expression flashed across his face as he watched her checking him out, then it passed and evolved toward something resembling annoyance.

"Sorry," she said, startled at how her voice echoed without the din of students. "I wasn't expecting to find anyone here. I didn't mean to interrupt."

Noah set his pen in the binding of his notebook. "Shouldn't you be home in New Orleans?"

"Shouldn't you?"

"Never been a fan of Christmas. What's your excuse?"

Colleen sensed, as much by his expression as through her own innate gift as a Deschanel, the unspoken pain behind his words. "My sister died a few years ago," she answered, startled at her instinctive willingness for truth with someone who clearly wasn't fond of her. "The last few holidays were very painful. I needed a pardon."

Noah's impudence faded to remorse in an instant. "I completely forgot about that. I'm sorry."

Colleen approached his table and set her satchel on a chair across from him, taking the next seat over. He glanced at the bookbag as if preparing to tell her the seat was taken. He didn't. "No reason for you to remember," she conceded. "You were in Charles' class, yes? When he spent his senior year at Jesuit?"

Noah frowned, nodding. She sensed a myriad of emotions in him.

His dumbfounded stare turned the moment awkward for her, and she broke the silence. "My brother isn't always a very nice person."

Colleen caught him regarding her closely, and she broke a rule of hers and decided to read his mind.

Until she sat across from him, the distractions of a classroom and other demands missing from the equation, Noah had never evaluated Colleen beyond her genetic link. He'd noticed details about her face and saw Charles staring back, sneering, calling him a poor Mick, an orphan, anything degrading that fit the moment.

She didn't really resemble her brother at all, though. Colleen's dark hair, normally strangled into a tight bun at the nape of her neck, flowed in waves over her loose, cable-knit sweater. Her chocolate eyes, free of makeup, were tinged in thoughtfulness, not hatred.

Her heart sank. She understood Noah better now, but she'd had to betray him to do it. This was a wrong she could never apologize for, just as Charles *would* never apologize for his.

"Have you had much of a chance to see Scotland yet? Outside of Edinburgh, I mean?" Noah asked.

Colleen crossed her legs, folding both hands over one knee. "No, though I've been dreaming of Skye," she confessed, then blushed, wondering, once again, what had gotten into her. Why she was telling this man, who had no care for what she dreamed about, such personal things. "I have a terrible suspicion I'll spend the next few years at the university without ever getting out of the city."

And then his words came from seemingly nowhere. "Then let's go."

Colleen blinked. "What? To Skye?"

"Professor MacDougal has a summer home near Portree, and he's urged me to use it many times. I don't know why I haven't."

She understood, though. To venture there alone felt lonelier than staying on campus, where they were surrounded by familiarity.

There was a loneliness in Noah not so unlike her own, and she was sad not to have seen it until now.

Colleen tucked a strand of hair behind her ear, re-crossing her legs. This boy—no, man. There was nothing the least bit boyish about how he looked at her now, nor in his invitation. No, he'd spent the last few months reproving her for her studiousness, punishing her, she felt, for something her brother must have done years past. And now he was asking her to go away to Skye, alone, together?

Everything rational within Colleen Deschanel appealed to her to say no.

She said *yes*.

CHARLES SLIPPED UP THE STAIRS OF HIS MOTHER'S townhome, wearing the pathetic, downtrodden look of the repentant guilty. He managed to avoid his mother *and* her overbearing excitement at his pending fatherhood, but he would've almost preferred that to what awaited upstairs.

Elizabeth passed him on the stairs. She shook her head, and he waited for her to say something, but what was there to say, really? The dark yellow moving truck parked outside said it all.

"She in her room?" he asked, when Elizabeth kept walking. He knew the answer, but he just needed a normal human moment with someone else before seeing Maureen.

Elizabeth nodded. "Yeah."

"Alone?"

"Mama went to the storage unit to get the rest of her things."

"Makes sense." He didn't move forward. He was stalled, in his actions, his words.

"You know nothing you're going to say to her is going to make this better," Elizabeth said. She looked back, down the hall. "She's not capable of reason right now. Or ever."

"I didn't come here to reason with her," Charles insisted.

"Why did you come? Penance?"

"Maybe," he said. There was so much more; their unusual alliance after that night by the river. The secret partnership at Franz Hendrickson's. Few words ever passed between the siblings, but they didn't need to, when you'd experienced these things together. Charles was the one Maureen could trust, and Charles had let her down. Maybe one day she'd see it differently, but he expected the full weight of her wrath for a lot longer than he thought he could handle.

"Well, she's in her room. Proceed at your own risk."

It was only after Elizabeth was downstairs and banging around in the kitchen that he realized how much weight she'd lost.

"You have a lot of nerve, Huck," Maureen said. The screech of packing tape filled the room. She was using more than she needed, and the way she snapped the tape against the teeth of the roller made him think she was doing it just for the sound.

"I didn't come here to fight."

"How nice for you, that you get to roam the world freely and decide *for yourself* what's best *for you.*" *Screech. Snap.*

"I know you're mad..."

"Mad?" Maureen's laugh was that of an old woman, and he remembered how she once fancied herself that old hag from the Dickens novel. "Why would I be *mad*?"

"I know Edouard isn't the man you saw yourself marrying." Though he was a huge step up from that loser Evers. "But maybe you can still have that life you've always wanted. Raising your kids while your husband works."

Screech. "Keep telling yourself that." *Snap.*

"He's not a bad man, Maureen."

She sniffled, hunched over a box that was covered so heavily in tape there was hardly any cardboard showing. "You don't know what happened the night he got me pregnant, and after what you, and Colleen, and Aggie did to me, I can't trust you to tell you."

Charles sat at the edge of the bed. His hand hovered above her shoulder, not quite connecting. "Did he hurt you?"

"With Peter, at least I had a choice," was all she said.

A powerful force pushed at the back of his eyes. They blurred with the force of it, and he knew, though it had happened only a few times in his life, that he was on the verge of crying.

He'd only wanted to protect Maureen. To temper his anger this time, and not leave her with an even bigger trail of regret at the end of his rage. But in not acting impulsively, had he missed the point entirely?

"I didn't know," he whispered. He did touch her, then, but she recoiled and rolled forward and away from him. "I wish you'd told me."

"Not everything is your business, Charles."

"You're my business, Maureen. You always will be."

"Not anymore. You may be the Deschanel heir, but I'm a Blanchard now. Or have you forgotten?"

His mind snapped back to the dingy lighting of the courthouse. The smell of old, cracked leather and furniture polish. The persistent cough of the judge, who clearly had somewhere better to be.

Maureen's silent, streaming tears paired next to Edouard's stoic resolve.

I now pronounce you husband and wife.

Maureen, fleeing back down what should have been an altar decorated in her favorite flowers but was instead just an aisle with seats on either side. Seats that would house spectators for some court case or another, later that afternoon.

Do not even dare think of making my sister miserable, Charles had said to his new brother-in-law.

She'll have anything she wants, anything at all, except that which I cannot give.

Which is?

He'd shrugged, as if about to espouse one of the most basic facts of life. *My affection.*

"Maureen... do you want... do you want me to..."

Maureen threw her head back, alternating between sniffles and laughter. “Kill him? Little late for that, don’t you think? Although, *Widow Blanchard* has a nice ring to it.”

“I didn’t know. I didn’t know he’d hurt you.” He reached forward and tugged at her arm to turn her. No matter how it hurt, he needed to see her face. “I didn’t *know.*”

Maureen wiped at her face. “Not your fault, right? Nothing is ever the fault of Charles Deschanel. I never should have gone to that bitch Colleen. I knew better! I knew she’d never do anything if it didn’t involve protecting the family name!”

“Hey.” Charles almost didn’t say the words that came next, but his conscience, or whatever existed of such a thing, wouldn’t allow him not to. “Colleen didn’t make this decision, Maureen.”

She laughed. “Sure she did. This has Colleen written all over it.”

“No.” He shook his head. “Colleen called me, and her number one concern was you and your happiness. When I told her, after, what I’d decided, she was furious with me. She knew you’d hate it. She cursed me out and said if she’d thought I’d botch the job so badly, she would have flown home and handled it herself.”

“Then she should have!”

“Augustus and I, we sat down and agonized over the right thing to do. We didn’t just move the chess pieces around the board. We knew we were talking about your future, and both of us wanted what was best for you. All of us want what’s best for you.”

Maureen threw the box on the ground. The contents rattled, and something broke. She didn’t care. “Don’t you get it? Everything you’re saying is about how *all of you* chose what my future should be. Even if you’d gotten it right, would that make it okay? Would it?”

Charles didn’t have the answer to this question.

She turned back to her packing. He was dismissed.

When Charles got back to Ophélie, Cordelia’s car was in the drive, which wasn’t a surprise. They’d mutually agreed to spending Christmas together, even if they never entered the same room at the same time, was better for appearances.

The other car in the drive was a surprise. Darwin.

Cordelia and her brother were not especially close, though she'd been meeting with him more frequently since their father passed. Through her, Darwin tried to get Charles to part with more of his money by way of investments in their business, but even Cordelia didn't put too much effort into the task. She'd have lunch with her brother, come home and say, *Darwin needs a hundred thousand dollars for the factory down payment. Up to you.*

Charles paused at the bottom of the steps. He wanted to know what that bastard was doing in his house. Needed to know, dammit. Cordelia might or might not tell him later, depending on her mood, and her moods had become even more unpredictable since introducing pregnancy hormones to the equation.

Instead, he went around to the back of the house and entered by way of the old servant's door, between the two kitchens. He used to do this, years before, when he was a younger man who required privacy for his indiscretions, so the staff gave him nary a look when he did it now.

He stepped quietly through the house, and when he came around the side of the broad central staircase, he saw the doors open to the first parlor, and that's where the voices came from.

"You're a fool, Cordelia. If you didn't want to marry him, then you should have been more resourceful *before* you signed your life away. And now you're carrying his child?" Darwin made a disgusted sound.

"We're entirely incompatible."

Darwin laughed. "You think you'd be compatible with someone else? Does such a man exist?"

"I think Father is dead now, and this makes us free to do our own bidding."

"Free? We'll never be free, as long as this business is ours. And this business, Cordelia, it's *failing.* Failing, because of Father's foolish choices. Failing, because of that stupid brat, and her words that he was even more stupid to believe. It's failing, and your goddamn husband isn't living up to his end of the marriage."

"Charles is a paragon of faults, but our business failing is not one we can assign to him, brother."

"It may not be his fault it's failing, but he has the means to fix it!"

Cordelia snorted. "And why should he?"

"Because he's family now, and this is a family matter, Cordelia."

"My marriage to him doesn't make him family," she said. "Any more than you being my brother makes you my friend."

"You say the worst things sometimes, you know that?" His dress shoes clacked across the cypress of the parlor floor. "You really know how to cut deep, when you want to."

"I say what I mean, and what's true, Darwin. I can't help if you don't like it."

"What I don't like is that this marriage of yours has given us *no* advantage whatsoever! None! We're not only no better than we were before you married him, we're worse!"

"*Must* we continue to talk about this?"

"Don't you care?"

"About your sniveling?"

"About Father's business! He built it from nothing, Cordelia. Nothing."

Cordelia laughed. "Have we forgotten the two million dollars of Grandfather's money that he toted across the ocean from Germany? Or, other than that, you mean?"

"I just don't understand how you've been married to him half a year and haven't had *any* luck getting him to agree to help. You're his wife, Cordelia."

"We're back to Charles, again?"

Charles' heart leapt into his throat when Condoleezza came up behind him. "What trouble you into now, child?"

"Shh," he said and pointed at the parlor.

She nodded, winked, and headed up the stairs. "Carry on, then."

Darwin's pacing stopped. "I've done everything I know to do! I even had that no-account philanderer photographed with all the women he ran around with when you were engaged. Sure, he gave me money the first time I asked, but he was so *snide* about it. I asked him again at your party, and he told me to go service myself."

Nothing came from the parlor for almost a full minute. When Cordelia spoke, there was a thin line of rage seeding through the center of her words. "You come here. Talk about family. Espouse your bullshit about familial responsibility. When *all this time you've been bribing mine?*"

"The Hendrickson family comes first. You know that."

Cordelia's heels sounded. "To you, it comes first. But my child will be a Deschanel, and I will not have his name tarnished by your inability to save a failing business without resorting to blackguard tactics. You take those pictures and you burn them, and if I hear you've been peddling them anywhere but your imagination, I will murder you myself, Darwin. Do *not* fuck with my family."

Darwin blubbered in a series of fits and starts. "But... I'm your family, Cordelia."

"This is my family now. I don't have to love someone to understand the nature of loyalty. Now, go, and think very, *very* hard about what you decide to do next where my husband is concerned."

"Cordel—"

"*Go.*"

Charles crept back behind the stairs as Darwin stormed out of the parlor. He opened and tried to close the door, but underestimated the weight and had to stomp back to finish the job, though not without a series of complaints.

Cordelia appeared in the parlor door. She pulled her shoulders back and straightened her skirt. Her face had the preternatural shine of a mythical beast returning from the slaughter of her greatest foe.

Her expression softened. One hand massaged her belly, and with the other, she pulled herself up the stairs by the bannister, one step at a time.

Charles didn't have the emotional fortitude to process what he'd heard, and he resisted the urge to go to Cordelia and ask. She wouldn't show the same loyalty to his face. They were not friends. They were hardly partners.

But loyal she was, nonetheless, in her own way. In the same way, perhaps, as sworn enemies who found themselves in the same military company on the eve of deadly battle.

Now he knew but didn't yet understand what this meant for their future.

CHAPTER 18
The Lockbox

Evangeline knew. She'd known all along, she just couldn't bring herself to accept the truth.

She'd known as soon as she checked the lockbox under the false board on her bedroom floor.

She'd known when she picked up the faintest whiff of patchouli, which was not her scent, and never had been, not even when she was playing around with Ethan's gang.

She'd known when Amnesty reappeared at the house, showing up at a time Evangeline would not normally be there, and gaped at her with that deer-in-headlights gaze.

And really, she'd known before that. Known something was amiss with Amnesty, maybe *very* amiss, and it went well beyond whatever speculations Evangeline had cast, and then cast aside, in order to make the relationship fit her world. Amnesty was everything Evangeline needed coming off a year that left her wondering if life was even worth all the damn trouble. But even though she'd known much of what passed between them was as elusive and unpredictable as Amnesty herself, she'd nonetheless convinced herself that the one true thing about her was her affection. She could be an heiress or a laundress, but when she kissed Evangeline, she was kissing with her whole, true self.

And no one else knew about Amnesty. Evangeline had no one to talk to about the pain eating at her heart, because she'd designed the secrecy around the relationship. In refusing to define it, she'd accepted it was more than what she felt others around her would understand and drawn the line in the sand, circling them.

If Evangeline couldn't even have an honest conversation with herself about what she was feeling, how could any of this have existed in the real world?

She'd told herself she was playing around. That if you didn't define something, it was fluid and movable, and there was nothing to be afraid of. They'd never gone much further than kissing... and some petting. Love was love, right?

It didn't make her a lesbian. Even thinking the word terrified her; just last week, a gay man had been beat to death in Crescent Park for his sexuality, and that wasn't an isolated event. If she was a lesbian, then she was different. Other. Exposed. Evangeline was not so narrow-minded to believe there was anything wrong with how humans were biologically made, but she was smart enough to understand that science and society were not often in synch.

And anyway, she still liked men. She might not be jumping to date them, but she still turned to look when a hot guy passed, and when she was alone, it was men who occupied her fantasies, not women. But then, why did Amnesty ignite something so powerful within her? She would've said it felt like fireworks, but everyone said that about love, and she was tired of hearing it.

Evangeline rocked in the chair on the front porch of the house she now owned, but didn't live in. She'd left the note, suspecting Amnesty still slipped in for shelter in the early hours of late nights, and wasn't surprised to see it missing.

We need to talk. You can keep the money, but I need closure. You owe me that much.

So she sat, waited, using the tips of her toes to move the rocker back and forth, back and forth.

. . .

This wasn't happening. It couldn't be. Not when she'd gotten better over time. Her precision at timing, her skill at hiding. If Connor was going to catch her, it would have happened a long time ago, not *now*.

But he hadn't caught her, exactly. He hadn't dug up any of her drug paraphernalia, or walked in and caught a whiff of something scandalous. It was a feeling, he said, but he wouldn't let it go.

"Elizabeth." He sat at her desk, not at the edge of her bed, or even next to her. He folded his hands over his lap, but it seemed so unnatural, as if he was doing something he'd watched adults to.

"Connor."

"Stop smiling. This isn't funny. It's not a joke."

"Who's laughing?"

"I knew something was up that day we..." Connor sighed. "I didn't know how to put my finger on it. The way you talked about the drugs, and then there was something, I don't know, I guess, maybe in the ease of how you lit that joint and smoked it. You didn't even choke, it was like... like you do it all the time."

"Well, I don't."

"What are you doing with your jaw?"

"Nothing." She'd been rotating it to alleviate the soreness from coming down off of a larger-than-usual high the night before. But she'd seen and touched Charles, and that snowballed into terrible visions, and now that she was blocking them, she found she no longer had any of her natural defenses anymore. She wasn't desensitized; she felt every last thing.

"I'm not asking you if you're doing drugs, Lizzy. I'm telling you..." He rolled his lips tight. Looked down at his lap. "I'm telling you I already *know* you are, because I know *you*, and I've known for a long time, I think."

Elizabeth shoved her trembling hands under her bottom. "And I'm telling *you*—"

"Stop," Connor said. "You've been lying to me for months. I can't bear to hear you lie to me now. I love you too much for this, Elizabeth. If you love me, you'll stop lying."

Elizabeth scoffed. She turned her head, but this dislodged one of her hands, and Connor spotted what she was trying to hide before she could stuff it back under her. God, she hated him right now! Hated him! He could sit there and live a normal life! He wasn't plagued by horrible visions. He didn't have to see everyone he loved in constant pain, pain he couldn't prevent. It was so easy for him to judge, when he never had to deal with *any* of that.

"You don't know anything, Connor. You never did."

"I'm the only one who knows, Lizzy. Which is the only reason I agreed to touch the stuff with you earlier this year, even though it went against everything I believe in. Because I believe in you, and I have watched you suffer for years." Connor blinked through the growing damp film in his eyes. He looked toward her, but not at her. "I would've robbed a bank, or killed a man, or *anything* to help you. Anything, Lizzy. Anything except watching you slowly kill yourself."

"Quit being dramatic, Connor." The tremor wasn't limited to her hands anymore. It traveled up to her elbows and now they were quaking at her sides. "You've always been like this, overreacting about stupid shit."

"That won't work on me, Lizzy. Not today." He leaned forward. "What the hell are you doing with your arms?"

"Nothing, Jesus!"

"You're practically inverting over there, Elizabeth."

"I *told* you to *stop* calling me Elizabeth!"

Connor looked at his feet and then, reluctantly, stood. He shuffled toward her, his stance tilted slightly to the side as if afraid to come too close. "I didn't come here to fight with you."

Elizabeth shot to her feet before she could think too much about what that would do with the visibility of her hands and arms. She didn't like feeling so vulnerable as he towered above her. She didn't like any of this. "Then try not to pick fucking fights with me by throwing around all this bullshit!"

Her foot caught something, probably the shag carpet, and she launched forward, arms flailing. Connor leapt forward just in time and caught her, but she felt his tight recoil as their flesh touched.

"Elizabeth... you're burning up." He eased her back onto the bed. He leaned his hand against her forehead, like her damn mother would do, as if he had a clue what he was doing.

"Stop babying me, Connor." She wiggled away from him. "Why are you even here?"

Connor looked stricken. "Why do I ever come over, I guess?"

"To torment me!" She didn't know when she'd started crying. "To harass me and tell me all the things you think I'm doing wrong, while you sit on that Sullivan pedestal of yours and—"

Two things happened, almost exactly in tandem.

Connor kissed her.

Elizabeth slapped him so hard she saw stars at the moment of impact.

Connor fumbled backward off the bed. He staggered toward the desk, wearing a look that was both incredulous and devastated, and Elizabeth felt, for a moment, vindicated, and then she was lower than she'd ever been in all her life.

She wanted to apologize... needed to. She had to take it back. No, this was all wrong, all of it. Connor was her anchor, her only peace.

Tears appeared on his stung cheek. He took one last look at her and then stumbled out her bedroom door.

AMNESTY SHOWED UP SHORTLY AFTER MIDNIGHT. Evangeline didn't see the bruises at first, but they flickered to light under the dim porch gaslights, and as Amnesty stepped closer, the full extent of the damage was evident.

Evangeline stood, but didn't approach. She wanted to, but she couldn't make herself. "What the hell happened to you?"

"My father," Amnesty said, sniffling. When she wiped at her nose, her hand came away with blood.

"Is that bullshit?"

"No. No more bullshit."

Evangeline waved her hand. "Doesn't matter anyway."

"Doesn't it?"

"You stole my money. You lied to me. I'll never know if you're telling the truth, and don't think I care at this point."

Amnesty nodded. As she turned her head, the dark purple ring around her eye came into view and Evangeline gasped.

"Hey, why don't we get you cleaned up," Evangeline said, pointing to the door.

Amnesty shook her head. "It's not as bad as it looks. I've had worse."

Evangeline rolled her eyes. "Of course you have. You've had a whole life you don't want me to know about, so why change that now?"

"Why did you call me here, Evangeline?"

Evangeline sat back down, this time on the porch swing. She squished to one side of the bench to allow Amnesty to sit, too; to show her it was okay.

"I don't really know. I didn't like how it ended. I still don't."

"I did take your money," Amnesty said. "I know you know, but I don't want to lie to you anymore."

"Thanks for confirming, I guess." Evangeline clutched her hands over her belly, which felt hollow with wanting. Wanting answers. Wanting absolution. Wanting *her*.

"Don't you wanna know why?"

"You can tell me, but how will I know if it's true?"

"Because I have no reason anymore to lie." Amnesty wrung her hands in her lap. She kept to her side of the bench. "I didn't meet you that night by accident."

"What do you mean?"

"I was looking for you," Amnesty said. She played with the bruise forming at the side of her chin. "You, specifically."

"That doesn't make any sense. We'd never met before. You didn't even know me."

"I didn't know you, but I knew who you were. Or, my father did, and he's always been the one to choose."

None of this made sense to Evangeline. She decided not to interject until she had a specific question to ask. "Okay."

"My mother died when we were little. I was five, or six. Old enough to miss her, but not old enough to understand what it meant. My sister was two, and still attached to Mom's hip all the time, and so she came to be attached to mine instead. My dad wasn't around much then. He changed jobs like most people change outfits, and he was often on the road, which was better for us, because when he was home, my mother was always scared. We were scared, too, but back then, he didn't take it out on us. Maybe he thought we were too young to get beat. I guess even monsters have some standards."

Amnesty wiped at a fresh spot of blood on her knuckles. "Once Mom was gone, that all changed. He put me to work within a year. Taught me how to pick pockets. You know, it's really not that hard to steal from an adult when you're a child, because they're not expecting it. You tell them you're lost and they take that very seriously. They *want* to help you, and they're so focused on that, they don't see or feel you slip the wallet from their purses or back pockets. They just don't. But, you know, word gets around and you gotta keep changing neighborhoods, because folks start looking out for the poor, little thieving kids in Tremé, or the 8th Ward. They stop feeling sad for you and start being wary."

Evangeline was too shocked, too enraptured with what she believed *was* the truth, finally, and she said nothing at all to break the spell.

"I got boobs when I was eleven, and bully for me, because that meant a whole different kind of work, in my father's eyes. He had to be careful, because eleven is too young even for the assholes who like the young ones, and so it wasn't all the time, not at first. When I was around fourteen, that's when I was turning tricks every day and night. And my sister, I couldn't bear it happening to her, so I begged, I *begged* my father to let me take the work for her. I'd do twice as much, so Cara didn't have to do any. I had half a fear that he might instead make me do twice as much and then still turn her out, but he didn't. At least not at first.

"On my eighteenth birthday, I thought that made me free, but my father wouldn't relinquish Cara. He said if I left he'd turn her out, and he knew that would make me stay. It did. How could I leave? And she was fifteen by then, and I knew I was on borrowed time. I knew he wouldn't let her beauty and innocence be a waste to him and his drug habit. And I was right. One day, he came to me and said, the money isn't enough. That sex with strangers four times a day wasn't enough, and that I either needed to do more, or Cara was going to hit the streets.

"Evangeline, believe me when I say I wanted to do more. I even tried to for a while. But once a day is hard for most of us, and four was already impossible. I was sore all the time. Half the time, the johns complained about the bleeding, I was so worn down. What could I do? Nothing. Just laugh and smile and make them forget about it, while I was dying, inside and out. The only thing that kept me going was knowing that my time on the streets kept Cara in school.

"My father was never one to be moved by anything sentimental. He never saw us as his children, I don't think, only, first, his burdens, and later, his opportunities. But I do think he appreciated, in his own way, the work ethic I'd conjured up to make protecting Cara possible. Even his shitty friends made comments about it, like *Hell, Carl, I wish I could get my daughters to do half as much!* He knew I was burning the candle at both ends, and he knew I couldn't pick up Cara's slack. And so, he gave me another option."

Amnesty reached into her beaded bag and pulled out a bottle of Coke. "I have two. Want one?"

"No, thanks," Evangeline said, although she was powerfully thirsty. Her mouth was a bed of cotton.

The bottle hissed as Amnesty opened it. She took a deep swig, offered Evangeline a sip, and went on when she shook her head. "He told me the money wasn't as good as it used to be in whoring me out. His words, not mine, but I knew what I was, and I was used to what he called me. A buddy of his was talking a good talk about how he'd get in with some of the upper crusts in New York, get to know them, and then squeeze *real* money. Not fifty here and there, and not hundreds, but *thousands.* Real money. And, I suppose it was his way of complimenting me when he said I was young enough and pretty enough to do the same kind of hustle here in New Orleans. So I did."

Amnesty swallowed more of her soda and closed her eyes. "It wasn't as hard as I thought it would be. I'd never been around decent men, so all I knew were men like my father, but decent men are easy to charm. They like flattery and conversation, and the married ones made it even easier because they couldn't tell anyone about me. If no one knew, then what could they do, later, when the money went missing, except fess up and ruin their lives? Or look like fools?

"My father didn't let me keep much of these big scores, but he dished out enough cash to make sure my clothes were nice enough to be in these fancy hotels, and that I could get my hair and nails done every few weeks. How generous, right?"

"I..." Evangeline swallowed. Her mouth was so dry. Her head felt even worse. *Listen, then process.* "How, or why, did he pick me? If you were out there bamboozling men..."

"I asked the same thing. He'd had his eye on your family for years, I knew that, but I thought he was out of his mind for thinking he could come anywhere near any of you. But then, he said, he had a plan. I asked if you were, you know, a lesbian, and he said he didn't know what you were into, but he knew you'd been..." Amnesty's eyes flashed wide with guilt, and she trailed off for a moment. "He knew what happened to you, and he knew other things, too, like the fact you hadn't gone to college, which, to him, was a sign you were vulnerable. He said you were the smart one, and there was trouble in paradise. I didn't think he was right, but..."

The spell broke. Evangeline threw her body sideways, to face Amnesty. "Are you trying to tell me you both thought I was vulnerable enough, after being *gang raped,* to fall in love with you? Do I have that one-dimensional crap right?"

Silent tears streamed down Amnesty's cheeks. "I agreed to it, like I agreed to everything he asked. For Cara. But then I met you, Evangeline, and there was this spark between us."

"Sure." Evangeline choked out a laugh. "A fucking spark. Which is *impossible* by the way, from a scientific perspective. Just some bull-shit people say."

"Then call it whatever you want! The *very night* I met you, I knew I had second thoughts. After a couple weeks of meeting you at night for our walks, my father pushed me for progress, and I knew then I couldn't do it. It's why you didn't hear from me for a while." Amnesty dropped her eyes. "I went back to turning tricks. I just couldn't do it. I liked you, and I kept wishing I'd met you under different circumstances."

Evangeline pulled herself off the bench. She needed distance from Amnesty, who was finally, *finally* telling her something that was true, and now Evangeline wished more than anything she could go back to a time where all her knowledge of Amnesty was a wish and a whim.

"But you did come back," Evangeline said slowly. "And you made up a story, and you played to my compassion. You accepted a *house* from me, pretended to have genuine feelings for me—"

"I wasn't pretending, Evangeline, I swear on my mot—"

"I don't care," Evangeline said. She put her hand up. "I don't care who you swear on. You led me on and led me to believe that I was... something to you. Something special. You know, I guess the joke's on me for trying out the human condition." Her hoarse laugh faded to a cough. "I don't care, Amnesty, or whoever you are, because if you really had felt remorse, and really wanted to make this right, you wouldn't have come back. You wouldn't have made me feel safe. Let me fall for you. And you wouldn't have taken my money and broken my heart."

Amnesty bowed her head and sobbed. She didn't protest again. Maybe, Evangeline thought, she understood that would make it worse, not better. Or maybe there was nothing more to say.

"You know the worst part," Evangeline continued. She was almost done. Not just with this conversation, but this chapter. This city. The whole fucking enchilada. "If you had told me this earlier, before we went down the rabbit hole we couldn't climb back up, I would've given you the money. *Any* amount. I would've gone to your father and asked him what his price was, to buy you and Cara out of his grasp. I don't have access to all my money yet, but Charles does, and Augustus does, and either one of them would give me anything I asked for. I would've done it for you, to save you."

Amnesty cried silent tears, mouth agape, slightly, in horror. She looked like she was screaming, but no sound came out.

I know how you feel. The whole thing is a shit po'boy.

"I feel horrible for you, and the life you've been forced to lead," Evangeline said. "Your father is a monster. If I believed in hell, he'd be the type of man the place was created for." Evangeline reached forward and pulled the empty pop bottle from Amnesty's hands. She dropped it in a nearby bucket, where they used to drop their sodas, in happier times. "I admire what you've done for your sister. I'm telling you all these things, because they're facts, and I work best with facts."

Amnesty nodded. Evangeline couldn't tell where her running mascara stopped and her bruises began.

"So the last thing I'll say is also a fact. Go ask your father what that number is. Come give it to me, and I'll give him that amount. For you and Cara."

"No, Evangeline, no, I don't want any—"

"I didn't ask what you wanted, just like you never gave me that chance," Evangeline replied. "I love you, and I can't walk away from this and sleep at night knowing what's ahead for you and your sister. So I'm going to clear my conscience with this last bit of blood money, and then we're going to go our separate ways. Do you understand?"

Amnesty could have fought harder. Evangeline half-expected

her to, even though she'd already hardened her heart, and her mind, against further vulnerability. There just wasn't room for more damage, and so there was no room for Amnesty's sad story, or her potential redemption. Evangeline could love her and still desire never to see her ever again. Those things could co-exist. They had to, for her survival.

And she had to leave New Orleans. She knew that now. Understood it, which was even more important. She'd thank Amnesty for that, if the girl hadn't taken so much more than she'd given.

"I'm truly sorry for everything, Evangeline," Amnesty said. She paused to the side of Evangeline, as if there was one more lasting hope they could find accord, but then continued down the stairs and was gone.

"Yeah," Evangeline said, when she was again alone. "Merry Christmas, Amnesty."

CHAPTER 19

A Band of Heather

Noah offered to drive the six hours to Portree. He rented a car and they left before either of them would question the insanity of the suggestion. Colleen wondered if he felt as lost and exhilarated as she did, sitting beside the last person in Scotland she ever expected to be going on a rendezvous with. After her first invasion of his thoughts, she swore never to do it again. Not on this trip, nor any shared experiences they might have when it was over.

Their route wound them past the fortress of Stirling. Colleen had pleaded with him to stop, like a spoiled child, to walk the steps of her idol, Mary, Queen of Scots and see the statue of Robert the Bruce. They passed through the ice-age glaciers of Glen Coe, and the Highland stronghold of the Jacobite Mackenzies, Eilean Donan.

Colleen internalized the majority of her rambling contemplations as she surveyed the volcanic carving of the Highlands. She was only just getting to know it, but she loved it, in a way she never thought she could love anywhere that wasn't New Orleans. Whatever thoughts danced through Noah Jameson's mind remained as hidden as her own, thanks to her promise to herself, and, though he didn't know it, to him.

How long did he intend to whisk her away? They'd never

discussed details, as if dissecting might break the spell and sway them from their course. The subject never came up; not the strangeness of it, nor the fact that with each mile passing from Edinburgh, both of them eased into themselves more and more.

"I've never seen anything like this. Not in all my life." Colleen exhaled, after speaking the words in a rush, one of only a few she made on the long journey. With the entire world passing by her window, casual conversation seemed inadequate and inappropriate. More, the silence between them felt comfortable. A peace had settled between them.

Noah smiled from his peripheral. He rested a hand briefly on her knee, then he removed it again and continued his focus on the road.

COLLEEN AWOKE AS THE CAR EASED UP THE GRAVEL driveway to a small cabin in Sligachan. The Cuillin Mountains set the backdrop, their foggy peaks lit by the full moon. She exited the car in a daze.

Continuing his stint as a gentleman, Noah took her bag from her. She entered the cabin ahead of him, stumbling a bit in her sleepiness. He instinctively reached out to steady her as her drowsy smile met his.

Is this really happening? Am I really here? With him? Me?

She spent so much of her life interpreting and analyzing every good thing that happened to her, that she couldn't prevent the inevitable comparisons to Rory. To Philip. Noah possessed some of Rory's thoughtful kindness, and he held his own intellectually, like Philip. But to compare Noah to either of these men was a disservice to both him and herself. Colleen had chosen to live in the moment by accepting a spontaneous proposal with all the potential for disaster, and now she must see it through.

This included, she realized with a sigh, letting go.

Colleen intercepted the potential for awkwardness by selecting her own room, a point she capped with the light comment, *You okay if I take this one*? Noah exhaled in relief, and she wondered at the strange sadness she felt at this. She was the one who'd chosen the separate room. Did she really expect him to look disappointed?

And, really, had he hoped she might stay in his room... a girl he hardly knew? Had she hoped he would hope for that? He had invited her to go away with him, though other than the light touch of his palm on her knee, he'd given her no sign his interest was romantic.

You don't play games, and though you don't know him, you don't think he does either. Stop overthinking. Stop all of this.

Let go.

"Good night, Noah," she said and pretended not to see the smile that followed her to her room.

Colleen turned off the overthinking for the night, using her careful system of compartments, and allowed herself the tempting lure of sleep.

Tomorrow was Christmas Eve, but she didn't think about that, or anything.

For once, Colleen's mind was clear.

Colleen rose to the pleasant aroma of strong coffee. She slipped her sweater on over her pajamas and went to meet Noah. This caught her off guard, that he rose before she did, as she was always the earliest riser back in New Orleans. There was comfort in greeting the world before the chaos hit. Yet here he was, pushing her farther away from the neat lines she'd drawn around her life.

His hair was a mess, the mane of someone who'd gone straight from her bed to her tasks. When sunrise hit the snarls, dancing across the ends, he swayed slowly in the old rocker. Colleen's heart bounced.

"There's more in the dining room," he called to her. Turning to face her, his green eyes caught hers. "Do you like picnics?"

"Would you believe me if I told you I've never been on one?"

"Never? A travesty, Miss Deschanel!" he teased, employing the same moniker he'd used through the term to give her a hard time. Before, when he'd said it, she'd heard no fun in his tone. Now... now, she didn't know. The man was an enigma, but one she'd have the opportunity to solve as they explored the quiet island together.

She blushed. "Well..."

"I found a picnic basket, so I thought we could make good use of it. We don't have any groceries, but we could stop in Portree for some wine and snacks."

"Sounds lovely," she said, and it did.

NOAH TOOK HER TO GLENBRITTLE, SITE OF THE FAIRY Pools of Skye. Despite the chill in the air, the sky was free of clouds other than the low fog settling over the Black Cuillins. Colleen had an image of sitting down at a bench here to write a novel, even though she'd never entertained such a whimsical, fruitless idea in her life.

They started down the uneven path. Fields of heather and peat moor flanked both sides of the rocky trail, though the heather wouldn't bloom again until the spring. They meandered the passage, which crossed the River Brittle in several spots, jumping the stones like children. Noah squealed when he missed and landed a foot in the ice-cold water. Colleen offered a hand, smothering an impolite giggle while pulling him back to the safety of dry land.

When, at last, the blue-green waterfalls cascading from pool to pool came into view, Colleen's knees buckled. Magic flourished in this place. Perhaps it had been born here. If anyone would know such a thing, it was a Deschanel. She suddenly wished Evangeline were here, and even Maureen and Lizzy, and even her brothers. They would know what she was feeling. It would knock them off their feet.

Colleen turned to see Noah cresting the rise ahead, shaking out the blanket. She moved to join him.

"Why is no one else here?" she marveled, helping him assemble the assortment of cheeses and meats on the tartan spread. All the food looked so incredible, and she knew it was the setting. It was this *place.* Things were amplified here, beyond their capabilities anywhere else.

Noah grinned. "It's Christmas Eve. Most people are celebrating with their families."

Colleen sighed. "Not us."

"I would love to be home right now," Noah said. "My dad couldn't afford it."

Her gaze dropped. She hadn't considered this and assumed he had his own demons he was running from. "I'm sorry."

"Why are you sorry?"

"You wish you were home but had no means. I had every means and chose not to go. I should have thought before I said something. It was insensitive."

"We shouldn't apologize for who we are," Noah said with a shrug, handing her a plastic cup half-filled with chardonnay. "That would be exhausting and pointless."

As he spoke the words, she realized the release of them came with his forgiveness of the wrongs her brother had done. They didn't matter now. Charles couldn't touch him here, and Colleen hoped Noah could see she was nothing like him. She wasn't like anyone, except herself.

"Why is it we always feel the need to apologize anyway?"

Noah gave her question the consideration it deserved. "Maybe we're afraid to be happy with ourselves? Or to admit as much to others."

"That's a heavy dose of wisdom." Colleen smiled. "Wasn't expecting that from you."

"I suspect we'll both feel that way by the end of the trip," Noah rejoined.

She was again hit with the awareness of how reckless she'd been *—oh, won't Evangeline be surprised when I post my next letter—* coming halfway across the country with this man who, not even days ago, had rued her very existence. And yet, her racing heart had nothing to do with fear or contrition. Her flushed face held no embarrassment.

He reminded her of here, and he reminded her of home, and he did this in a way that made her ache for what she left behind as much as what she'd run toward.

She didn't know this man at all.

And yet.

She did.

"I love my family," she said in a rush. "I don't want you to think I'm here because I don't."

"I didn't think that."

"I told you about how I adore Mary, Queen of Scots. She was a stubborn queen, but she put her family, the crown, and her country above all else. Only when she stumbled on what her heart wanted did she falter." Colleen studied the amber liquid in her cup, swirling it. "I want to be like her, but I don't. Does that make sense?"

Noah's cheeks were aflame. She sensed in him the fear of giving her the wrong answer to a question, one that was among the most important she'd ever asked.

"You... you want to honor your family and do the right thing, but you're afraid you'll lead with your heart instead of your head. Right?"

Colleen watched him, learning more about the man sitting in front of her with every passing moment. She nodded slowly, swallowing. "I want to serve them." She couldn't elaborate, no matter how Noah put her at ease. He could never know everything about her family. What they could do. What *she* could do. "I don't want to simply exist and rent space on this planet. I want my life to matter, for them."

Noah exhaled. "And you said *I* was doling out the heavy wisdom today."

Colleen was unfazed. "You said we shouldn't apologize for who we are, but if you'd prefer I keep these things to myself—"

He reached a hand forward, and, for a fleeting moment, she thought he was about to rest it against the back of it on one of her flushed cheeks. Or was that only that she wished he would? Instead, it gently landed on her arm. "No. I enjoy listening to you talk."

Her gaze traveled to his hand. It was a strong hand, and she liked the soft weight of it on her skin. "What about you, Noah? What do you want from life?"

"I want to matter, too, Colleen, but my family is no bigger than my father and me. I have a mother, and sisters, somewhere... Ireland, I think. But I've never met them. To hear my father speak of my ma, I might not want to."

Colleen's chest hurt at the idea of any mother who could walk away from her child. For all of Irish Colleen's faults, she always put her children first, over everyone and everything. "What happened?"

"She was a witch."

Colleen couldn't help but chuckle. "I take it the separation wasn't a happy one."

"No, not in the pejorative sense," Noah clarified. "Dad said she was... an actual witch." Noah shook his head in embarrassment. "Hearing the words out loud, I realize how ridiculous that sounds. Just something my dad used to say, but he believed it. Deep down, he honestly thought she was a witch."

This didn't sound ridiculous to Colleen at all, a witch from generations of sorceresses. If anything, she wished she could ask Noah more, but it was evident he shared his father's prejudices. Which meant she had to tread very carefully with her own behavior. "It's amazing to me our paths never crossed until now. That it took crossing an ocean."

"Colleen," Noah said in a soft, gentle tone of voice, choosing his words with evident caution. "There may as well have been an ocean separating us in New Orleans."

She parted her lips, moving to apologize, once again, for her upbringing, her heritage, but Noah's wisdom about apologies still resonated. "Do you still feel that way?"

Noah's fingertips traveled to her face. The gesture felt as if it contained more than what he permitted himself, but so much had transpired between them, beneath the surface, behind their words, unspoken. She feared it and felt the fear in him, too. "I truly don't know how to describe what I'm feeling."

Colleen leaned into his touch, allowing her own temporary surrender to a man she hardly knew, and yet her soul had danced with him in a past life, another time. As she closed her eyes, she was sure of it, and had no care at all for how unlike her this feeling was. She'd taken a leap of faith. She'd let go. "Maybe we don't need words."

LATER THAT NIGHT, WHEN THE CLOCK CHIMED THE witching hour, she slid under his cotton sheets, wordless.

He moved within her, silent, demanding yet soft, like the whisper of silk.

"Merry Christmas," Colleen murmured against his chest, as she fell into sleep against the sweet scent of her lover's musk.

CHAPTER 20

I Would Die, I Will Die

Elizabeth froze at the sight of Connor in the family room with her mother. Irish Colleen had called her down, and Elizabeth assumed she'd been summoned for chores, or some favor or another. She had her driving permit now, and though it wasn't the same as a license, Irish Colleen had no trouble breaking rules when it suited her. She'd sent Elizabeth to the grocer four times already that week.

She stopped breathing. She remembered doing these, these... interventions for Charles, when he was much younger and there was still a remote chance of correcting his course. It was much smaller than the one Irish Colleen arranged for her oldest son, but Charles' drug problems had been no secret in the family, whereas Elizabeth's were at least somewhat well concealed. Enough that it had apparently taken Connor snitching on her to reveal them at all.

Elizabeth said nothing. She'd say nothing when they confronted her. They couldn't prove it. Even Connor's suspicions were only that.

"Well, are you going to stand there catching flies with your tongue, or are you going to help Connor with his school project?" Irish Colleen chided.

"What?"

"Remember?" Connor said. He strained his eyebrows from behind Irish Colleen, urging her to play along. "The one where I have to go to City Park and find one of each tree listed with the Audubon Society?"

Oh, Connor. You can do better than that.

Elizabeth didn't want to see him. She should, because she was the jerk, not him, but there was nothing easy in making amends and she didn't have the words for whatever he was going to say. She'd imagined apologizing to him for striking him, and nothing she conjured sounded close to adequate. Maybe because she was still sore from it all herself.

But she was curious why he was sitting in her family room after how things had ended, so she forced herself to smile. "Right. Let's go stare at trees, then."

Connor waited until they were a block away before he said anything. "Sorry for the surprise in there. I figured if I called, you wouldn't want to see me."

Elizabeth swallowed a lump in her throat. She didn't deserve him. Not now, and maybe not ever. "You might've been right."

He smiled sadly. "It's okay. Everything will work out, Lizzy." He started walking again, and she followed, but noted they were headed in the opposite direction of the park.

"Where are we going? Not the park, obviously."

"No, not the park."

"You're not gonna tell me?"

"No, and you're not gonna ask anymore."

"Oh? I'm not?"

"No," Connor said. His smile was tight, but warm, as was his gentle look from his peripheral. "Because you owe me."

Elizabeth pouted as his side, but she let him take her hand, and even laced their fingers tighter.

They rounded onto Decatur, and she hardly had time to read the sign outside the building before Connor ushered her in.

But she caught enough.

Methadone Clinic.

"Connor, no." She tugged her hand away and started back for the door. "This is bullshit, you tricked me! What's wrong with you?"

Connor's expression didn't change. He took her face in his hands and looked her in the eyes. "Elizabeth Deschanel, I love you more than anyone else in the world. More than my parents. More than Thomas." He spun her around, and she found herself before a mirror. She wondered, later, if the clinic put it there for everyone else who'd been coerced into coming. "Look at yourself."

"I know what I look like, Connor! I see myself every day!"

He rubbed the outside of her arms. She saw him behind her left shoulder, in her reflection, but he pressed his face to hers and made her look directly into her reflection. "No, you see what you wanna see, whatever keeps you from seeing the truth. I'll leave here with you, Lizzy, I'll walk you home, but first I'm asking you to look."

"You're ridiculous," she hissed, shifting around from foot to foot. He wasn't going to leave until she did it, though, so Elizabeth sighed and focused her eyes directly forward.

What she saw shocked her.

She blinked, looked again. Blinked until her eyes hurt.

She couldn't make it go away.

And how hadn't she seen it until now? She looked at herself every morning in the bathroom. The house was full of mirrors, and she must have caught her reflection four, five times a day, easily.

It wasn't so jarring that she saw someone else. She had the same mousy brown hair and wide eyes, and her cheekbones were still soft and round. But there were hollows beneath them where none previously existed. Dark bags rimmed the underside of her eyes, which seemed to—there was no other word for it—*droop.* The spots around her mouth were new, like freckles, but they weren't freckles.

"I would die if you died, Elizabeth. It's as simple as that. So you can't die. I swear on my *life* I will help you find another way to stop the visions, but it can't be this. *This* is killing you. And it's killing me, because you die, I die."

Elizabeth wouldn't cry. She *couldn't* cry, or every last bit of what she'd stopped from hemorrhaging into her life these past months would break through the dam holding it back. She wanted to say something to this hag in the mirror; this woman who was her, looked like her, but wore the weight of the world in every sickly pore.

"Irish Colleen never has to know. None of them ever have to know, Elizabeth. Just us. Only us."

What hell had she delivered herself to, in the name of peace? What had she traded, in exchange for harmony?

Everything. The answer was everything.

"I'm afraid," she whispered, finally.

Connor kissed her cheek, but his eyes never left hers in their shared reflection. "It's okay to be afraid. We can be afraid together."

"What if I can't do it?"

"You can," Connor answered. He looped his arms around her waist from behind, as much hug as promise. "Because we can."

ETERNAL DARKNESS SHROUDED THE LUMBERING mansion. Everything about the Blanchard home gave off the impression of the utter absence of light. From the way Edouard kept the dimmer switches at their lowest settings, even in the middle of the day, to the dark, imposing curtains, always drawn, and the furniture from another, earlier era, made of dark, heavy wood, half of it covered in plastic. The prevailing scents of old cigars and lemon furniture polish rounded out the measure of the man who had inherited the old home and treated his birthright like a mausoleum.

Maureen tried to unpack her things, but even lifting a shirt from her trunks felt like a monumental effort. Everything in her life was weighted by the quickness in which everything had changed. She was, so recently, young, free, and on the verge of her whole life. She didn't know what awaited her, but the potential was a bright light beckoning from the beyond. The hopefulness of options.

It wasn't *so* bad, at least not at the outset. Edouard was nice enough. More than she expected from the man who had so calculatedly seduced her, used her, and then discarded her when he was finished and ready for the next. He never outright mentioned that her brothers had forced him into the commitment of marriage, but she knew, and he knew she knew. She wished she could tell him it wasn't her fault! She never wanted this. Maureen, sophisticated in the art of seduction in her own limited ways, knew all along they were only playing a game and was fine with it. She wanted to link hands with her new husband and rail against the injustice of two brothers who couldn't mind their own business when the adults were talking. She hated the underlying insinuation that she was a child who needed others to intervene and hated even more the message this sent to the man who was now her husband.

It didn't matter. Edouard either knew this, or didn't, but he showed no signs of wanting to take out his displeasure on Maureen. To the contrary, he was resigned to his fate, in a way she wasn't yet and might never be. He dutifully explained where she could find everything in the house and then told her she was the mistress and could run the household as she pleased. The staff answered to her direction. She wasn't limited by money, which was hers to spend as long as she stayed within the generous budget set, and he wouldn't stand in her way when she made decisions about such things as décor and meals.

He had only two rules, and he conveyed them with an earnest graveness.

One, she wasn't to ever disturb him when he was in his office. This included his office downtown, as well as the one in what he called the east wing of the house. If she absolutely required his attention while he was working, she could leave a message with his secretary and indicate the urgency, though he cautioned her never to express urgency if one wasn't warranted.

And two, she should never show her displeasure or sadness over his inability to be a loving, doting husband. Love, for him, he said, came from the access to discover her happiness through other means. She would never want for anything else, and that had to be enough. He had nothing more to give, and her satisfaction within the marriage was hers to decide.

Maureen understood she should be happier about this. She'd been willing to settle for a lesser man, Peter Evers, in exchange for a quiet, nuclear life that fit her narrow expectations of contentment. And here was Edouard, a man of great means, telling her she could have whatever she wanted. Could run her home however she wanted. A man who had no desire to control her, or guide her. A man who would turn the other way as she took lovers, as long as her whims never caught the attentions of others. A man who was giving her permission to be a man, but with a woman's touch.

But it was not until faced with the realization she would never be loved that Maureen finally, utterly, craved it.

Chelsea called earlier, to give her the news that she'd done exactly as she said she would and eloped with Mason Landry. No fancy wedding for Chelsea, either, but the difference was, Chelsea was married to a man she loved, and who loved her. Her impertinence might cost her favor with her family, but she'd traded it for a future no one could sully.

Maureen dropped her blouse on the bed. She'd hung no more than three things in the past hour, in a closet that was hers now, and would be, for all of time. Edouard had given Maureen her own suite, separate of his. She supposed that sent the message of what their marriage would be more than any words he'd said on the matter. But he'd also surprised her when he said, *Should you decide you want another child, give me ample notice of the expectation and I'll make sure to visit your bed until you're with child once more.*

Dutiful sex. This was what would pass for excitement in Maureen's new life.

She tried to engage him with news of her latest doctor's appointment earlier that evening, when he'd come home from work. She didn't ask him about his day, because that was still too raw. It was too distressing to think of those terrible old women running amok, gossiping about Maureen as if she was no more than a commodity.

Dinner awaited him, which garnered a light smile and raised brow. She took this as a good sign, though she'd done no more than choose the dish—pot roast—and instruct the cook to prepare it. But as soon as he sat down to eat, he opened the day's Times-Picayune and buried himself in the day's news.

"Husband," she'd said, from the opposite end of the long table. "How was your day?"

"It was fine," Edouard replied without dropping the paper. He turned the page. She couldn't see his face. "But don't feel burdened with the task of engaging me in small talk, Maureen. I don't require it."

Well, maybe I do. "I had an appointment today. About the baby."

"That's nice."

"Do you want to hear about it?"

"Was there anything newsworthy?"

"Not especially, except—"

"Then, no. Feel free to update me when there is something notable to discuss."

"I didn't finish. I only meant that the baby is fine, but there *is* news, about the sex."

"Oh." He lowered the paper, just slightly.

"We're having a girl."

"Is that news?" he asked. "You'd said before you were having a daughter."

"No, I only thought that. Mother's intuition and all."

"I see." Edouard folded the paper and set it next to his plate. "I'd like you to consider naming her Olivia."

Maureen set her fork and knife on the plate. This was the closest she'd had to interest in anything she'd said or done since their wedding day. A light thrill passed through her at the possibility of an actual conversation. "Olivia? Why's that?"

"Olivia was my mother's name. She passed away when I was eleven."

"How?"

Edouard drew his lips tight. "Cancer."

Maureen tried not to frown. Olivia. It sounded so old-fashioned; she was sure, somewhere, she had an old spinster aunt with that name. There was nothing youthful or fun in it, not like Rebecca or Claire, which were the names she'd been toying over.

Edouard wasn't commanding this decision, though. He was asking. He'd expressed no emotion whatsoever about becoming a father, other than inconvenience, and everything he'd said on the matter conveyed that Maureen would be handling the parenting duties solely on her own, unless she counted the nannies he was more than happy to pay for.

If she gave him this, would it make him care? Would he see his daughter and think of someone dear to him?

"Or not," he said quickly. "This is your choice."

"I like the name Olivia," Maureen said. She smiled. She hoped he could see in her how easy life could be. How acquiescent Maureen was, and how she would live to please him, if only he'd let her.

"Good," Edouard said. He returned to his paper, the moment passed.

All moments would be like this, Maureen knew. Fleeting, with the whisper of potential, but the reality of emptiness and false starts. If Edouard had more in him, it was not hers to receive. She was nothing more than the game gone wrong.

She doubted he would be so reckless in the future, though she harbored no illusions that he'd stop hiring young girls and using them for his peculiar pleasures. Whatever he owed her now, it was not fidelity. The best she could hope for was that he wouldn't end up impregnating another young woman and bringing shame to their home.

Maureen wondered if she was the first, or just the first whose family wouldn't let it go.

She abandoned her unpacking and stepped into the hallway. Her bare toes recoiled at the aging red and gold carpet, which had long ago lost any semblance of softness. It felt like straw against her bare flesh, as if reminding her that everything here came at a terrible price.

"Daddy," she whispered. "You can come out now. He's not home."

Nothing in response. No sound, or sign, of August Deschanel. No passing wind, or whisper from the darkness.

"Maddy? You around?"

In the days since she moved in, her ghosts had gone quiet. She didn't expect Jean, or the Ophélie crew, because they'd been gone for a while now, ever since she moved back to New Orleans with Mama. Daddy and Madeline had followed her everywhere, though. Peter, too, though she couldn't fathom why he'd want to hold on to Maureen, the girl who'd gotten him killed, instead of, say, his children. But none of them had followed her here, to her marital home.

But, no, that wasn't quite accurate either.

August and Madeline had both quieted just before Maureen learned she was pregnant. She'd been too caught up in her depressive spiral after losing her job, and her freedom, to notice. She was even *grateful* for the space she assumed they were giving her to breathe.

What was it Pansy had said to her, in what now seemed a lifetime ago? That she might wish for a time when the dead still talked to her? Maureen couldn't grasp ever missing that constant intrusion in her life, but now here she was, calling for the dead in an empty house.

Even Peter's obnoxious refrain felt like a loss.

Maureen had never known real silence until now. She'd never understood how *loud* the complete absence of sound could be; how it screamed at her until she wished for nothing more than the cacophony of competing voices of Ophélie.

Maureen scanned the line of portraits in the endless hall. All dour, serious men vaguely resembling her husband. Joyless faces, all of them, stretching back through time. And where were they? Did they not haunt the halls of their old manor? She didn't especially yearn to meet them, but they were better than the expanse of nothing where the noise had been.

She didn't know why, or how, but she *knew,* somewhere, she'd traded motherhood for her access to the dead.

She gasped as Olivia kicked. Her hands wrapped around the outside of her belly, which no longer looked so incredible in short skirts, and might never again. "You're my girl, aren't you, Olivia? My sweet girl? My baby? Daddy might not ever need you like I do, but I'll always need you. And you'll need me, won't you?"

Olivia didn't answer. Only the dead had ever answered to Maureen.

And now, even they'd gone silent.

Epilogue: Irish Colleen and the Seven

Colleen Deschanel, known as Irish Colleen to her family and friends, ran her eyes down the row of pictures of her seven children, as she did each night of her life.

Pictures seemed all she had now. Four years ago, all seven of her children lived under the same roof, sharing their lives, both joys and failures, with one another. With her. For better or worse. Now, she was left with only one, and it wouldn't be so long now before Elizabeth was gone, too. In some ways, she already was.

Her children were scattered now, and this was the first Christmas where they'd chosen to remain that way, instead of rallying around the tree, and one another. The holidays were the one time of year where the family was unified, no matter their rifts or faults. She didn't know if they'd ever, really, be whole again.

Charles had his own family now, though she guessed he'd never felt lonelier. Her oldest, her larger-than-life firstborn, was reduced to an unhappy marriage and a coming child that may or may not prove to be a blessing. Irish Colleen imagined the cold gift exchange between husband and wife. The lack of eye contact, or the warmth of small talk. They'd retire to their own rooms and fall asleep joyless, loveless. She no longer found comfort in her belief that settling her son was best for him. She knew better now.

His changes were not for the good, and she'd set him on this path.

Her second son, Augustus, dropped by with his wife for Christmas dinner. They were more united than Charles and Cordelia, but she detected little in the way of contentment. That Augustus loved her was almost painfully obvious in the ways he doted on her, hanging on her words, watching her actions with cautious love. But Irish Colleen didn't sense the same from the enigmatic Ekatherina, and she wondered, not for the first, or last, time, what her motivations in marrying Augustus had been. Irish Colleen prayed for a child to bless their house, for she knew a child healed most ailments.

Colleen stayed in Scotland for Christmas. There was no scholastic reason. Classes were on hiatus, the students all gone home to be with their families. So why hadn't she come home? Irish Colleen couldn't ask this question of her daughter, for it was her who'd made it clear Colleen's loyalties to the family were a burden to her. She couldn't take this back, and while Colleen's absence was painful to bear, the alternative was worse. When Colleen called, from somewhere in Scotland, with some friend she didn't name, Irish Colleen heard the first hint of happiness in her eldest daughter. She wouldn't allow her bruised feelings to get in the way of that.

Evangeline came with Augustus to dinner, and her announcement was surprising, though not shocking. She would be leaving for Massachusetts in the spring, to attend a fancy technical college Irish Colleen had never heard of. Augustus assured her there was no more prestigious institution for someone science-minded, and Irish Colleen declined to remark that there was no future in science, and if they'd spent enough time in church, they'd know that. But one thing was for certain: Evangeline needed a change as much as Colleen had. Whatever her future held, she required a shake-up to find it. Irish Colleen knew when she was outmatched.

She hadn't spoken to Maureen at all since the courthouse nuptials. She'd called the Blanchard house, and the staff was apologetic in their contrived excuses, but Maureen never came to the phone. Was she hosting her own Christmas dinner? Did her very odd husband even care about such things as tradition? She couldn't decide if she was more upset that Maureen's future had taken such a sudden turn, or that her eldest children had made the decision without consulting her.

Irish Colleen blew her smiling picture a kiss, because even though Maureen was out of her house now, forever, it was still their thing.

Only Lizzy needed her now, and even that was up for debate.

Connor had come over that evening, as they were washing the dishes and cleaning the last of the dinner mess. He'd just gotten his driver's license and was proud to come on his own, swinging his keychain with adorable bravado. By then, Elizabeth had retired to her room, and Irish Colleen started to tell him this when she realized he was someone she needed to see.

"Connor, if something was amiss with Lizzy, you'd tell me, right?"

Connor opened his mouth, then closed it. He said nothing.

"No, dear, of course you wouldn't." She swung her dishrag over one shoulder and patted his arm. "But you know, don't you?"

He still said nothing. He seemed rooted by his loyalty, his silence painful for them both.

"I understand," she said, to him, or perhaps herself. "You don't have to tell me. I don't worry about her much, because of you, you know that?"

Connor tried to smile, but it came out more like a twitch. "Thanks, Mrs. Deschanel."

"I know if there's anyone who cares for our Lizzy as we do, it's you," she went on. He wouldn't tell her anything. She'd known that all along. "She's not been right all year, but you've been at her side, and so she hasn't been alone, has she?"

Connor hesitated before he said, "No, ma'am, she hasn't."

"I'm going to venture a guess that what she's dealing with is more serious than I can imagine, and no, Connor, don't look so concerned. I won't torture you for answers, I only want to help."

"I know," he said. "She knows, too."

Irish Colleen leaned in. "How *can* I help her, Connor? What can I do for my baby that I've not already done?"

He shuffled in place as he mulled this over. When he looked at her, he wasn't so much a boy anymore, as a young man, full of promise and weighted by life. "Give her space."

IRISH COLLEEN CLIMBED THE STEPS, MEANDERING PAST the row of empty bedrooms. She stopped at the end of the hallway and pressed on the door to Elizabeth's room. The creaking sound was the only sign of life in the quiet house. There was no sneaking around up here.

She wouldn't ask the question. Connor's reticence, and then advice, was a form of wisdom, and to press Elizabeth for something she wasn't ready for would risk losing her, too. Instead, she'd kiss her good night, and if after, Elizabeth should want to talk... well, she'd do her best to be there. Tough conversations were not Irish Colleen's forte, but she'd avoided too many in this family, and they'd paid the price for that silence.

"Lizzy?"

She crept through the darkness, toward the curled lump under the comforter. Elizabeth was rarely asleep so early, though she tried. More likely, she was faking it, or reading with her flashlight.

When Irish Colleen peeled back the covers, though, she was greeted only with the soft snores of Elizabeth's deep sleep.

Elizabeth was, for the first time in as long as she could remember, already asleep. She hadn't waited up for her mother's visit.

Give her space, Connor had said. But what good had space done for Madeline? Charles? Augustus? Evangeline? Maureen?

How, now, was she to know the way, when the path behind was littered with irreversible failure?

Give her space.

Was the wisdom of a teenager better than her own mother's intuition?

The wisdom of another came back to her.

Her husband. August.

You are the mother of a perfectly imperfect clan, and what will be will be. Do you remember my family's motto, Colleen?

She hadn't. Such a thing seemed so far less important than keeping them alive and fed. What good were mottos when Colleen was colicky and Charles suffered from repeated ear infections? When she battled her own illnesses while tending to those of eight others?

The strong shall rise again. Remember that, when you're carrying the weight of all of them, and afraid of what the future holds. I have lived through things you can't imagine, dearest. Things I hope die with me. But I know... I know we will always rise. The sun will rise, and we will rise, like a phoenix from the ashes, and nothing, nothing can keep us down. Not for long.

Irish Colleen kissed the top of Elizabeth's head and let her sleep.

Maureen is a mother now, and her brothers prepare for their own children. Colleen knows her love is real, but equally fears what will happen when he, inevitably, discovers she's the witch he fears.

Don't miss a minute. Download 1975 today.

Also by Sarah M. Cradit

KINGDOM OF THE WHITE SEA

Kingdom of the White Sea Trilogy

The Kingless Crown

The Broken Realm

The Hidden Kingdom

The Book of All Things

Blackwood Cycle

The Raven and the Rush

The Poison and the Paladin

Southerlands Cycle

The Sylvan and the Sand

The Flame and the Forsaken

Guardians Cycle

The Altruist and the Assassin

The Belle and the Blackbird

Darkwood Cycle

The Melody and the Master

The Hand and the Heart

Sceptre Cycle

The Claw and the Crowned

The Duke and the Disciple

THE SAGA OF CRIMSON & CLOVER

The House of Crimson and Clover Series

The Storm and the Darkness

Shattered

The Illusions of Eventide

Bound

Midnight Dynasty

Asunder

Empire of Shadows

Myths of Midwinter

The Hinterland Veil

The Secrets Amongst the Cypress

Within the Garden of Twilight

House of Dusk, House of Dawn

Midnight Dynasty Series

A Tempest of Discovery

A Storm of Revelations

A Torrent of Deceit

The Seven Series

Nineteen Seventy

Nineteen Seventy-Two

Nineteen Seventy-Three

Nineteen Seventy-Four

Nineteen Seventy-Five

Nineteen Seventy-Six

Nineteen Eighty

Vampires of the Merovingi Series

The Island

and more

The Dusk Trilogy

St. Charles at Dusk: The Story of Oz and Adrienne

Flourish: The Story of Anne Fontaine

Banshee: The Story of Giselle Deschanel

Crimson & Clover Stories

Available as a single collection, The Shorts

Surrender: The Story of Oz and Ana

Shame: The Story of Jonathan St. Andrews

Fire & Ice: The Story of Remy & Fleur

Dark Blessing: The Landry Triplets

Pandora's Box: The Story of Jasper & Pandora

The Menagerie: Oriana's Den of Iniquities

A Band of Heather: The Story of Colleen and Noah

The Ephemeral: The Story of Autumn & Gabriel

Bayou's Edge: The Landry Triplets

For more information, and exciting bonus material, visit www.sarahmcradit.com

The Family

Deschanel Family (Line of August)

The Deschanel (*pronounced Day-shah-nell*) family are the line of heirs of the great Charles Deschanel of France, who settled the Deschanel dynasty in Louisiana in 1844. All current day descendants of this original Charles are either of the line of August or Blanche. Deschanels are of the line of August, and all others (Fontenots, Broussards, Guidrys, etc.) come from Blanche. August, with his wife "Irish" Colleen Brady, had seven children: Charles, Augustus, Colleen, Madeline, Evangeline, Maureen, and Elizabeth. Madeline, their fourth child, tragically passed in an automobile accident on Christmas morning, 1970.

Irish Colleen was August's second wife. His first, Eliza, he married for love, but she was unable to bear children and eventually passed away from cancer.

The rights of inheritance of the Deschanels follow the tradition of the eldest son, so Charles, son of August, is the current heir.

August (1905-1961) & "Irish" Colleen Brady (1932-)

Charles b. 1950
Augustus b. 1951
Colleen b. 1952
Madeline b. 1953
Evangeline b. 1954
Maureen b. 1956
Elizabeth b. 1959

Deschanel-Broussard Family (Line of Blanche)

The Deschanel-Broussard family (*pronounced Brew-sard*), are cousins of the Deschanel family, equal in wealth and prestige. Where the Deschanels are descendants of the line of August, the Broussards are descendants of the line of Blanche. Claudius Broussard is Blanche's third husband, and the children from this union are considered her most favored. She also has a son by her second husband, Johnson Guidry, but her relationship with Pierce is fractured.

Blanche did not have children by her first husband, Ellis Kenner. Both Ellis Kenner and Johnson Guidry died of "mysterious circumstances."

Blanche Deschanel (b. 1906) & Johnson Guidry (1890-1930)
Pierce b. 1926

& Claudius Broussard (b. 1900)
Eugenia b. 1940
Pierce b. 1926
Cassius b. 1942
Wyatt (1943-1955)
Noble (1944-1955)

Guidry Family (Line of Blanche)

The Guidry family are those descended from Pierce Guidry, first son of Blanche Deschanel-Broussard. Although the first son is the heir on the Deschanel side, Blanche does not recognize Pierce as her heir. Instead, she sees her second child and eldest daughter, Eugenia Fontenot, as her heir. Pierce represents his line of the family as one of the seven Deschanel Magi Collective Council. His two daughters, Pansy and Kitty, are also on the Council.

Of Pierce's children, only Pansy, so far, is married.

The Guidrys, for no reason other than Blanche's disdain for her second husband, Johnson, are considered the black sheep of the clan.

Pierce Guidry (b. 1926) & Winnifred Babin (b. 1926)
Pansy b. 1949
Alton b. 1950
Kitty b. 1954

Pansy b. 1949 m. Placide Lafont b. 1945
Rex b. 1973

Fontenot Family (Line of Blanche)

The Fontenot family are those descended from Eugenia Broussard-Fontenot, second daughter of Blanche Deschanel-Broussard. Although Eugenia is a second child, and a daughter to boot, Blanche recognizes Eugenia as her heir. Eugenia is married to Wallace Fontenot, and they have three sons. Eugenia represents her line of the family as one of the seven Deschanel Magi Collective Council.

The Fontenots are well-respected in the community, with a similar prestige as their Deschanel cousins.

Eugenia Broussard (b. 1940) & Wallace Fontenot (b. 1939)
Luther b. 1962
Llewellyn b. 1963
Lowell b. 1964

Broussard Family (Line of Blanche)

The Broussard family are those descended from Cassius, third child and second son of Blanche Deschanel-Broussard. Cassius is married to Helene Barrow, and they have two children, a son and a daughter. Cassius represents his line of the family as one of the seven Deschanel Magi Collective Council.

The Broussards, like the Fontenots, are well-respected in the community, with a similar prestige as their Deschanel cousins.

Cassius Broussard (b. 1942) & Helene Barrow (b. 1944)
Jasper b. 1963
Imogen b. 1965

Sullivan Family

The Sullivans are one of the oldest and most trusted families in New Orleans. A family of attorneys, a majority of Sullivans, most notably males until recently, join the family law firm, Sullivan & Associates, which has been a New Orleans staple since 1839. The family came up through the ranks, by their bootstraps, with humble beginnings as Irish immigrant laborers. The Sullivans are both the attorneys and friends of the Deschanel Family. Like the Deschanels, the designation of heir follows the eldest son, and so Colin Sullivan Sr. is considered the head of the family. His father, Patrick, still lives, but in quiet retirement.

Colin Sullivan Sr. (b. 1932) & Josephine Bartleby (b. 1931)
Colin Sullivan Jr. b. 1950 (m. Catherine Connelly b. 1948)
Rory Sullivan b. 1952 (m. Carolina Percy b. 1953)
Patrick Sullivan b. 1953
Chelsea Sullivan b. 1956

Sullivan & Associates

Sullivan & Associates is a family-owned law firm, and one of the oldest and most trusted in New Orleans, founded in 1839 by Aidan Sullivan. Comprised mostly of Sullivans, the firm is considered something of a birthright for any Sullivans looking to go into law. They have represented the Deschanel interests for over a century. Charles Deschanel's best friend, Colin Sullivan Jr., as well as Colin's two brothers, Rory and Patrick, all plan to join the family firm one day. Colin Sullivan Sr. is the current Senior Partner, following the retirement of his father, Patrick. Colin Sr. and his brothers, Jerome and Jamie, are the figureheads of the firm.

Homes & Properties

Oak Haven

The old Victorian mansion Irish Colleen and seven used to live in, on Chestnut and Sixth in the Garden District, just beyond Lafayette Cemetery No. 1. Although there are larger (Magnolia Grace) and more storied (Ophélie) homes in the family possession, August Deschanel chose this particular property to raise his family in with the thought of giving them a more "normal" upbringing than he had.

The Gardens

The colossal mansion of Ophelia Deschanel at Jackson Ave., taking up an entire square block between Coliseum and Prytania in the Garden District. The Gardens also houses the cavernous chambers where the Deschanel Magi Collective and the Collective Council meet to discuss family business. The architectural style of the estate is Italianate, and the most notable feature is the extensive, exotic garden wrapping around the property, shielding the home from outside view. This house will be inherited by the future Deschanel Magi Collective Magistrate.

Ophélie

A large plantation and surrounding lands purchased by Charles Deschanel I, built in 1844, and currently occupied intermittently by the Deschanel family. Charles will inherit the property as the heir to the estate. Located near Vacherie, an hour west of New Orleans, the Greek Revival ivory mansion on the Mississippi River is secluded from the road by gates and foliage. The estate has forty-five rooms and large ornate gardens, as well as two hundred outbuildings from when the property was a working plantation. Charles, as the heir, has inherited this property.

Magnolia Grace

A beautiful, traditional Greek Revival mansion in the Garden District that once belonged to Fitz Deschanel (the second son of Charles I), and has ever since been passed down through the second sons. Augustus Deschanel inherited this property, which is located on Prytania, near Eighth.

Deschanel Media Group

The brainchild of Augustus Deschanel, who had dreamed of starting his own company since he was a young boy. The company's vision is a magazine for locals, which both catered to the elites but also offered an opportunity for aspiring writers to get their short stories published and in front of potential patrons.

Femme Forte

A sprawling Northshore mansion along Lake Pontchartrain, considered the birthright of Blanche and her descendants. The property will be inherited by Eugenia Fontenot, her favorite child.

Weatherly Estate

The vast, columned Uptown home of Daniel Weatherly Sr., gifted for his patronage of Tulane. His son, Dan Jr., is a good friend of Charles Deschanel. The estate is located near the sister universities of Tulane and Loyola, by the Ursuline's Academy.

About the Author

Sarah is the USA Today and International Bestselling Author of over forty contemporary and epic fantasy stories, and the creator of the Kingdom of the White Sea and Saga of Crimson & Clover universes.

Born a geek, Sarah spends her time crafting rich and multilayered worlds, obsessing over history, playing her retribution paladin (and sometimes destruction warlock), and settling provocative Tolkien debates, such as why the Great Eagles are not Gandalf's personal taxi service. Passionate about travel, she's been to over twenty countries collecting sparks of inspiration, and is always planning her next adventure.

Sarah and her husband live in a beautiful corner of SE Pennsylvania with their three tiny benevolent pug dictators.

www.sarahmcradit.com

www.ingramcontent.com/pod-product-compliance
Lightning Source LLC
Chambersburg PA
CBHW020334310726
48979CB00015B/2369/J

* 9 7 8 1 9 5 8 7 4 4 2 7 7 *